THE
HOUSE
OF QUIET

BY KIERSTEN WHITE

Paranormalcy
Supernaturally
Endlessly

Mind Games
Perfect Lies

The Chaos of Stars

Illusions of Fate

And I Darken
Now I Rise
Bright We Burn

The Dark Descent of Elizabeth Frankenstein

Slayer
Chosen

The Guinevere Deception
The Camelot Betrayal
The Excalibur Curse

Star Wars:
Padawan

Hide

Mister Magic

Lucy Undying

The House of Quiet

THE HOUSE OF QUIET

KIERSTEN WHITE

DELACORTE PRESS

Delacorte Press
An imprint of Random House Children's Books
A division of Penguin Random House LLC
1745 Broadway, New York, NY 10019
penguinrandomhouse.com
GetUnderlined.com

Text copyright © 2025 by Kiersten Brazier
Jacket art copyright © 2025 by Marcela Bolívar
Pattern used under license from Shutterstock.com

Penguin Random House values and supports copyright. Copyright fuels creativity, encourages diverse voices, promotes free speech, and creates a vibrant culture. Thank you for buying an authorized edition of this book and for complying with copyright laws by not reproducing, scanning, or distributing any part of it in any form without permission. You are supporting writers and allowing Penguin Random House to continue to publish books for every reader. Please note that no part of this book may be used or reproduced in any manner for the purpose of training artificial intelligence technologies or systems.

Delacorte Press is a registered trademark and the colophon
is a trademark of Penguin Random House LLC.

Editor: Wendy Loggia
Cover Designer: Casey Moses
Interior Designer: Ken Crossland
Production Editor: Colleen Fellingham
Managing Editor: Tamar Schwartz
Production Manager: Tracy Heydweiller

Library of Congress Cataloging-in-Publication Data is available upon request.
ISBN 978-0-593-80657-9 (trade) — ISBN 978-0-593-80658-6 (lib. bdg.) —
ISBN 978-0-593-80659-3 (ebook) — ISBN 979-8-217-12261-5 (int'l edition)

The text of this book is set in 11.5-point Fairfield LT.

Manufactured in the United States of America
10 9 8 7 6 5 4 3 2 1

The authorized representative in the EU for product safety and compliance is Penguin Random House Ireland, Morrison Chambers, 32 Nassau Street, Dublin D02 YH68, Ireland, https://eu-contact.penguin.ie.

Random House Children's Books supports the First Amendment and celebrates the right to read.

For Cassie and Josh for providing an escape

And for Steph and Jade for providing a rescue

PROLOGUE

The dizzy game was Magpie's one request before Birdie goes.

The room whirls and blurs around them as they spin in circles, hands clasped, until little Magpie can't hold on anymore. She flies away. Birdie realizes a moment too late that this isn't going to end well.

Magpie watches with those knowing green eyes as Birdie wipes the blood from her split eyebrow. She's only six, but she's the calmest, sweetest child in the world. Birdie loves her more than anything. It feels unimaginably cruel that in order to help Magpie, Birdie has to leave her.

"It's all right," Magpie says.

"It's not," Birdie answers through her tears. "You're going to have a scar."

"Then you'll always know it's me, by my scar."

Birdie laughs, sniffling. "I'll always know you, my Magpie."

Magpie's expression gets somber, and the lip that didn't so much as tremble as Birdie cleaned the cut begins to wobble. "But you'll be gone so long. You might forget me."

"Never. Never ever. I'm only going away now so we can be

together forever later. Once you get the procedure, we'll have a little house. Just you and me."

"With flowers," Magpie says, even though flowers don't grow in Sootcity.

"And books," Birdie adds, even though neither of them can read.

"And cupboards full of candy," Magpie finishes, even though she doesn't like sweet things. Birdie does, though.

Birdie's counted it out. With their mother and father both working and Birdie going away to serve in a big house, it will take six years for them to earn enough for Magpie's procedure. Birdie will be sixteen and Magpie will be twelve then. Maybe Magpie is right. Maybe Birdie won't recognize her anymore. But she'll still *know* her. She'll always know her. Birdie blows gently on the cut and then holds her baby sister as tightly as she can.

Six years isn't that long. Six years, and then nothing will ever separate them again.

CHAPTER ONE

A House Is Not a Home

The House of Quiet sits waiting, the only firm, immovable point in a landscape of rot and treachery. Deep within it, a heart beats. The heart of the house feels everyone scurrying around above it, all those little points of heat and life and *noise*. The heart hates the noise, and it needs it, all at the same time.

Inside the house, tucked not where they belong but instead in the bedrooms downstairs, young people sleep. They're so *loud*. The people who used to lie in those beds were old. They took the noise away; they didn't bring it with them.

But now the young things are there and the house can never rest. Its heart beats too hard, agitated and twitching, and the House Wife feels it and knows that agony but cannot help it.

Yet.

The House Wife, eyes and hands of the house, drifts down the hallway. The heart squirms and thrashes somewhere beneath them all. She wants to soothe it, to promise that soon, soon, things will go back to how they were. Soon, they'll always have enough.

They just have to deal with all the bodies sleeping fitfully around them first.

She stands over them, staring, hating them. Knowing they must hate themselves, too. She presses a hand to a fevered brow and shushes, but it does no good. She's not the one who can take this burden from them. She glances upward in longing toward the second floor.

That used to be the noisiest place in the house. There was an order to things then. An even, predictable ebb and flow. Nothing like the strain of how things are now.

They explained the change to her so many times, but words are hard to hold on to. All she knows is now she must be careful. But the house isn't built to care, and neither is she. She thinks she might have been once, but it's too hard to think of anything before the house.

She's always been in the house, and the house has always been in her.

The House Wife returns to where she belongs, standing in front of the red circle. She stares into that scarlet abyss and waits, listening to the cries coming from somewhere far beneath.

"*Shh, shh, shh,*" she whispers, like the whoosh of blood pumping through a heart. "Soon."

CHAPTER TWO

A Bird in Flight

Maids aren't supposed to be seen, but they're always supposed to see. Birdie tugs on the carriage curtains once more. They're sewn firmly in place. It makes her feel unsettled and vulnerable to have no idea where she is. The driver could be taking her anywhere.

She used to watch carriages pass by and dream of what it would be like to ride inside instead of clinging to the back like a tick, but right now she'd give anything to be hanging on, breathing in the familiar burning stink of Sootcity. Able to anticipate anything coming for her. Able to jump off and flee, if she needed to.

She can't run away, though. Not now that she finally has a destination to run toward. She takes deep breaths and closes her eyes. They're picking up two other maids. She has to calm down first. The worst thing she can do right now is look suspicious.

"Magpie in the tree, are you looking for me?" Birdie sings, voice so quiet it's lost to the clattering of wheels on cobblestones. And then she sings the answer, even though it's Magpie's part, not hers. "Birdie in the bush, will you learn to shush?"

She closes her eyes at the memories of Call and Answer,

Magpie's favorite other than the dizzy game. The way Magpie always giggled singing her response. She was *convinced* she could throw her voice when it was Birdie's turn to look. Birdie bumbled through cupboards and stoves and cabinets in the neighborhood junk pile, never getting close to where she knew her little sister was.

Birdie knows where Magpie is again, at last. And nothing's going to stop her. Birdie's heart rate calms. She retreats into herself and becomes a perfect maid once more.

The carriage stops, and two young women climb in. One has light brown skin, black hair, and eyes as round as buttons. The other has pale white skin, with an abundance of freckles the same reddish color as her hair. They're both in sturdy gray dresses nearly identical to Birdie's own.

At the minister's house, the maids were required to wear white dresses to blend in better with the walls. Which meant they stayed up every night scrubbing and cleaning their own dresses after scrubbing and cleaning everything else. Most nights Birdie barely got three hours of sleep, between waiting for the other maids to drift off and visiting her friend.

Despair and guilt litter her mind at the thought of that last locked door that never opened for her, but Birdie sweeps those emotions away with ruthless practice. She's a maid. Maids don't have feelings.

"Hi!" the redhead says. She must not have gotten the same training, because her feelings are written all over her face. Excitement and nerves both conveyed in a brilliant smile. She has a gap between her front teeth that Birdie finds immediately charming. "I'm Rabbit!"

"Minnow," the round-eyed maid says, keeping her gaze on her

lap. They both have animal names, which means they're from the same lower class Birdie is.

Was, she reminds herself, flooded with bitter anger. Somewhere up in the hills, her parents sit in a cavernous, empty house. She hopes they rot there.

But it's good they're Rabbit and Minnow. She was worried with prime positions in the House of Quiet, the maids might have had plant names, indicating families with healthy prospects for growth. The upper classes always use more abstract names. Geological features, seasons, nonsense like that. Birdie almost laughs, thinking about Nimbus, the boy from the first big house she worked in. Such a silly name for such a sweet person.

After she left Nimbus's house, she went to work for the minister of finance. Six months of fear and deception and struggle, with only one safe place in the whole house. But she's here now. That's the only thing that can matter.

"What's your name?" Rabbit prods.

"Birdie." Birdie was the nickname Magpie gave her, though Birdie often daydreamed of being named after a plant. Someone with a name like that would have been able to earn enough money to keep her family together. If she were Rowan, and Magpie were Willow, they would have had enough to get by. They never would have sent Magpie to get the procedure, hoping to buy a new future for all of them.

"Where are you from?" Rabbit asks the third maid. "Name like Minnow, it isn't the city."

Birdie can't tell if Minnow is scared or alert or simply always looks that intense thanks to her large, round eyes.

"The coast," Minnow says at last, her blunt delivery making it clear she's not interested in elaborating.

Birdie doesn't need to be best friends with her, but she does need both maids on her side. Maids cover for each other. It saved Birdie from being caught more than once, in the minister's house. Hopefully Rabbit and Minnow follow the same unspoken code from the lower quarters of Sootcity: *We help our own, because no one else will.*

"I've never left the city," Rabbit says breathlessly, trying and failing to peer out the curtains. "I've never worked as a maid before, either. I was in a laundry."

A quick glance at Rabbit's hands shows hints of blue under her skin. Before, when Birdie thought her mother was there to protect them and keep the family together, before she knew so devastatingly otherwise, Birdie used to hold her mother's hand and trace the blue creeping outward from her veins. A few more years in the laundry and Rabbit's hands would seize up and stop working, just like Birdie's mother's did. Which is the luckiest possible outcome. Unlucky is the chemicals finding their way to the heart and stopping it outright.

But obviously Rabbit's lucky, because she's here.

"How did you get a position in the House of Quiet?" Birdie tries not to sound as shocked as she is. After all the scheming and spying and extorting Birdie did to get here, a laundress got the same position?

"Oh, I had the procedure last year." Rabbit's smile fades a bit. "It was supposed to be my cousin, but she died three weeks before. Run over by a cart, crushed her legs, it was terrible. All my other cousins were too old and had already joined the military to pay for her procedure. So my family stuck me in instead."

"How old are you?" Birdie asks. Rabbit doesn't look much younger than Birdie, but fourteen is the cutoff for the procedure.

Any older, and the brain doesn't have enough room to adjust to such violent changes.

"Sixteen."

Birdie's jaw drops in surprise. "It didn't kill you?"

Rabbit giggles at the absurdity of the question. Even Minnow cracks a smile but wipes it quickly away and stares blankly at the floor.

"I'm a late bloomer, as my da says. I was barely fifteen then. We just lied about my age. The procedure didn't kill me, but it didn't take well, either. I'm an inward empath."

Minnow stiffens almost imperceptibly, shifting away from Rabbit as though distance will help. If Rabbit can sense their feelings, she'll know when Birdie's not being truthful. This is a disaster. She's going to fail before she ever even gets to the house.

There are two categories of abilities—inward and outward. An inward empath means Rabbit can feel other people's feelings. An outward one would have meant Rabbit could send her feelings out to others. That was the one Birdie always hoped for with Magpie. Outward empaths were employed taking care of children, or as nurses, or as companions. Birdie always thought Magpie would be good at it, and she didn't want Magpie to have to endure the intrusions of inward abilities.

She has no idea what the procedure did to Magpie, though. Another thing her parents refused to tell her. Birdie spent years obsessively gathering lists of abilities—the broad categories of empath, thought reading or thought projection, and future sensing, with more specific specializations depending on what the procedure triggers—all while dreaming of what Magpie would be able to do.

What did Magpie become when she went into that building with its enormous machine? And why is she gone now?

Rabbit laughs. "You two shouldn't look so nervous. Like I said, it didn't take well. I can guess more about how you're feeling from your faces than your actual emotions. But the government certification meant they assigned me to a spot in the House of Quiet. And they paid in advance! My little brother can go to school." Rabbit beams. "I made him promise to write me as soon as he knows how. Do you think someone there will read the letters to me?"

Birdie nearly volunteers before she catches herself. The more people underestimate her, the easier it is to hurt them. Birdie didn't need the procedure to get a position in the House of Quiet. She just needed several months of picking locks and reading tedious correspondence until she found something she could use to manipulate the minister.

Thinking of what she did and whom she left behind makes her sick to her stomach, though. Or it could be the claustrophobic carriage interior. Birdie's tempted to bang on the door and ask if she can ride on the back, but then her new dress would be mud-splattered.

After a couple of tortuous hours with nothing to do—a situation deeply unfamiliar to all three girls, as evidenced by their fidgeting—the horses stop. The driver, an older man with lines so deep in his forehead they look like fissures in a stone, opens the door. Birdie can't see anything past him but trees. They're out of the city; that much is obvious by how fresh the air is. But there's nothing around them.

It looks a little like where the minister's country manor was. Birdie tenses, half expecting the minister of finance himself to appear, that oily smile on his face. The same one that seeped across his features when Birdie informed him that she'd stolen a letter plotting against the minister of defense and demanded he recommend her to a position in the House of Quiet.

That smile has haunted her. Why wasn't he upset?

The driver holds out a canteen and three mismatched mugs. "Tea," he says. As soon as Birdie takes the offering, the door closes once more.

"Least he could have done is tell us how much longer," Rabbit grumbles. She pours for herself, then offers the canteen to Birdie.

"None for me, thanks." Birdie's stomach is still unsettled by the ride, and she'd prefer it empty. Maids aren't allowed inconvenient bodily functions.

Minnow and Rabbit split the rest. Within minutes, their heads bob in unison. Birdie wishes she could join them. Sleeping during the day is a luxury she's never imagined for herself. She used to indulge in dreams of working in a shop, only ten or twelve hours a day, leaving her time to meet up with Magpie for a pastry or sweet. Listen to the details of Magpie's day doing important work wherever the government assigned her.

A whole life, planned around Magpie's procedure. Birdie never stopped to wonder if Magpie *wanted* the procedure at all. None of them did. They were all too focused on saving to pay for it, in the hopes that Magpie would lift them all out of poverty.

Birdie hates her parents for what they did, but she hates herself, too.

The carriage jolts and bumps. Neither girl so much as startles awake, and Birdie eyes their empty mugs with suspicion. Nimbus's mother had a special tea that rendered her unconscious every afternoon. Why would the driver want to do that to them, though?

When the carriage stops again, Birdie closes her eyes, just in case, every muscle tense and ready to run. She doesn't want to leave Rabbit and Minnow behind, but if this is the trap, it's for her, not them.

The door opens. Someone grunts in approval. Not the minister, then. Birdie can't imagine him doing something as unsophisticated as grunting.

"Delivery tomorrow, too?" the driver asks.

"Busy season," a second man says. His voice is new. Where did he come from?

The driver speaks again. "Where *is* the house?" There's a long pause before the driver forces a laugh and says, "None of my concern, I know. Just curious."

"I wouldn't be, if I were you," the second man says. It's less a threat than a weary warning. The door clicks shut. No one has come for Birdie, but she doesn't relax until the carriage begins moving once more.

Birdie pops a few of the curtain stitches and gets the corner open. The twilight world around them is unfamiliar. She'd expected well-tended countryside like the minister's estate. Instead, she finds a flat and near-featureless landscape. She wishes she'd been able to take Nimbus's lessons on geography. It's upsetting that she has no idea where they might be.

The sun's last rays illuminate surprising pools of water. Not contained and orderly rivers or lakes, but a mess of ponds and quagmires dominating the ground all around them. The carriage slows, then slows more, until Birdie could walk faster. Even though the land is perfectly flat, their path is winding and strange. Finally, in the distance, Birdie sees a darker black against the nighttime horizon. It looks more like an absence than a presence. A hole, waiting to swallow them.

But as the carriage tugs them ever closer, the lines resolve into something comprehensible: a building, standing sentinel. It's at least three stories tall, with ornamental towers on both sides.

The structure feels forbidding, like the mausoleums on the hills overlooking the city, where the wealthy families inter their dead. A reminder that even their rotting corpses deserve better than people like Birdie.

The House of Quiet, at last. Birdie shouldn't be surprised they wanted it far, far away from the city. After all, sometimes the passage-ways the procedure opens in young brains are weak, like Rabbit's. But sometimes they're too powerful for the mind to stand, or too dangerous for anyone to be around.

"Too much noise," Dr. Bramble had said when Birdie asked about it. *"The House of Quiet eases the discomfort. A kindness, provided by the Ministry of Health and Progress. You'll find your sister there; I'm sure of it. We just have to get you inside."*

A *kindness.* That phrase jabs Birdie like a thorn in her shoe. There are no kindnesses. Not for people like Birdie and Magpie.

At the minister's house, there was a footman. Footboy, really. The minister wanted his heavy trunk brought down to his carriage, but of course he couldn't see it being taken there. So little Herring did his best to balance it as he navigated the dark, treacherous servants' stairs. When he fell, breaking too many bones to easily fix, the minister dismissed him to die at home. Instead of sending his own personal doctor, or payment, or even just condolences, he sent Herring's family a bill for the cost of the damaged trunk.

That was the type of man who ran this country. He had no kindness in him. And, even more troubling, the Ministry of Health and Progress paid Birdie's parents an astonishing sum in place of returning Magpie after her procedure. If anything, the Ministry should have demanded Birdie's family raise another impossible sum in order to fix her.

The carriage comes to a stop. Rabbit and Minnow nearly tip

over with the movement, but they're still out cold. Birdie peers at the house. On the first floor, in the corner, a dark figure stands behind a window. Waiting . . . and watching. Birdie pushes the curtain hastily back in place, hoping she wasn't noticed.

Birdie's here. She made it. And she's not leaving until she's stolen her sister back from the House of Quiet.

CHAPTER THREE

Asleep in an Unquiet House

The darkness breathes in and out, softly sighing.

Up ahead is the only light: a candle, held by a girl. She's pale, skin practically white, hair blending and bleeding into the darkness around them. In the flickering, desperate illumination, she's small and fine-boned, plain-featured except for her bold eyes turning up sharply at the outer corners. Her face is a determined mask over absolute terror as she moves forward, unable to see beyond the tiny circle provided by her candle. The flame is sputtering, about to go out.

But she keeps walking without hesitation. Out of sight, taking the light with her.

The darkness shifts. It becomes contained in four cramped walls of rotting gray wood that lets in weak, smoke-filtered light. A sour prickle of anxiety permeates the tiny shed as a freckled, red-haired girl tries to gather several mewling kittens into her arms. Every time she has almost all of them, they tumble free and she has to start over.

"Please," she whispers with tears in her vivid brown eyes as she looks over her shoulder at the door. "Please, he's going to drown you."

Sometimes things can change. With a very great amount of effort, an apron appears over the girl's dress. She laughs with relief as she quickly loads all the kittens into her apron and runs out of the shed. The light outside cuts through the dream, splitting it in two, so bright it hurts, so loud it turns into a roar.

The ocean, roiling and gray and infinite. A girl is sitting on a rock, perched as pretty as a picture, staring at the infinite waves. She's soaked in blood.

No. No, thank you.

Spinning, spinning, spinning into the arms of a tall, pale boy. His eyes are as blue as cornflowers. He has full lips, cheekbones like monuments, and a charmingly boyish nose in the middle of such striking features. He's dazzlingly, distractingly beautiful.

Until he opens his mouth. Tar sludges out, sticky and black. He's choking on it, silent tears streaming down his face. His chin is stained, then his chest. The tar pools around his feet, reaching for everything around him.

No.

A different boy prowls ahead, mouth cruel, eyes narrowed, stalking through an endless forest of perfectly straight trees. In his hand is a knife. Whatever he's hunting, it doesn't sound like something scurrying, or something on four legs. It sounds like someone running. There are cries, too, soft, pathetic ones. Soon he'll catch up, and then—

Blood. Blood is better. At least the blood was only on the girl. And there's the ocean, too. The ocean is nice. But the girl, sixteen, maybe seventeen, tall with light brown skin and long black hair and gray eyes so round they look like the smooth stones of the shoreline, isn't looking out at the waves. She's looking down at something beneath the rock she's sitting on.

Her dress is soaked in blood. Even her feet are dyed red, like she's been wading through the stuff. But she doesn't move toward the water to wash it off. She keeps staring at the space under the rock she's perched on.

"Have you heard the story of the Fool and the Bog Mansion?" she asks. Her voice is low and melodic, soothing in the same way the waves are. "There once was a man who had only enough food to keep from starving, only enough peat to keep from freezing. But he *wasn't* starving, and he *wasn't* freezing. One night he had a dream. In this dream, he was a wealthy man who lived in a beautiful mansion. It felt more real than real life, because he wanted it more than he wanted anything he already had. He became convinced the mansion was out there somewhere, waiting for him. Leaving everyone who loved him, he wandered into the wilderness in search of the life he now felt was his due. One night he came upon a peat bog with a light burning deep beneath it. He dived into the brackish, hungry water, tangled in roots and plants and dead things. And there, beneath the bog, he found it at last: his mansion. But the roots and the plants and the dead things had hold of him. He was stuck. He couldn't get back up, and he couldn't dive any deeper. All he could do was stare at what he was owed until he starved and froze to death."

The girl lifts a hand and points. There, at her feet, where there should be only shoreline, is a pool of murky water. And somewhere deep inside, a light burns. A red light, behind a circular window, in the middle of a black, quiet house.

"I think it's been waiting for me all along." She looks up at last, and her eyebrows, fierce and expressive, draw downward. "What are you doing here?"

"Am I real?"

"Aren't you?"

"I never know. I'm just visiting."

"Me too."

"Whose blood is that, on your hands?"

The girl on the rock shrugs her broad, sharp shoulders. "I don't know yet. We'll find out soon." Her head is tugged downward, the lure of the house beneath the water too much to resist. But then, surprisingly, she does. She turns toward the ocean as though noticing it for the first time. "You can sit with me, if you want."

She sounds tentative. Almost hopeful. She's not as striking as the boy, but she's lovely in a way that triggers a shiver of warmth and longing. If one can get past the sight and scent of so much blood.

At least no one's vomiting tar or killing kittens. It's as good a place as any to spend the night. Dreamers can't be choosers.

CHAPTER FOUR

A Bird on the Hunt

Birdie hasn't slept until dawn since she was ten years old. That was the year she went to work at Nimbus's house and learned that maids live not in tandem with the sun but in weary defiance of it. So when Birdie opens her eyes to a hint of light outside the leaded diamond windowpanes, she panics. This is the worst possible start to her time here.

After the strange woman in charge led them to their rooms last night, Birdie crept out to explore, but there was someone in the hallway. Lingering, silent and anonymous in the dark near the stairs. It unnerved Birdie so much she retreated and tried to rest, but the fear that at any moment the unknown figure would come for her, combined with the idea that somewhere under this same roof Magpie was sleeping, left Birdie shivering for hours.

She's *never* slept alone. Her family all shared the same room, with Birdie and Magpie in a single bed. In the houses where she worked, she was always with at least one other maid, though more often it was three or four of them packed in together. She feels so vulnerable, being alone.

Taking a deep, shuddering breath, Birdie pokes her head out.

The hallway is clear. Whoever was standing sentinel last night is gone. Good. Birdie needs to get out of this room. Despite the windows and the solitude, it feels airless and claustrophobic. It's so narrow that Birdie can touch the far wall with her feet while lying in bed. Her bed, her trunk, and a rickety table with a washbasin on it are all lined up against the wall leading to the door.

At least it's morning now, and Birdie can look for her sister under the guise of getting to work. She washes, pins her chestnut-brown hair into a bun, and dresses. There's nowhere for her to store clothing, so she rearranges her trunk to air out her spare dress and make sure it doesn't wrinkle too badly.

Her packet of drawings is still safe, wrapped in the scarves she brought from their neighbor Mare. Blue for her, green for Magpie. A hopeful gift. One Birdie will do anything to deliver. She places the scarves reverently onto her bed, then runs a finger down the bundle of papers.

The first, a sheet slid under the mysterious locked door as she sat outside it her first night in the minister's house. She'd been weeping quietly, certain she was alone on the abandoned third floor, until the art landed against her feet: a drawing of a dog so absurd it made Birdie laugh. And the last, the final sketch her friend passed to her before Birdie left them behind forever. She takes that one and props it up on the table. It feels lucky, and she needs all the luck she can get.

Her door opens without a sound, and Birdie lets out a sigh of relief that she's still alone. The woman who greeted them last night had been undeniably strange. She called herself the House Wife and drifted ahead of them vacantly before giving them each a key to the stairs and leaving without a good-night or instructions for the morning.

Birdie half suspected the minister had sent word ahead and

the House Wife already knew she was a liar and a thief. But her door isn't locked, no one has caught her yet, and the whole house is waiting. Birdie will do exactly what she should, so she can be free to do what she shouldn't.

That familiar terror of disobedience tugs on her as soon as she thinks about breaking rules. It whispers that she'll cost her family everything, that she'll be thrown out, that she'll lose what little she has. But she's already lost everything. Besides, she's doing *exactly* what she's supposed to. Maybe not as a maid, but as a sister. And as a secret employee of someone other than the house.

Rabbit and Minnow have rooms next to Birdie's, but neither of them is awake yet. They were groggy to the point of delirium last night. The tea the first driver gave them was definitely meant to make them sleep. No one is allowed to know where the House of Quiet is. Including the first driver, who didn't know where the second driver was taking them.

Her secret employer, Dr. Bramble, has been trying to get into the house for years to discover its secrets. The doctor kept telling her he couldn't *guarantee* Magpie would be here, but Birdie's sure her sister is under this roof. Her heart races looking at the line of doors marching orderly down the hallway.

Birdie tries the doorknob of a room near the stairs. It's locked. Pressing her ear to it, she hears nothing inside. No soft breathing, no rustle of bedding. Why lock an empty room? She tries a few others—all locked, all silent. Magpie was so loud at night. She whimpered and snored and ground her teeth with a terrible creaking noise that made Birdie dream of voyages on wooden boats in stormy waters. Birdie misses that sound so much.

There's nothing else she can do here for now. Daytime will reveal whether the rooms are empty or filled with deep sleepers.

The stairway goes up past this floor. Are there more bedrooms above her? The stairs seem to go on forever as she creeps carefully upward to the third floor. But there are no doors or hallways in the cavernous space. It spans the entire footprint of the house, ceiling so low she can touch it. Round windows, the only source of illumination, are set close to the floor instead of at eye level. It makes her feel oddly precarious, like she's standing on a table. The tower above the stairs is hollow; doubtless its twin on the other side is, too.

There's nothing to discover here. Hurrying down the stairwell past the maids' floor, she sees no other exits until she reaches the bottom. The door out is locked. The woman who gave them keys last night told them it would be, but it still makes Birdie nervous. She feels trapped. With shaking hands, she inserts the key she was given, then lets out a breath of relief when it turns easily. She pushes the door open onto the ground floor of the house. She debates leaving it unlocked for her fellow maids, but they have keys, too.

Last night Birdie had to pretend to be sleepy and confused, so she couldn't pay close attention to her surroundings upon entering the building. That was frustrating. Part of her job as a maid is to know the house better than anyone—not just the layout, but the patterns and rhythms of everyone living there. That way, she always knows where she can be and when she can be there. Convenient for spying as well, as the minister found out.

She's in a hallway. To her right is the entrance foyer, and to her left is a fogged-up glass door leading outside. The scent she noticed last night is still here, a little stronger downstairs than it was up. It's like a dog coming in after rolling in cold, wet mud and grass.

Every doorknob on the way to the foyer is locked. The House

Wife might have seemed distracted and vacant, but she doesn't overlook details. She hasn't been cleaning well, though. It perks Birdie up. She's necessary, and she'll prove useful so no one suspects her.

The floor is polished black tile, which means it shows water stains if not cleaned and dried correctly—and constantly. Pale white marks show the pattern of a sloppy mop. Someone had no idea what they were doing. Maybe another maid like Rabbit, working here because of an ability, not because of any actual skill or training.

The walls are paneled and painted a sickly yellow gray, like an egg yolk boiled too long, and lined with paintings that make Birdie's arms preemptively ache. They're in intricately textured gold frames, perfect for catching dust in hard-to-clean places.

Her eyes snag on the images. Children reach up in supplication, grateful and eager smiles on their cherubic faces. And standing over them, almost as though walking on top of them, is the figure of a man. As Birdie trails a finger down each progressive painting, the man's depiction changes from stooped and old to straight-backed and radiant.

The paintings are bad but still aren't quite as upsetting as a portrait of the minister's late wife. She had ice-blue eyes that tracked Birdie wherever she was. Why can't all art be like the drawings her friend made to illustrate her stories, with boldly whimsical ink lines and cheerful characters?

The entrance foyer features a few stiff leather chairs, set up like a sitting room where no one wants to talk to each other. The front door, heavy and imposingly carved with somber children reaching hands upward in supplication, is also locked. Birdie doesn't have a key for that one.

From this central point where the hallways intersect, all Birdie can see are closed doors. Except one, on the opposite end of the house as the stairs. It's cracked open. The scent of fresh bread drifts tantalizingly free.

The kitchen has none of the grandeur of the wide halls with their high, wood-paneled ceilings. The walls are rough, with no plaster or paint covering the planks and the dried mud packed between them. The ceiling slopes downward toward the exterior wall. There's one long table with several chairs and a bench beneath the small, warped windows.

An older woman at the counter looks surprised to see her. She's stout in a way Birdie finds reassuring, with a round face and tired eyes. Her gray hair is tucked into a kerchief, and her sleeves are rolled up to reveal strong forearms covered in flour. Birdie likes cooks. They're the busiest person in any house, but generally pleasant, so long as you make their life easier rather than harder.

Birdie takes a deep breath. Her nose wrinkles in distaste as she gets a whiff of the earthy scent instead of bread. How can a smell be soggy and charred at the same time?

The cook doesn't miss her expression. She points with her chin toward a large stove in the corner.

"I save wood for the ovens," the cook says. "Means we have to burn peat for warmth, though." Next to the stove is a door to a small room. Inside, Birdie sees an unmade bed. So that's where the cook sleeps.

"I'm Birdie," she says.

"Cook," the woman answers. Not a name, just a title. Interesting.

"What do you need?" Birdie assumes she'll be working for the House Wife, but there's no reason not to ingratiate herself to the cook. Want to know if guests are coming, residents are leaving, or someone's ill, pregnant, celebrating, not sleeping well? Watch what's going in and out of the kitchens.

"Any experience cooking or baking?" Cook asks.

"No, but I can follow directions."

Cook stares at her, eyes heavy and sad but distant, like she's not really seeing Birdie at all. Then she blinks and comes back to herself. "Right. That's most of it anyway. Come knead this dough while I get breakfast ready." She demonstrates the technique.

Birdie takes over with far less assured movements. But it's good to have something to do. The wait is agonizing. Magpie could walk in at any moment. Her baby sister, green eyes wide, eyebrows raised, one with a bright white scar through it. That scar is all Birdie would need to recognize her sister even though they've been apart for seven years. Six and half years of that time because Birdie was working in a grand house with no days off to visit her family. Six months of that time because no one could or would tell her where Magpie went after the procedure.

Instead of feeling guilty about the scar being her fault, Birdie holds it like a promise: She marked Magpie, and because of that, she'll be able to find her again. She'll have to be careful when they're reunited not to give anything away. But Birdie just wants to *see* her. To know she's here, and for Magpie to know that Birdie's come for her at last.

Birdie and Cook work in silence as the kitchen fills with morning light. It's odd that Cook hasn't asked about the other two maids. Maids are never allowed to sleep in. Unless . . .

Understanding descends like a rock dropped right into her stomach. Birdie eyes Cook with a new wariness. If the woman isn't annoyed by two new maids being lazy, it's because she knows exactly why they're so sleepy. No wonder she seemed surprised by Birdie's early appearance.

Is Cook the person who was standing at the end of the hallway last night? And why are there no other maids already in the house?

"Right, that's enough." Cook puts the dough into a bowl, covers it, and sets it aside before going back to the stove. The smell of sizzling bacon is almost enough to cover the peat stink. Birdie's stomach audibly growls. Cook lets out a dry laugh, then hands her a day-old hunk of bread. "After breakfast we can have whatever's left. That's how it works now. You understand?"

Birdie makes a show of yawning and nods.

Cook sighs as she pulls out a tray of baked apples. "That's how it works now," she repeats, more to herself than to Birdie.

Birdie wants to ask how it used to work. Before she can, Cook hands her a key ring with one key selected. "Go unlock the bedrooms and then knock once, sharply. Don't open any of the doors, though. Not all the rooms are occupied, but you'll learn which are soon enough. Unlock them all, except the door at the end of the entry hall. Then come right back."

Birdie does as instructed, going up and down the hallways, unlocking and then knocking with her heart in her throat.

The hallways meet like a T, with the foyer in the center, so it's easy enough to know which one Cook told her to avoid. Birdie fights the urge to linger and watch for Magpie to come out. It would be so much easier to greet her quietly, where she can warn her sister not to reveal their connection.

As jittery as on her first morning serving in a big house, Birdie hurries back to the kitchen. Cook has a tray waiting. Instead of the baked apple, poached eggs, bacon, and bread, it has only a bowl of mush drizzled with honey.

"Take this to the bedroom closest to the stairs, on the right side," Cook says. "You might have to spoon-feed."

THE HOUSE OF QUIET 27

Birdie frowns down at the tray. That sounds like nurse work, not maid work. Is everyone in such desperate condition? But Cook shoos her out before she can ask any questions. "Hurry now. If it takes too long, there might not be anything left for you after breakfast."

Birdie rushes out, fully intending to follow instructions, but she slows and then stops. One of the bedroom doors is open. She can hear voices inside.

"What's that front area called? Right inside the door?" Minnow. She's already in the room, talking to one of the residents.

"You mean the foyer?" a girl answers. "I always forget the word for it, too. And I can never remember *wardrobe*, either. I'm forever referring to it as my dress cupboard. It aggravates my mother to no end. Or I should say aggravat*ed*. I suppose it doesn't matter what I call it now, since she can't hear me. But it makes me wonder, if it's a ward for robes, what are the poor robes being treated for?"

Birdie takes a step forward, peeking through the door opening. The girl inside is extremely pretty, probably Birdie's same age, wrapped in a fall-leaf orange silk robe that sets off her honey eyes, brown skin, and shiny black curls. Not Magpie.

When Minnow doesn't respond to the nonsense question, the girl keeps talking. "My name's River."

River. What is someone named River doing here?

"Hurry, we don't have much time. Breakfast is always right after Cook unlocks our doors. Before she claims you, could you help me with something? I want to light my fireplace, but there's no wood. Do you know what this is?"

Birdie dares to get closer. Minnow notices the movement and looks up sharply. Birdie offers a flat smile. "Need help?"

Minnow shakes her head. "Peat briquettes." She turns back to

River, who is seated casually on the floor for a prime view of the fireplace. "You burn them. For heat."

"Really!" River picks up a brick and examines it, incredulous. "I thought it was dried mud."

"It is. But it's peat mud. It lights quickly and smolders even longer. It even burns when it's wet."

"You know," River says, "I kind of like the way it smells."

Minnow raises an eyebrow. "It's all you'll smell soon. How many fires will we need to start this morning?"

Birdie pauses midstep. That's information she wants, too.

"I couldn't say. Maybe the others have figured it out on their own, given how chilly we've been. I doubt it, though. We've all been trained to have no functional value whatsoever."

If everyone on this floor is useless at something as simple as starting a fire, then they must all be wealthy. As lively as River seems, there are dark circles under her eyes and a slump to her shoulders that implies deep exhaustion. Why is she here? Is she alone, or are the rest of the residents her family? It makes no sense.

"How long have you been here?" Minnow asks.

Birdie gives Minnow a sharp glance. Minnow's taking too long and asking too many questions. She's going to get in trouble.

River tucks her feet to the side and leans on an outstretched arm. "Oh, don't worry. You won't catch what we have. It's not even considered a problem by most of the country. Only by people like my parents." She says it breezily, but there's a sadness beneath her words.

Troubled by River's presence but also not wanting to get in trouble herself, Birdie steps out of the doorway as though leaving. But then she pauses to keep listening.

"That's easy enough to light," River says. "I can do that. You won't have to come in every morning to help me. Unless you *want* to."

"I can help however you need," Minnow blurts out.

"In that case, I'd like to go on walks. Outside. Cook hasn't let me, but I'm sure if I had *you* to accompany me, it would be fine."

"We're in the middle of the endless peat bog between north and south. It's dangerous."

The peat bog! That's where they are. Even Birdie knows about the miles and miles of bog splitting their country. The northern section is a violent, backward place. It's a constant drain on resources. Most southern criminals turn their sentences into military-service time, and many families where Magpie and Birdie are from enlist their older children so they can pay for the procedure for a youngest child. A lot of those with abilities are assigned to the military, sent up the coast to manage whatever nonsense is going on in the north.

Birdie's biggest fear used to be that gentle Magpie would be stationed there. Would that be better or worse? Surely if Magpie had been on northern patrols, Birdie could have enlisted alongside her. Not the life she'd envisioned, but still one together.

Troubled and annoyed at the delays, Birdie hurries down the hallway to the assigned door. She knocks, then pushes it open. It's too dim to make out any real details inside.

"Good morning. I have your breakfast." Birdie sets the tray on a table near the door and then throws open the heavy drapes. The bedroom is lush and elaborate, with plush, comfortable chairs and impractically large windows. Families like Birdie's can't afford that much daylight. The fireplace in here would need to be lit around the clock to keep the temperature bearable.

It's as fine a room as any Birdie's ever seen, fit for a minister or lord. Freezing, though. She'll get the fireplace going as soon as she's seen to breakfast. Even as nervous as she is, her maid-trained mind is already lining up tasks.

She grabs the tray and at last turns to the four-poster bed. There's a figure lost in the middle of it, staring with wide, blank eyes. Birdie nearly drops the tray.

She knows that face.

CHAPTER FIVE

A Bird Puzzled

"Nimbus!" Birdie rushes toward her old friend, buzzing with joy at this unexpected reunion. He knows what Magpie means to her. He can help her, and they can—

His expression doesn't change as she gets closer. He remains motionless, his gaze tracking movement somewhere behind her. She looks over her shoulder, confused, but there's nothing there. Something is wrong. Something is really, really wrong.

Why is he *here*? She sits carefully on the edge of his bed and takes one of his hands in hers. Nimbus is the same age as Magpie. He turned thirteen just before Birdie left his house six months ago, but he's still as small and delicate as a child. His brown cheeks are round with health, and his coiled black hair surrounds his head like a halo.

But his eyes, so lively and warm, don't settle on her. It's like Birdie isn't there at all.

"Nimbus?" she prods. He turns his head slowly toward her, like one of the automatons his father collected. Birdie always hated them, animals and clowns and sad children pantomiming life in a creepy, endless cycle. Each costing more than she would make in a lifetime.

"What happened to you?" Birdie whispers. She wants to cry. To rush back out and demand someone tell her what's wrong with Nimbus and why he's in the House of Quiet.

But that's not what a maid would do. She was given work, and she'll do it. Both because she has to be a perfect maid and because she always feels better with a task. Besides, maybe it'll help snap Nimbus out of whatever this is.

She retrieves his breakfast and sets the tray over his lap. Nothing changes in his demeanor. When Birdie takes the spoon and lifts it to his lips, he eats with rote, mechanical movements, sometimes pausing, frozen, for nearly a full minute at a time. Just like one of his father's toys.

Birdie bites the insides of her cheeks to keep from showing how upset she is. Most employers and their families are indifferent to maids—some even cruel—but Nimbus was *always* kind. They were as close to friends as two people in their opposite stations could be. It's because of Nimbus that she knows how to read. In more than one way, it's because of Nimbus that she's here at all.

Nimbus's tutor, Hawthorn, never so much as looked at Birdie, but Nimbus saw her interest and left out all his workbooks so she could learn alongside him. When she found out Magpie's name had come up for the procedure, Nimbus smiled as big as she'd ever seen him and made her promise to come back and tell him what ability Magpie had gotten. He knew how hard Birdie had worked to save up for it, and how much it would change her life. He even hugged her the day her parents sent for her to live with them again, which wasn't something Nimbus had ever done.

But the house Birdie's parents had was too large and too empty, and they wouldn't explain how they could afford it or where Magpie had gone. They looked nearly as empty and lost as Nimbus does now, telling Birdie to leave it alone and be grateful for what they'd received.

Birdie went back to Nimbus's house. But not to celebrate. To beg for an audience with Nimbus's wealthy father, her only connection in the city. To plead for someone, anyone, to help her find out what happened to Magpie and where she was sent.

That was where Hawthorn found her, weeping on the steps after being denied a meeting. And that was how she came to meet Dr. Bramble, an employee of the Ministry of Health and Progress. A man obsessed with getting into the House of Quiet, who set Birdie on this path as his own private spy. He was the one who got her a position in the minister of finance's house. Not even Dr. Bramble could pull enough strings to get her a job in the House of Quiet. It took extorting a minister.

Nimbus is so central to her presence here—he taught her to read, and he introduced her to Hawthorn—but she never thought she'd see him again, much less in the House of Quiet.

After Nimbus eats the last bite with the same lack of energy or attention as the first, Birdie carefully wipes around his mouth.

"I'll come back soon, okay?" It's more a promise to herself than to him; she doesn't think he can hear her.

His room is still cold, though, so she lights the fire. She hopes he doesn't mind the smell. Then she hurries back toward the kitchen, desperate to talk to Cook. Rabbit passes her with a tray of food. This one features the full range of breakfast options, plus a teapot and teacup. Rabbit's eyes are wide with alarm, her trembling arms held straight out in front.

"Use your hip, like you're carrying a heavy laundry basket," Birdie advises.

Rabbit adjusts, then shoots her a grateful smile. "At least with laundry, if I dropped it nothing was going to shatter." She juts her chin toward a room down the hall. "Apparently, we have a spoiled brat who can't be bothered to come to the kitchen for breakfast."

"Careful what you say about them," Birdie cautions. Minnow getting too friendly with a rich girl, and now Rabbit calling an employer a name. Who are these girls?

"I'm only repeating what Cook said in front of everyone else!" Rabbit widens her eyes like she can't believe it, either.

Birdie wonders what the condition of Rabbit's charge will be, and if they're someone from a wealthy family, like Nimbus.

Dr. Bramble was vague when he rubbed his hands together and said things were "shaking loose" at the House of Quiet, presenting an opportunity for Birdie to slip through the cracks and get in.

Maybe what was shaking loose was the old use of the house. The government finally realized it was uncharacteristically generous to take care of afflicted poor children, and they've started taking in wealthy invalids now, too. Maybe Nimbus was in some sort of accident or had a terrible fever. Sometimes those can burn so hot they damage the mind if they don't end up killing you. Mare lost both of her children to a season of fever that swept through Sootcity before Birdie was born.

Still, why use the House of Quiet, out in the middle of nowhere, cloaked in secrecy, and surrounded by a deadly bog? Surely Nimbus would be more comfortable in his own bed with a nurse using abilities to soothe him.

And the room Nimbus is in isn't new. It's lavish enough to belong in a minister's home, but the backside of the drapes was bleached by the sun and there were smoke stains around the fireplace. These rooms have been here for a long time, and Birdie can't imagine anyone from her quarter of Sootcity surrounded by velvet curtains, sleeping in a sea of silk pillows.

If wealthy families have been using the House of Quiet as a way to tuck away ill relatives they're ashamed of—the only explanation that makes sense to Birdie—the locked rooms upstairs must be where the poor people stay. But before Birdie can try to sort through all this new information, she's back in the kitchen.

Cook has barricaded herself beside the oven. Minnow stands near the door with her hands clasped, waiting to be needed. At the table are four teens. Birdie desperately searches their faces. No Magpie.

No Magpie. She wants to sink to the floor in despair. But she can't let herself. There's still a chance. She's about to volunteer to deliver food to the upstairs residents, but a look around kills the last of her hope.

Kitchens really are the best place to learn how a house works. And the food here makes it obvious: There aren't any unaccounted-for residents. No bowls set aside, no plain fare prepared to feed plain kids. Maybe it's going to be made later, but she sees no evidence to give her that hope.

Birdie always knew there was a chance Magpie wouldn't be in the house anymore. A reunion was never going to be as simple as walking through the door. But just getting to the door was so hard and took so long and cost so much, Birdie almost felt she deserved an easy resolution.

She should know by now she doesn't deserve anything, and that nothing will ever be given to her.

Birdie steels her spine and wills tears not to fall. Time to figure out how the house actually works, so she can find out where those who have finished treatments are sent. And to hope—there it is again, that cruel hope—that Dr. Bramble and Hawthorn will keep helping her. They were so interested in Magpie's plight and vowed to help Birdie run away with her sister once they were reunited. Birdie needs to be as useful to them as possible so they'll extend that promise now that it's going to take longer.

Cook messed up, though. There are plates for only three on the table. Birdie fixes one more and sets it in front of the tallest boy. Then she moves next to Cook and leans close. "Can I speak with you?"

"Introductions," a dreamy voice says from the doorway. The woman from last night stands on the threshold of the kitchen, as though there's an invisible line she can't cross. She's tightly buttoned into a red dress with a high collar and a skirt like a bell swishing to the floor. "I am the House Wife. At the table we have Sky, River, Lake—"

"I already know Birdie," Lake, a pale girl of twelve or thirteen in a simple white nightdress, interrupts. She wrinkles her cute, upturned nose.

"I don't believe we've met, miss," Birdie says.

"Why is Birdie back? She went down and never came up again. She *died*," Lake says, eyes tearing up. "Didn't she? She dies, and you scream, and my ears, oh, they hurt and they bleed and I run to the kitchen for a knife to jam into them to make it stop." Lake puts her hands over her ears, turning toward an older boy beside her, the one with the missing place setting. He's a full head higher than the girl even sitting and has the most remarkable eyes Birdie's ever seen, a brilliant cornflower blue. They're trained on her like he's seen a ghost.

Birdie waits, but no one responds to the girl's decidedly upsetting pronouncements. The House Wife continues as though she hasn't heard a word of it. "And in the bedrooms we have Dawn and Nimbus."

Lake looks down at her untouched plate and scowls. "The apples are mushy. I didn't like them." She picks up a fork and begins eating.

River smiles brightly, tossing her thick glossy curls over her shoulder so they don't get in her way while she eats. "Don't listen to Lake. None of us do."

Lake sighs. "You didn't, until it was too late."

"Why are we being introduced to *the help*?" the last teen boy says. He keeps his eyes on the table, shoulders moving up and down with barely repressed fury. River reaches out toward him. He pushes away as though burned, chair clattering backward onto the floor. "Don't touch me!" he screams, voice breaking. "Don't anyone touch me!"

He storms out of the kitchen, carefully twisting so he doesn't brush the House Wife.

"Sky is always that charming," River says lightly, but she looked troubled, watching him leave. "Though we've been together only a short while, we've all learned to treasure our daily sessions of being shouted at for existing in his vicinity."

Lake shrugs. "He's the first to leave."

River pats her hand. "Yes, dear. We can all see that."

"They're going to take the House Wife away," Lake says.

The Cook startles, narrowing her eyes. "What do you mean?"

Lake leans as though listening to someone whisper and nods along to whatever she's hearing.

The remaining boy hasn't stopped staring at Birdie. She resists the urge to fidget under the intensity of those blue eyes. He's the only one unaccounted for so far. One more name left that she hasn't heard. Maybe he's not rich. Maybe his name is Heron, or Turtle, and that means that Magpie could still be here, and—

"You didn't introduce Forest," River says to the House Wife. The House Wife tilts her head, blinking. River at last seems irritated. "He can't introduce himself; we need to do it for him. Your name *is* Forest, right? That's what Lake said. Though he only arrived yesterday and hasn't spoken at all, so how she knows is a mystery."

"Forest," Lake says, voice trembling with fear. Then she blinks and sees Minnow. A scowl replaces her look of terror. "You! You're no help at all with that knife."

Minnow startles. "Do you—do you need help cutting your food?"

Birdie wants to scream. Lake, River, Sky, Forest, Dawn, Nimbus. None of them are from the lower classes. None of them are poor, so none of them have had the procedure. Where are the kids who have?

She needs to find records. Documents. Histories. But even if she finds where Magpie is now, how will she leave this place and get to her? Her whole life has been waiting, and whenever she thinks the waiting is at last over, it gets even worse.

Rabbit rushes into the kitchen, nearly knocking over the House Wife. "Strangest thing," she says, hurrying over to Birdie. Rabbit seems to have only one mode of speaking, and it's *loud*. But her eyes are bright and she's flushed with emotion. "As soon as I opened Dawn's door, I was as sad as I've ever been in my life. Started crying and everything. Look!" She points at her tearstained face. "Maybe I'm more of an empath than we thought!"

Birdie knows all about the different abilities that the procedure can trigger. She collected information like shiny pebbles, daydreaming and wondering which Magpie would get. There were a number of stranger, more unusual abilities, but the one she wanted most for her sister was relatively common: the ability to send her own emotions outward.

Rabbit didn't get better at feeling someone else's emotions overnight. *She was forced to experience someone else's.* Dawn's.

And if Dawn has an ability, that means she's had the procedure. Sky's tantrum suddenly makes sense. Birdie knew a girl whose cousin could tap into other people's feelings and thoughts through touch. She has no idea what River, Forest, Nimbus, or Lake's abilities are, but she's suddenly positive they each have one.

Birdie's *never* heard of someone from a wealthy family having the procedure. It's unfathomable. Did it somehow become a fashionable trend? Was it not enough to have their children perform musical pieces or paint portraits—now they added abilities as parlor tricks, taking spots from families who'd waited for years for an opportunity to put a child through the procedure?

"Who's been moving my knives around?" Cook mutters, then bustles past them and into the pantry.

Birdie seizes her chance and follows. Rabbit and Minnow are right behind her. "I know that boy, Nimbus. His family has more money than everyone in the low quarter of Sootcity combined. Why would he have the procedure? Why would any of them?"

Cook pulls down a sack of flour and stares at it as though it's personally offended her. "That's just it. *None* of them have had it. Not a single one."

CHAPTER SIX

A Bird Listening

"Well, come in and close the door so they don't hear, at least," Cook snaps.

Minnow closes the pantry door and seals them all in the cramped space.

"What do you mean, none of them have had the procedure?" Birdie asks. "You can't have abilities without undergoing the procedure."

Cook looks exhausted. "I don't have any more answers than you do. Just be wary. Lake has no idea where she is and is prone to wandering and telling us we've all already died. River claims to be an empath, but she knows things she shouldn't. She's a liar. Don't listen to her or talk to her." Cook scowls, not feigning concern or affection for any of her charges. "Sky has something with touch. Avoid him, too. Dawn's feelings force themselves into you like an infection. You can rotate who has to deal with her room. I won't go in there. No one knows what's wrong with Nimbus. Just keep your thoughts busy while you work around them."

"What about Forest?" Birdie asks, haunted by those blue eyes. But Minnow asks a question on top of that one, interrupting her.

"Where are the others?" she asks.

Cook's scowl deepens. "What others?"

"The ones that use the bedrooms upstairs. They are bedrooms, aren't they?"

Birdie holds her breath. Maybe Magpie is still here. Maybe Cook lets the poor children wait to eat. Maybe they get only one meal a day. Maybe, maybe . . .

Cook's scowl disappears, smoothed away into a blank expression. "Those rooms are empty now."

Birdie feels the words like a punch to the gut. She gasps for air, trying to feign an appropriate level of interest and act as though she doesn't want to walk into the bog and never come back.

"And where," she says, voice calm despite the storm of despair inside, "do they send the children who *have* had the procedure and need help, if they don't send them here anymore?" She clenches her hands into fists behind her back so they won't betray her by shaking.

Cook shrugs. "They come and go. Less now than they used to, while we care for . . . these ones." She squinches her face like she has a bad taste in her mouth.

"*Where* do they go?" Birdie presses.

Cook raises her hands in a gesture of futility and annoyance. "Do I look like I'm in charge?"

She doesn't. But that doesn't make Birdie any less inclined to strangle her. Cook runs this house; it's obvious. She has to know everything that's going on under the roof, including the drugging of the maids. So she must have more information than she's letting on.

Minnow speaks up, which is probably for the best before Birdie attacks Cook and ruins everything. "We're maids to the residents here, then?"

"Oh no," Rabbit says, wringing her hands. "I've never worked with ladies before. Or gentlemen. I don't know how to be someone's servant, I—"

"You aren't their servants," Cook snaps. "You're here for the *house*. Not them. You understand? The house."

Birdie *doesn't* understand. The other two must not, either, because Cook rubs her forehead like she has a headache. "Our duty is always to the house," she says. "You're to tidy up their rooms and keep the bathrooms and communal spaces clean, but otherwise you help me by keeping them out of my hair. I don't want to see them except at mealtimes. I'd leave them shut in their rooms around the clock, but I was overruled. Make sure you keep the stairs locked, though. Don't want them wandering."

"Who overruled you?" Birdie asks. Whoever did that is actually in charge, and that's who she needs to find.

"What about the woman in the red dress?" Rabbit asks, infuriating Birdie with the interruption. "Whose wife is she?"

"She's not—" Cook starts, then shakes her head. "She's the House Wife. She helps the house. Do whatever she asks without question; otherwise leave her alone. Come directly to *me* with any problems with the residents. Better yet, don't have any problems."

With that, Cook bustles past them back into the kitchen.

Rabbit shrugs and follows. Birdie turns and meets Minnow's eyes for a heartbeat. Minnow is studying her as though trying to figure something out. Birdie doesn't like it.

She makes her expression go flat, erasing herself from her own face. It's a trick she learned a long time ago, taught to her by Cricket, a maid in her first house. "Best get back to work," Birdie says.

Minnow grabs a basket, seemingly at random, and disappears. Birdie didn't hear her get assigned to laundry—or anything, for that matter. But Cook is avoiding Birdie's gaze, so it's clear they're more or less on their own.

Birdie needs space. She needs to think. She needs to scream, but that's not an option. So she takes a bucket, a bottle of vinegar, some soap, and a handful of rags into the bathroom near the room she wasn't supposed to knock on. The tile in here is the same glossy black as the hallways, and she can see every footprint, fingerprint, and water droplet. Oddly, it's not as bad as she'd worried it would be, though. Which means this group hasn't been living here very long, or the previous maid was excellent at her job.

As she scrubs, she stews. Cook has to be wrong. There's no way this group didn't get the procedure. Their families must be lying. But why? Why put their own children through that?

What did River say? *It's not even considered a problem by most of the country. Only by people like my parents.*

River seems unusual. Maybe she got the procedure on her own, as a way of rebelling against her station. But Nimbus wouldn't have done that. And Birdie can't imagine his serious, distant father or his barely functioning mother choosing this for him.

It's a mystery. It's not her mystery, though. It doesn't matter. All she needs to do is find out what happened to the previous patients. Where did they go after treatment? And was Magpie among them?

She needs to talk to the House Wife. But just as Birdie steps out of the bathroom, she sees a flash of Rabbit's red hair and a swirl of the House Wife's red dress disappear into the room she was told not to knock on.

Birdie stomps a foot. It's childish enough to make her feel foolish, which deflates her mood a bit. If she had just stayed in the kitchen, she would have been taken back to help the House Wife instead of Rabbit. Now she's stuck in the bathroom.

Birdie leans against the tiled wall and sighs. She has to be smarter than this. She can't afford to have feelings.

A murmur of voices catches her attention. She leans closer to the wall, pressing her ear against it. The bathroom doesn't share a wall with the House Wife's room. It's River. And . . . Minnow, again.

What is Minnow thinking?

"Did you ask about taking me for walks?" River asks.

"That makes you sound like a prized dog."

Birdie would laugh if she wasn't horrified. How is Minnow so confident, talking to River like that?

"I feel like one sometimes. Though less pampered than I used to be."

"I'll ask; I promise," Minnow says. Then she asks something, too quiet to make out.

River laughs, the sound so bright and loud she could practically be in the bathroom with Birdie. "You thought I was pregnant, didn't you? I saw your eyes go to my stomach when we were talking by the fire. Did you know in the lower quarters of Sootcity, girls can have babies with whomever they want, and no one cares whether they're married or how advantageous the match is? Everyone in the community celebrates every baby and helps take care of each other. Isn't that lovely? And if girls want to be with another girl instead, or boys with boys, or anyone wants to be with no one at all, that's perfectly acceptable. Isn't it the same in the north?"

Birdie frowns. Why are they having this conversation at all? And why is River asking Minnow about the north?

The answer is once again too quiet to hear. If Minnow is going to waste her time talking to the rich girl, she should at least speak up for Birdie's sake.

"Mm," River says. "Anyhow, sorry, you asked me a question. The answer is three years. I was fourteen when it started. But I've only been here for three days. There was a girl here before me, but I never met her. She finished her treatment the day I got here. And the House Wife only treats one person at a time, unfortunately."

"What are all these desks for?" Minnow asks. Desks? Birdie doesn't care about desks. She needs Minnow to ask more specific questions about the House Wife and the treatments.

"For tutoring, eventually. My parents assured me my studies would continue, as though they ever cared about that," River says.

Birdie bites the inside of her cheek. Wouldn't Dr. Bramble and Hawthorn be annoyed, knowing they went to all that work to get Birdie in here when they could have just gotten Hawthorn hired as the house tutor?

"If you've had this . . . condition for three years, why did your parents send you here now?" Minnow asks. She's ignoring Cook's cautions not to speak to River. Birdie's grateful, but also puzzled as to why Minnow is so curious.

"I received a letter from the Ministry of Health and Progress, informing me that I'd be sent here for treatment. Dawn got the same. I haven't gotten Sky to talk to me, Lake makes no sense, and Forest and Nimbus aren't chatty, so I can't say for certain if they were also required to come. Anyhow, it ruined my parents' plan to marry me off as quickly as possible before anyone realized I was defective. But I suppose the House Wife will fix me so I'm acceptable again."

Their conversation continues, but River must have shifted positions, because Birdie mostly just hears the rise and fall of their voices. Until Minnow asks a sharper question.

"No other children here?"

Birdie presses her ear to the wall so hard it hurts.

"No."

She slides down the wall and sits on the floor, legs splayed out with no thought for decorum. At least the open door blocks her from view unless someone looks directly inside. She knew Magpie wasn't here anymore, but every new confirmation hurts.

River's voice gets louder, too. "No one here but us pampered pets, begging for walks and playtime and attention. Isn't this place odd, though? I know what hospitals for the poor look like. No privacy, no comfort. I imagined the House of Quiet would be the same. So why did they have such lovely rooms ready for us? What's upstairs like?"

If Birdie didn't know better, she would swear River was trying to get information out of Minnow. Neither of them is acting the way they ought to. Birdie will have to be careful around them.

"It's boring," Minnow says, walking by, that empty, pointless basket still balanced on her hip. She hasn't been doing anything at all. Just pretending.

Birdie nearly gets up, but a tall figure appears just outside the room Minnow left. Peeping through the crack between the door hinges and the wall, Birdie can make out the lean lines of Forest.

"Oh, hello, Forest," River says. "You're very upsetting. I haven't figured you out yet. At least you're not as bad as Sky. He wants to murder us all, did you know that? No, I suppose not. I'll have to take care of him myself."

With a swish of her robe, River pads by. Who *is* this rich girl? What is going on in this house? And how quickly can Birdie get the information she needs so she can leave it all behind and find her sister?

CHAPTER SEVEN

A Bird Trapped

The more Birdie works, the more she feels like a fist is in her chest, squeezing tighter and tighter.

Magpie isn't here.

Magpie isn't here.

The words repeat in her head like a cruel children's song, taunting her. Everything she did to get here, and she's just another maid in another house.

She doesn't even have her friend to comfort her. After that first night in the minister's house, when she felt so alone and so terrified anticipating what she was there to do, that barred door on the abandoned third floor became her refuge. Where she comes from, people look out for each other and help with what little they can. Whoever was behind that door had drawings, and Birdie had stories, and they traded them back and forth as comfort and companionship until the night Birdie left.

"*Come with me,*" she had whispered, and, as ever, there was no answer. Only a final drawing.

Just as well her friend didn't escape with her. Because Birdie didn't escape at all. She just traded the cage of one grand house for another.

Birdie is so tired and so sad, and that fist keeps squeezing so hard she can barely breathe. She cleans the bathrooms and then goes room to room building fires with the smelly briquettes. Minnow didn't bother. As far as she can tell, Minnow hasn't done anything. And Rabbit hasn't reappeared from the House Wife's room, either.

Birdie knocks on a door because she hasn't learned yet which bedrooms are occupied. She should have done this work while the residents were all at breakfast, anyway. She won't make the same mistake tomorrow.

Tomorrow. It stretches in front of her, vast and relentless and empty.

The door opens. Sky glares down at her, his lip curling in hatred. Birdie dips a curtsy and begins backing away. "Sorry, I'm lighting the fires, I'll—"

"Come in." He steps aside. It surprises her so much that she does as requested.

Sky stays where he is, posture rigid, one hand behind his back. He watches Birdie as she lays the peat briquettes. Nimbus's father never bothered maids, and the minister didn't seem to realize she existed until it was too late, but Birdie's heard enough stories to be wary. She keeps him in view out of the corner of her eye.

Sky begins pushing the door shut, slowly, so it won't make any noise and draw her attention.

Birdie stands. Sky pushes the door harder, but it bounces off a shoe. Forest is looming in the way, but he doesn't look at her. Only at Sky.

"Get out," Sky snaps at him.

Forest doesn't move.

Birdie won't pass up this chance. "Forgot matches, so sorry," she says. She dips another quick curtsy and squeezes out past Forest, who hasn't moved an inch. He's still staring at Sky, eyes narrowed.

Forest's issues with Sky just saved her from something. She doesn't know what, and she doesn't want to find out. And now, on top of everything else, she'll have to avoid Sky while cleaning his room every day and living in the same house. This cursed house. This house where her sister isn't.

Birdie can't take it. That feeling in her chest isn't sadness. It's anger. She's *livid*. She has to release it before someone notices. Her bedroom is too far away, and if she gets caught up there, she'll be accused of shirking her duties. Not that any other maids seem to care about those.

She rushes toward the glass door next to the stairs and finds it unlocked. But instead of being outside, she's in a steamy glass room filled with plants. Birdie flees to the far corner. Tucked between two potted trees, she crouches, wraps her arms around her legs, presses her mouth against her knees, and screams.

She screams and screams until her throat is raw. Six months. Six months, looking for the right material to use against the minister so she could get a recommendation for this position, and Magpie *isn't here*.

Maybe Magpie never came to the House of Quiet at all. Maybe her parents lied about Magpie being taken away. Maybe she died, and they knew it would break Birdie to find out.

If she lets herself believe that, though, she'll sink to the floor and never get up again. No, Magpie's out there, somewhere. Dr. Bramble was confident Magpie had been sent here. This is still the best place to find information on where Magpie ended up after treatment.

Look for the warm places, Magpie says in her memory. It's what Magpie would say on the grayest, coldest days, when the factory smoke choked out the sun and dirty ice crept in under the windows. Magpie could always find the one spot in their tiny apartment that the sun hit just right. The one spot they could curl up together and be comfortable. Birdie's repeated that saying to herself for years. There's always something good to find, in any situation.

The warm place in the minister's house was visiting her friend. Telling them stories through the door and always receiving a drawing slid underneath when it was time to go. She had to leave her friend behind, but she'll always have those memories. Someone who listened when Birdie felt the most scared and alone. Someone she was able to help a little even though no one else in the house seemed to care that they existed.

The warm place in Nimbus's house was Nimbus himself and his generosity. He can be her warm place here, too. Her chance to return the favor of his kindness. If she can do a little good for him while she tries to figure out where Magpie went, she should.

It's what her people do: find ways to ease each other's burdens. Other people's children fed when there's any food to spare. A coin from the neighborhood junk dealer, Mare, when things were most desperate. Factory or laundry shifts picked up when someone was too sick to report themselves.

She knows Nimbus isn't from her neighborhood or even her class, but he's one of them. He has been since the first day he left his workbooks out for her.

So: She'll work, and she'll do what she can for Nimbus, and she'll be a spy in the House of Quiet, looking for the information that will lead her on the next part of her journey to finding Magpie.

She'd hoped this was the destination. It's not. But it's not a dead end. She refuses to let it be.

Feeling better with a plan—and after the scream, another trick Cricket taught her long ago—Birdie checks the perimeter of the greenhouse extension. The glass enclosure has been built right against the exterior wall, and there's a fuzzy layer of green on the rocks thanks to the continuous moisture and warmth. Most of the plants are fruits and vegetables, but there are some that are merely decorative. A cushioned bench hides between bows of dense, spiky green trees.

Birdie pats the pillows. They're at least a couple of years old, the velvet worn down where a procession of bodies sat. More confirmation that rich people have been visiting or staying here long before this new twist of their children needing treatment. Why?

And how is she supposed to snoop and find information while cleaning a house this size with so many residents and so little staff? And why can't she find a door that leads outside? If the front door is always locked, she needs alternatives. Just in case. She pushes on one of the glass panels, wondering if there are hinges she's missed.

"I wouldn't," a voice says from behind her.

Birdie whirls to see Minnow standing in the center of the greenhouse. "Wouldn't what?"

"Try to go outside. It's a peat bog. Impassable, unless you know where you're going. Even then, they're treacherous. One step wrong and you're sunk up to your neck, trapped until you starve to death. Who builds a grand house in the middle of a peat bog?" She tilts her head as though waiting for Birdie to supply an answer.

Birdie shrugs, irritated. "I only build grand houses on the moon. That way I can look down on everyone."

To her surprise, Minnow laughs. It's like a flash of barely glimpsed silver beneath a calm surface, much like her name. Minnow turns to leave, then pauses. "I suppose this means the rumors are true, then."

Birdie's intrigued. "What rumors?"

"That whatever the procedure does is contagious. You haven't heard that? No whispers in Sootcity?"

"That's impossible," Birdie scoffs.

Minnow gestures toward the house. "You really think any of *their* parents paid to have their children's minds pried open like tin cans just to see what might come out?"

"They could have sneaked out. Got it done on their own."

Minnow lifts a doubtful eyebrow and sits on the edge of a planter. Seeing her do that is like the fire bells ringing through the quarter, clanging a warning that something is wrong. Even when Birdie was in here alone, she wouldn't have dreamed of sitting. There's no pretending to be working if you're caught sitting.

"I'll bet that's why they didn't have any maids when we got here," Minnow continues. "They figured it out and left. Probably why they hired Rabbit, too. Can't be infected if she's already had the procedure. Did they tell you anything before you came? Warn you?"

Birdie shakes her head. The risk of infection doesn't matter. She doesn't care about herself. She can't. She can only focus on Magpie, or this will all fall apart.

"Ever heard of anything like this before?" Minnow presses. "We don't have a lot of kids get the procedure where I'm from."

"Families save up for it for years, sometimes lifetimes. If there were another way to gain abilities, if you could be infected just by proximity, everyone I know would be trying to make it happen that way." But what if Minnow's right and none of the residents have gotten the procedure? Birdie can't even begin to grasp the implications.

"What's the procedure like?" Minnow asks.

Birdie frowns. Everyone knows that. Minnow's town must be incredibly small and isolated. And why wouldn't she ask Rabbit, who's actually been through it? The more Birdie is around Minnow, the less sense the other maid makes. Birdie gives the most basic answer she can. "There's a building in the center of Sootcity, between all the other Ministry buildings. Inside is a machine, bigger than this whole house. You save and save and hope and wait, and if you're very lucky, your name comes up and you go inside and get changed forever."

"So it can't happen by accident."

"No, it can't happen by accident."

"Infection, then. Unless you have another explanation."

Birdie shrugs. "I don't. And it's not my job to. Are you leaving? So you don't get infected?"

Minnow shakes her head and sighs. Her eyes drift to the windows, looking for something neither of them can see in the impenetrable landscape of fog. "I can't."

"Neither can I. Let's get back to work."

"Floors first?" Minnow asks.

Birdie waits for Minnow to laugh or indicate she was joking. They can't clean floors during the day when the residents are walking around. It inconveniences them and makes the maids unavoidable. Another thing Minnow should know.

"Bedrooms. Then the kitchen," Birdie says. "And then everything else."

She walks out, hoping against hope that cleaning this place top to bottom will reveal its secrets. But also resolving to keep an extra eye on Minnow. Because Birdie's certain now she's *not* a maid.

CHAPTER EIGHT

A Bird at Work

As soon as Birdie enters another beautiful bedroom with another spoiled rich kid inside, she's overcome with rage again.

All the pain and the injustice and the loss, all the anger she's never been able to feel: It's *everywhere*. It's boiling inside her, screaming that she needs to do something. Anything. Someone needs to hurt because of how badly she hurts, and the red-faced, shouting girl in front of her is the perfect encapsulation of everything that has ever been taken from Birdie. Her childhood, her sister, her future. She's the reason Birdie has nothing.

Minnow balls her hands into fists and steps forward. It's enough to jar Birdie out of her own mindless rage. Minnow's about to do something terrible.

"Enough of that," Birdie snaps. Minnow whirls, ready to turn her anger on Birdie, but Birdie's looking only at Dawn, the final resident and the source of the feelings roiling in Birdie and Minnow.

Dawn is a short, pleasantly rounded girl wearing a frilly pink dress with a matching hair bow, awkwardly placed on a sloppy brown braid. "I know you were all talking about me!" she shouts.

"Everyone talks about me! The only person who ever loved me was my nurse, and she made me like this, so—"

Birdie holds up a hand and cuts her off. "Stop acting like a baby."

The girl gasps. "You can't talk to me like that!"

"I can talk to you any way I wish when you're making us feel like this for no reason."

Minnow staggers backward, trying to physically distance herself from the feelings. At least she's finally clued in to what's happening and Birdie can focus on improving the situation rather than preventing disaster.

Dawn stomps a foot. "I have plenty of reasons! I'm trapped here, and my family abandoned me, and no one likes me, and—"

Birdie takes Dawn's hands. Her voice is quiet, but her words are direct and unflinching. She's never spoken to anyone from the upper classes this way, but it has to be done, and her anger—Dawn's anger—makes her bold. "You've every right to be upset with your circumstances. But you have a bed, and food, and a roof. Which is more than many where I grew up. And even those without would have used what they had to help those around them. Because that's what we do. When we feel trapped and miserable, we don't let it poison us. We *help*. You've been given an amazing gift to do just that, if you decide to use it."

It's like someone pulled a plug. Birdie can feel all the outside anger draining away. But now that she knows the border between her own anger and Dawn's, Birdie realizes just how much is left behind.

Birdie dips a light curtsy, at last able to respond how a maid ought to. "I'm Birdie, and this is Minnow."

"I'm Dawn." The girl is a little sheepish. Birdie feels embarrassment rising and refuses to indulge it.

Birdie smiles. "It's lovely to meet you, Dawn. I'm sorry for how I spoke, but I was angry. I think you understand?" She definitely crossed a line. Cook doesn't seem to care about the kids or how they're treated, but Birdie won't risk losing this position until she knows where Magpie is.

Dawn nods eagerly. "I do understand. It's fine. Thank you for being so nice."

"If it's all right with you, I'm going to clean while Minnow starts your fire. You'll feel better once your room isn't so cold."

Unlike River, Dawn just stands around awkwardly, watching them work instead of learning to do things herself. But it's hard to be annoyed because Birdie's feeling better. Hopeful, even.

Once the fire is crackling in the fireplace, Minnow slips out into the hall without a word. At least the atmosphere is pleasant now. Birdie leaves with a spring in her step that quickly tamps itself down when she sees Minnow waiting with a bored expression in the hallway.

Minnow follows Birdie into the next bedroom. It's empty at the moment, but inhabited. Birdie assumes it's Lake's room, given the absolute chaos of the space. There are random pieces of clothing abandoned in odd places and a washbasin turned upside down in the middle of the floor as though trapping something.

After picking up, Birdie sweeps out the fireplace while Minnow makes the bed.

"You're doing it wrong," Birdie says.

The glare that flickers across Minnow's face makes Birdie glad the other maid doesn't have the same ability as Dawn. "No, I'm not."

"You have to tuck the corners, like so." Birdie pulls back all the bedding and redoes it in a fraction of the time it took Minnow.

"Why?"

Birdie glances at her from the side. "Why?"

"Yes. Why? Why do we have to tuck the corners *like so*?"

"Because we do." Further confirmation. Every maid knows how to properly make a bed and can do it in ruthlessly efficient fashion. Minnow isn't incompetent, but she isn't practiced. She's never been a maid before. And without an ability like Rabbit's, why would she have gotten this position?

"So," Minnow says, "we can't skip tucking the corners, but we're allowed to yell at the residents? That will make working here a lot more pleasant."

Birdie snorts a laugh. "We probably shouldn't make a habit of it." She leans back on her heels and shakes her head. "I couldn't stand how selfish it was. Dawn in there, moping about how terrible she has it. When she can see that Nimbus is—" Her voice cracks.

"You know him," Minnow says. She's too perceptive for Birdie's comfort.

"I used to work in his house." Birdie sniffs to get her emotions back under control and continues. "And with the wages for that specific ability, Dawn would be able to support an entire family. Anyone from my quarter would be *overjoyed* if the procedure resulted in that. I might have taken it a little too personally, though. It's the ability I hoped for with—well, it's a good one."

Birdie shakes her head, trying to clear it. Some of Dawn's eagerness for approval is lingering. She shouldn't say anything to Minnow that isn't strictly necessary.

Minnow shrugs. "Probably would have gotten her shipped north immediately."

Birdie stops mid–pillow fluff. "What?"

"With her ability. You know, they send people who can project emotions to the north for crowd control and interrogation."

Birdie frowns. "*What?* No, they end up working in hospitals. Or with children. That's what all the pamphlets say. Where did you hear that?"

"Just a rumor," Minnow murmurs.

"Who told you that, though? Do a lot of people say it?" If more young people are sent north than Birdie thought, maybe that's where Magpie ended up, after she left the house.

"You're doing that wrong," Minnow says, pointing to the fireplace. She seems happy to be the one correcting Birdie now.

Birdie's stacking the peat briquettes the same way she always has with wood. Minnow clearly relishes the correction as she crouches next to Birdie and edges her out of the way, efficiently arranging the peat and then lighting it.

"I don't understand why Dawn's here," Birdie says, drifting to the window and staring out at the blank white mist softening the deadly landscape around them. "It's not such a terrible ability."

Minnow stands, wiping her hands on her apron. "Because her family thinks it's shameful, so she does, too. Can't have a daughter with the same ability as the *help*."

"No wonder she's so sad and angry."

"Not anymore. You felt how much she likes you now, right? All it took was that nonsense about everyone helping each other."

Birdie frowns, hurt. "That wasn't nonsense. That's what we do in my quarter. Why, what's it like where you're from?"

"It's not like that on the coast," Minnow says, voice flat. "We're too spread apart."

Minnow grabs the remaining scattered clothing, but pauses in the middle of the room, turning in a circle. "What do I do with these? Rabbit should know whether they go in the laundry, but I haven't seen her all day."

Minnow isn't in a position to complain about another maid not pulling her weight, but Birdie decides not to comment. "Just hang them for now. But . . . there's no closet." Birdie glances around the room, puzzled. "No drawers, either. Almost nothing for storing clothes or possessions. These rooms weren't meant for long-term occupation."

Minnow lets out a noncommittal hum. "That's odd, isn't it?"

Birdie sighs. "Everything about this place is odd."

All morning and into the afternoon, Minnow shadows Birdie, watching and imitating her. She might not be a maid, but she's a quick study. Each room is tidied, each fireplace tended to. They avoid the rooms when they're occupied, darting in as soon as the residents leave.

The work is simple enough, but there's so much of it that Birdie barely has time to think. A sickly yellow glow suffuses the house as afternoon lengthens to evening and the sun at last pierces the ever-present fog.

"I'll pop upstairs and make sure everything's good there," Minnow says, darting off before Birdie can tell her upstairs isn't a priority.

It's nearly suppertime, so Birdie heads toward the kitchen to offer to help Cook. She freezes and ducks back behind the hall corner, though. Cook is standing outside the kitchen, grasping Lake by both her arms. Birdie carefully peers around. Cook's back is to her, and Lake isn't tall enough to see over Cook's shoulders.

"What did you mean?"

Lake says nothing. Cook shakes her. Birdie watches in alarm, unsure what, if anything, she should do.

"Tell me what you meant when you said they were going to take the House Wife away soon! Who? When? This is where she belongs, where she's safe."

Lake speaks at last. "Do you still see their faces?"

"Whose faces?" Cook demands, practically shouting.

"The children in the bog."

With an animal moan of despair, Cook shoves Lake aside and slams into the kitchen. Birdie stays where she is, heart racing. Why does everyone in this house have secrets, and why can't any of them be the secrets that Birdie needs revealed?

CHAPTER NINE

Rabbit Awake

Rabbit wakes up.

No, that's not right. Rabbit already woke up today. But now there's an enormous red sun around her, pinning her in place. She doesn't like that sun. She's tired, so tired, and she wants to be back where it's soft and dark again.

Rabbit wakes up. No, that's not right. Rabbit already woke up today. She must have dozed off. She can't do that again. She sits up, trying to look ready to help. The House Wife is in the red sun now, and she might need Rabbit. But she doesn't look like she needs anything. She looks happy, and she smiles at Rabbit, and Rabbit feels happy, too.

Rabbit wakes up. No, that's not right. Rabbit already woke up today. She's sitting with the House Wife in the window seat of a room filled with velvet in every shade of red imaginable. It's nice. Like being in the middle of a human heart. The House Wife hums, soft whooshing noises like the heart is beating around them. She holds Rabbit's hand, absently stroking it as they both gaze out the window at the setting sun, red and terrible on the infinite horizon.

"Thank you for your help today," says the House Wife. They

walk into the hallway together. Everything feels vague. Like Rabbit hasn't slept in days, or has slept *for* days. What has she been doing? She turns and sees the House Wife smiling at her. That's right! She helped the House Wife today. That's what she did. And if the House Wife is telling her thank you, it means she did a good job.

The House Wife is kind, and she doesn't mind that Rabbit fell asleep. Rabbit's sure it'll be their little secret.

The next thing Rabbit knows, everything is loud and strange in the kitchen. She feels like she's underwater, watching it all happen above her. She might be sick. Hopefully no one notices. She can't lose this job. Everyone she loves gave everything for the procedure, and she disappointed them, even if they said it was fine. She won't disappoint them again. She's being paid so well, and it's all going directly to her family.

She did that. Her! Helping everyone.

"Where were you all day?" Birdie whispers. Then she pauses and puts a hand against Rabbit's forehead, frowning. "Are you feeling well?"

Rabbit doesn't know how to answer either question. She giggles, thinking how funny it would be to say she was in the middle of a small red sun, and it feels like the sun is still inside her, burning away. Then she tries to get serious again, tries to remember where, exactly, she was so she can give Birdie an answer. But the second question. Is she feeling well? She's feeling soft and fuzzy and quiet, like the pillows in the House Wife's room.

Rabbit bats away Birdie's hand. "I'm fine. I helped the House Wife."

CHAPTER TEN

An Unquiet Sleep

Cook and a man sit in a meadow. She's nearly unrecognizable. Gone are the lines gouged into her face by time and strain. Her hair is thick and dark, her jawline firm. Between them is a child. Their posture is angled toward her, shielding her, looking only at each other and their girl. Which is important, because all around them on the edges of the meadow, unseen children are crying and screaming and begging for help.

"Would you like cake?" Cook asks, stroking the girl's hair. But Cook's gaze isn't filled with love. It's filled with desperation. "Tell Mum what you want, love. Anything for my little mouse. Anything." Cook keeps whispering *anything* over and over like she's trying to drown out the sound of suffering and terror all around them.

But the cries are inescapable. They threaten to swallow everything, to take over. With a sickening ripping sensation, at last another dream appears. It's not much better. A girl with freckles and a scar like a chalk line through her eyebrow is carried past. She's covering her ears, screaming and incoherent with pain. The

House Wife rushes forward and takes her into her arms, carrying her gently back toward her room.

Lake watches it all happen, curious.

"She has hair like yours," Lake says to the maid Birdie, who is suddenly standing next to the girl. Birdie doesn't answer.

"Are you dead?" Lake asks. "Or are you not even here yet?"

"Lake, honestly." Birdie sets down an armful of sheets and takes Lake's hand. "Let's get you set up with Dawn and Nimbus. I have too much to do today to keep an eye on you. I'm sorry."

"Arrow has a knife." Lake watches as Minnow, covered in blood, walks past them. Right through Birdie.

"If I meet an arrow, I'll be careful," Birdie says.

"You already have." Lake throws her hands in the air, exasperated. "Being stuck makes everyone so *stupid*. It's exhausting."

And then Birdie's gone, as are the walls and the house. It's just a vast and empty bog. But Lake is still there. She sits where she is, contentedly humming to herself. "It's peaceful before everyone gets here," she says, turning and staring, inviting conversation. "Don't you agree?"

It *is* peaceful. So peaceful the dream can't be held on to. Relaxing is always a bad idea.

Back in the shed. *Not the kittens again.* But this time Rabbit sits on the floor, glassy-eyed, petting the stationary creatures. Everything is muted, like the world has been padded with cotton. There's none of the fear or frantic energy of last time. Rabbit doesn't need help.

Does she?

A red circle appears behind her.

No. No no no, not that. *Not that.*

It's brilliant and burning, getting closer and closer. The darkness and the crying were bad, but this is worse. It's so much worse. The red circle will swallow everything. It's not Rabbit's dream. It's not anyone's dream.

A dream without a dreamer. And now it knows someone's here, and it doesn't want to let go. It doesn't want to let any of them go.

CHAPTER ELEVEN

A Bird Observed

Birdie wakes up slowly. Something is different, but she can't quite tell what. The maid next to her is breathing in a deep, even rhythm, no other sounds disturbing the night.

The maid next to her. She's in the House of Quiet, and she sleeps alone here. Birdie freezes and cracks one eye open.

The House Wife looks down at her with a peaceful smile. Birdie sits up, heart racing. How long has the woman been standing there? What is she doing in here?

"Do you need help?" Birdie asks.

The House Wife's smile doesn't shift. It's less an expression of happiness and more one of vacancy. Like Nimbus's mother once her sleepy tea started taking hold. She wasn't present enough to be truly happy.

"It's quiet up here now," the House Wife says.

Birdie waits, but nothing is added. The House Wife just stands there, breathing, for so long Birdie wonders if maybe she didn't really wake up. Maybe this is still a dream. And she very much wants to wake up from it.

At last, the House Wife tilts her head to the side. "Shhh," she cautions, though Birdie hasn't said a word since her question. And then, with a sigh, the House Wife nods. "She needs me." With a whisper of her skirts, she slips out of Birdie's room and into the hallway.

Is Birdie supposed to follow? How long was the House Wife in here, watching her? And is this the first time, or does she come up every night? It must have been her in the hallway, that first night.

Birdie envies the residents downstairs in their locked rooms. They might not be able to get out, but at least no one else can get in without making noise. Birdie climbs out of bed. Either the House Wife is expecting her to follow, in which case Birdie will at last have time with her, or the House Wife isn't, in which case Birdie can snoop with a perfect excuse of already having been awoken.

Though she would dearly love to sleep more. Last night she and Minnow staggered to bed late, having stayed up to finish the deep cleaning of the bathrooms and kitchen that would make maintenance easier. Minnow isn't actually a maid—Birdie's sure of that—but at least the girl knows how to work hard. Unlike Rabbit, who was half-asleep through dinner and then stumbled right up to bed.

Rabbit's going to get in trouble, and Birdie's worried it'll reflect on her, too. But hopefully Birdie will be the House Wife's assistant today. She can't imagine Rabbit was all that effective cleaning whatever's behind that locked door.

Speaking of locked doors. Does Birdie dare risk it? She knows she should rush down to make certain the House Wife isn't expecting her to follow. But this is too good an opportunity to pass up. And surely the House Wife will expect her to take a few minutes to get dressed, not knowing Birdie can get dressed in mere seconds.

Birdie picks one of the doors at random, halfway between her room and the stairs. She crouches in front of it and pulls the simple tools out of the side of her worn leather boot. Lock picking is easy with enough practice; she used to work on her friend's door every night, while she told stories and they sat on the other side, silently listening.

Whenever she got it unlocked, though, her friend would slip another drawing under the door. Always a bottle of poison. A warning that if Birdie broke the unspoken house rule that no one could go into that mysterious room on the third floor, she wouldn't survive. And she had to survive, for Magpie. So Birdie stayed on one side, and her only friend in the world stayed on the other.

But they kept each other company in their isolation, and she got very, very good at picking locks.

This one isn't difficult. With a few deft twists, it clicks open. Birdie pushes the door, heart hammering. But inside is disappointing. Illuminated by the wan moonlight creeping in through a window too narrow to climb out of, there's a cot, not much different than hers. The thin mattress is slightly off-center, like someone stripped it quickly and never came back. Nothing else.

Birdie closes the door, disappointed but not surprised. This isn't where she's going to find information about where Magpie went.

But . . . something nags at her. The bedroom isn't at all like her maid's quarters. She pushes the door open once more. It's an empty bedroom. Empty, but *bad*. Bad in a way that makes her want to step back into the hall and not look closer. Magpie isn't in here, so Birdie doesn't need to know.

She steps inside anyway.

There, scratches where someone would have lain in the bed and dragged their fingers down the wall, over and over. There, metal loops on the bed frame for chains to be run through. Maybe it's just this room, though.

Birdie closes the door and opens the next one. This tiny bedroom—*cell*, Birdie's mind whispers to her—has a poem gouged into the wall next to the bed, the only place someone chained to the frame could reach.

> *I pray for death*
> *Before I wake*
> *That way there's naught*
> *For them to take*

Birdie's hands tremble with horror. This was a hospital. A place of healing. Her tools clink to the floor and she crouches to retrieve them, grateful to look away from that terrible poem. One of the picks has rolled beneath the bed. Birdie's fingers feel marks on the floorboards. Someone's written down here, too. The metal bed frame's legs shriek in protest as she moves them, and Birdie freezes, holding her breath and waiting.

It's so dark she has to press her face almost into the wood to see what's written. There's a date. More than a year ago, so before Magpie would have come here. Beneath it, a list. *Fox, Badger, Turtle.* But then Birdie frowns. Because the next names are *Stone, Hammer, Obsidian, Silver.*

Those are *northern* names. The list goes on and on, more northern names than anything else.

They don't have the procedure in the north. They'd never risk giving it to such a rebellious and violent group. So these can't be the names of children staying in the house for treatment—can they?

Between the northern names and the wealthy children downstairs, Birdie's beginning to wonder if anything she knew about the house and the procedure is correct.

"Magpie," she whispers firmly as a reminder to herself of the only thing that matters. She closes the door without bothering to relock it. No one is using these rooms anyway. Maybe they haven't been used in ages. Or maybe this was briefly used as a detainment space for northern rebels. They hear rumors of them in Sootcity. The occasional explosion, a robbery, a boat of coal sunk so no one can benefit from it. Mindless destruction.

It's not her concern. Birdie tiptoes down the stairs and hurries into the central hallway that runs from the foyer to the House Wife's room. She expects that door to be left open, a light burning beyond it. But the only lights are the dim gas lamps on the wall, barely flickering from when Birdie and Minnow turned them down before going to bed.

Just in case, Birdie tries the House Wife's door. Locked. And she knows better than to pick a lock if she's not certain the room beyond is empty.

Maybe she should have just gone back to sleep. Now she's downstairs, cold and hungry and frustrated. And haunted by what she saw in that room. She can't help whoever wrote those things, but it's not her job to, anyway.

Judging by the marginally softer quality of darkness coming from the greenhouse, it'll be dawn in an hour anyway. Birdie steps into the kitchen. Cook startles, dropping several buns. She eyes them grouchily, then wipes them with her apron. Birdie doesn't bat an eye—why waste good food?—but it's clear Cook isn't used to serving in a big house. Something like that would guarantee she'd never work again.

Another inconsistency. The grand rooms paired with a cook who has none of the skills required for someone catering to that level of wealth and privilege. Birdie wants to ask who used to stay in the bedrooms down here and who stayed in the ones upstairs. Why did the House Wife say they used to be noisy? That detail hits Birdie in a different way now that she's seen what was behind the locked doors. Were those children screaming? Crying? Begging for help?

Maybe they got the help they were begging for. Maybe they were so upset by their overwhelming abilities that they were in constant agony. Maybe they were locked up for their own protection, until they could be treated.

Maybe, maybe.

You're always trying to maybe *the world into a kinder place,* her mother had once said to her on a cold morning in the sleeting rain. A carriage had passed by and splashed them rather than offering to let them hop on. Birdie had consoled herself by listing reasons why it wasn't cruel. Maybe the person inside was sick and being rushed to the doctor. Maybe the driver didn't see them. Maybe it was a minister inside on a very important mission for the good of the country.

There are no maybes. The world isn't kind.

Birdie knows it isn't. If the world were kind, families like hers wouldn't have to save for the procedure, since the government claimed rights to all abilities anyway. If the world were kind, she wouldn't have had to go to work at ten years old and could have been with Magpie on the day she went into that terrible building. If the world were kind, she wouldn't have had to lie and cheat in order to have any hope of finding her sister again. If the world were kind, rooms like the ones she saw upstairs wouldn't exist.

There's no point in wondering about maybes. Birdie needs to put her head down and work. "Would you like me to unlock the doors while you prepare breakfast?" she asks.

Cook's hand immediately goes to the front right pocket of her apron. "No."

At least Birdie knows where the keys are now. Too bad she learned to pick locks, not pockets.

"Why did the previous maids leave?" Birdie asks, thinking of Minnow's suggestion that they fled rather than risk infection.

A look of frustration mingled with—pain?—flickers across Cook's face before she turns away. "Maid. Only one. She knew how to mind her own business; you'd do well to follow her example. Also, there's no need for you to come down before the sun. There's nothing for you to do this early."

Birdie shrugs, pretending she doesn't care about what happened to the maid before her. "Didn't get the floors yesterday. I'll start now." She reaches for one of the dropped buns but hesitates, asking silent permission. Cook gives her a gruff nod, and Birdie shoves it in her mouth before going back out to the hallway to retrieve her supplies from the linen closet she tucked them into.

She pauses, staring at the locked door to the House Wife's room. *Is* she in there, or is she looming over some other sleeping person?

"I have a question," Minnow says.

Birdie startles, practically leaping in the air. She puts a hand over her racing heart. "Where did you come from?"

"The coast," Minnow says with that same flat affect.

"No, I mean, right now. Never mind. What is your question?"

Minnow's enormous round eyes drift casually around them.

"In big houses, are there usually more than one set of stairs? I worked in a much smaller house before."

No, you didn't, Birdie thinks. Why is Minnow lying? Why not tell the truth that she's never been a maid before, like Rabbit? Is she embarrassed, or is there another reason?

Birdie answers the question. "Yes. A grand one for the owners, and hidden ones for the servants."

"And the stairs we use here? Those are the servant stairs? That's why we have to keep them locked?"

Birdie frowns, not paying much attention to the conversation. Her eyes are glued to the House Wife's door. She's getting through it at some point today, but it's agony waiting in the meantime.

"They're much wider than most servant stairs," Birdie says. "But it's not the same as a manor. This isn't a real residence."

"What do you mean?"

"No storage. The bedrooms don't have closets. They aren't meant for long stays. Don't forget the seams of the foyer chairs when you clean them; dust can gather there."

Birdie's hoping that their strange encounter earlier will lead to the House Wife choosing her today. But Birdie can't leave anything to chance. The surest option is to go up and make sure Rabbit doesn't appear at breakfast. Birdie can lock a door as easily as she can unlock it. No one would hear Rabbit's cries for help, and Birdie could rescue her at lunch *after* she'd claimed her place working in the House Wife's room. Given the layout, that door leads to the entire back end of the house. It must be where they treat the afflicted. Which will also be where they keep their records. After all, this is an official part of the Ministry of Health and Progress, and they keep records on everything.

Even though Birdie knows guaranteeing Rabbit won't be

available is the best idea, she feels sick just imagining doing that to another maid. Maids protect each other. They step in to cover when someone needs help, because they all know what it costs to lose a position.

She's not like her mother. She knows most of the world isn't kind, but she also knows kindness is a choice. It's one she always tries to make. But can she afford to make it here?

CHAPTER TWELVE

A Bird Rejected

"So," Minnow says, missing the obvious cues that Birdie isn't interested in chatting, "why are there so many rooms upstairs? Were they for more servants, or for kids affected by the procedure? Was it that common to have problems? Do you know anyone sent here?"

Birdie is irritated at the constant interruptions. "Why are you asking me?"

"You're from the—from Sootcity," Minnow says, stumbling a bit on her words. "I assume you know more people who have had the procedure than I do."

"I've been working. I've barely been home in six years." Just the one time, breathless with excitement because Magpie's procedure had finally happened. She burst through the door only to find her apartment empty and a new address left with Mare. Mare had given Birdie the two knit scarves and kissed her cheeks, crying with happiness for their good fortune.

But the new address was a house too big for them to possibly afford even after the procedure, holding only two hollow-eyed, silent parents who refused to tell her what had happened to Magpie.

Not Birdie's home. *Never* Birdie's home.

Birdie lugs the bucket of water and bottles of vinegar into the foyer and measures out what she needs.

Minnow sits on one of the stiff leather chairs, tapping her fingers on the arm of it. Again with the sitting. "Don't you wonder, though—"

"Why you aren't helping? Yes, I do wonder that."

Minnow smiles, genuinely delighted by Birdie's snark, and retrieves a mop. But then she picks up right where she left off. "If rich kids needing treatment is a new development . . . why are there so many nice bedrooms down here?"

Birdie dips a rag into the mixture, exasperated, because of *course* she's wondered that. "Doctors, attending to patients. Visiting ministers, checking up on the house. Wealthy donors, wanting to be shocked and horrified and entertained by suffering before going back to their own comfortable lives." She could see Nimbus's mother doing that, at least until her own son was one of the suffering. "I don't know, Minnow, and it's not our job to know."

Minnow nods, lips pursed. "Hmm. But back to the staircases. You said the servant staircases were hidden. Ours isn't hidden, is it? It's just behind a door. Is that what you meant?"

"No, that's not what I meant," Birdie snaps. She's running out of time to decide whether or not to go up and lock Rabbit in. "Servant passages are hidden behind things like wall panels. But this isn't a normal house. There's no reason for a hidden staircase."

"No reason at all," Minnow says, and at last there's a hint of a smile on her inscrutable face. "Thanks, Birdie." Then she leans the mop against the wall and walks away toward the kitchen.

Birdie doesn't have a headache, but she feels like she will by the end of the day. With one last look at the House Wife's door, Birdie gives up on her plot to trap Rabbit. There would be no way to explain how Rabbit's room got locked when none of them have those keys.

That's what Birdie tells herself, at least. She does a quick mop of the foyer floors. The hallways will have to wait until after bedtime tonight; there's just not enough time. Especially without help. Plus, this keeps her in full view of the House Wife's room for when she comes out. Unfortunately, Cook beats the House Wife. "Doors," she calls, holding an arm out of the kitchen door with the keys dangling from it. Why can't Minnow do this?

Trying not to show how annoyed she is, Birdie takes the keys and does the unlock-and-knock round, same as the day before. She doesn't knock on Nimbus's door, merely unlocks it as quietly as she can, hoping abrupt noises don't scare him.

When she takes the keys back, Cook is still working on the breakfast trays for Nimbus and Dawn. Birdie wants to be back in the hallway, but the House Wife came into the kitchen during breakfast yesterday, so it makes sense she will again today. Birdie waits, eyes glued to the door.

Sky walks in first. What will he do after whatever happened—or didn't happen, thanks to Forest—in his room yesterday? At least there are other people here.

His glance ricochets off her like he can't physically stand to look at her. But Sky doesn't look angry. He looks ill. He gives her a wide berth, scooting around the perimeter of the kitchen before taking the farthest seat from anyone.

River and Forest come in next, River chatting happily and Forest saying nothing. Birdie avoids looking at him, afraid she'll be pinned in place by those remarkable blue eyes again. Getting too familiar is dangerous. Maids who view employers as friends or even family always end up hurt. She made that mistake with Nimbus, assuming his kindness would be shared by his parents. What would she have done if Hawthorn hadn't found her on the steps of their house that day?

It's nearly impossible not to notice how handsome Forest is, though. She wants to look at him in a way that surprises her. But it's the same as art hanging on walls: not there for her to enjoy. Her eyes stick firmly to their safe view of the hall.

"Who moved the door?" Lake shouts angrily as she walks in, rubbing her hip. She glances at Birdie, and her brows draw even lower. But then she turns her head sharply to the left, toward the pantry. "No," she whimpers. "No, please, don't let them take you down there. Don't." Lake's face drains of color as she tracks *nothing* across the kitchen and through the door to the house. "They never listen." Tears begin rolling down her face.

River stands and guides Lake to sit next to her. She leans close and talks softly, but it's not clear whether Lake can even hear her. The mood in the kitchen is as clammy as the air outside the windows.

"These are ready," Cook says, gesturing to the trays for Dawn and Nimbus. Birdie desperately wants to volunteer to be the one to help Nimbus. Both because she's worried about him and to get out of this gloomy space. But she can't afford to miss the House Wife's appearance.

"I'll take them," Minnow volunteers cheerily, grabbing the trays and leaving. Once again Cook has miscounted place settings for the table, so Birdie adds one.

Rabbit stumbles in a few minutes later. Birdie tries not to show her disappointment. Or her annoyance when, rather than helping clear plates as everyone finishes their food, Rabbit just leans heavily against the counter. Her gaze is glassy. Maybe she's actually sick.

"Go back upstairs," Birdie whispers. "I'll cover for you."

Rabbit turns and blinks slowly at her. "Why?"

"Because you're going to get yourself in trouble!"

A dreamy smile spreads like a spill across Rabbit's face. "No, I'm not. She said I did such a good job. That I was the most help."

That can't be right. Before Birdie can press for more details, the House Wife appears in the doorway to the kitchen. Her expression isn't severe so much as it's *empty*. Her ornate dress reminds Birdie of drapes, or bed-curtains. The House Wife feels like a furnishing, not a person. Birdie can't explain it better than that. Maybe she used to be a maid or a nanny. Being physically in a room without having any presence is a valuable skill. But then why would they put her in charge of treatments?

Another odd thing: The House Wife was wearing that same dress in Birdie's room. Did she get ready for the day long before the sun came up, or did she never go to bed at all?

The House Wife has that strange look on her face again, like she's listening to something Birdie can't hear. "Sky," she says at last, her voice as soft as if she's talking to herself. "You're very noisy today."

Birdie looks over in surprise and meets River's equally puzzled expression. Sky hasn't said a word since he got in the kitchen.

"We'll start your treatment now," the House Wife says.

Sky stands, his expression simultaneously hopeful and angry. "Fine," he says.

Of course it would be the last person Birdie wants to be in confined spaces with. But hopefully the presence of the House Wife will prevent him from doing anything bad.

"Do you want breakfast?" Cook asks, her voice softer and more tentative than Birdie knew it could sound.

"Come along, Rabbit," the House Wife says, as though she didn't hear Cook's question.

Birdie steps forward, blocking Rabbit from view. "She's not feeling well. I'll assist you today."

"No!" Sky edges next to the House Wife like he's trying to hide. "No, I can't be alone with her; I *can't*."

Birdie risks a glance at him. He's not looking at her, though. He's looking at the House Wife, desperation contorting his features from haughty to surprisingly young and frightened. What happened between Sky and Forest yesterday? Did Birdie read that whole situation wrong? Maybe Sky wasn't trying to trap her in his room alone with him at all.

The House Wife waves a slim, pale hand through the air. Her skin is nearly translucent, no evidence the sun has touched her in years. "Rabbit," she says, then crooks a finger. As though connected to the House Wife by an invisible line, Rabbit's feet stutter forward. She follows the House Wife and Sky out of the kitchen.

Sky managed to hurt Birdie after all. He kept her from getting into the rest of the house. Birdie turns toward Cook to plead her case, hoping against hope that Cook will intervene, but Cook's on the verge of tears. The older woman turns and stomps into the pantry.

It's all Birdie can do not to scream in frustration. *She* should be the one with the House Wife. Rabbit is clearly sick or useless or—oh no. Rabbit's been drinking. That explains the lack of balance, the pallor, the sleepiness. She must have hidden spirits in her trunk.

If that's the case, she'll be gone as soon as the House Wife or

Cook realizes. Hopefully it's soon enough for Birdie's needs. Then she'll just have to deal with Sky.

There's a feeling in her chest, though. It takes Birdie a moment to figure out what it is. It's not just frustration over this missed chance. She's . . . *jealous* of Rabbit. Being a maid is the only thing Birdie's good at, the only reason she's ever had a place in the world. Rabbit has no idea what she's doing, and yet she's getting opportunities just because she was lucky enough to have the procedure. She's not a good maid *or* a good empath, and she's still more valuable than Birdie.

It's why so many families sacrifice everything and risk the rare but possible catastrophic results to get their children abilities. Otherwise, there's no hope for any of them to do more than merely survive.

Minnow pops back into the kitchen, setting the trays on the counter next to the dishes. "Dawn's in a better mood," she reports to Birdie. "And I got Nimbus to eat almost all his food. I'll clean the top floors today; been a while since they've seen a broom. Then I'll do the dishes. Is that all right with you?"

"Why are you asking my permission? I'm not in charge."

Minnow shrugs. "Who is? Near as I can tell, we're on our own. I'm only asking you because it leaves you down here with all the spoiled monsters."

"It's fine." If Birdie's down here, that's more opportunities to see the House Wife or get through that door.

"Golden! See you at lunch."

Golden? Before Birdie can ask what that means, Minnow darts away. She was right to leave. Today feels much worse than yesterday. Yesterday Birdie still had hope—hope that she might find Magpie, or at least find easy answers. Today she has none of that.

The residents are bored and restless, as well. Dawn isn't angry anymore, but there's a fog of sullen energy in her room. It's a struggle to do anything in there. Sky's thankfully empty room is a mess of clothes and bedding that takes too long to sort through. No one has said anything about laundry; Birdie adds it to her list. Forest's room is completely tidied. If anything, it's cleaner than Birdie left it yesterday.

River's room isn't messy, but she chatters at Birdie the whole time Birdie's working, then follows Birdie out, still asking questions. Where Birdie's from, what it's like, whether she knows where Minnow's from, if they were friends before they came to the house, on and on.

Birdie does her best to answer without actually answering, heading straight to Nimbus's room in the hopes that River will leave her alone. Doesn't she know she shouldn't talk to maids?

Unfortunately, River comes in, too. But at least she stops talking. Instead, she sits on the edge of Nimbus's bed and takes his hand, stroking it gently. It softens Birdie a bit.

"I never find Nimbus, you know," River says, frowning at the boy. "I've looked, ever since he arrived. It's like—it's like he's not here anymore."

"What do you mean, you've looked for him?" Birdie asks, intrigued.

"*Now* you decide to listen to me." River squinches up her nose, then grins mischievously. "Even my family doesn't know what I can do. I worked very hard to make my ability alarming but still mysterious enough that they had to send me away. I thought it would be to our country estate. All my grand plans to dashingly rescue myself from my own window in the middle of the night, ruined when they sent me here instead. Oh, well. Still better than facing betrothal to the minister of defense. He's in his *thirties*, Birdie. Can you imagine?"

"I—no?"

"Exactly. It's too wretched to think of. But the truth is, my ability isn't terribly clever. *I* am, though. I made it seem threatening. After all, what good minister of defense wants a wife who can read his thoughts?"

Birdie opens her mouth to ask if it's true, then, that River can read thoughts. The way she phrased it makes it unclear. But before she can ask, River answers herself.

"Trick question! There *are* no good ministers of defense. But the moral of the story is that I didn't end up in the House of Quiet on purpose, but I still want to be helpful. If you think of anything you need, or if you see some way to break through to Nimbus, please let me know. Or if Minnow needs any help." River looks down, idly picking at the gold thread woven through the dark blue coverlet on Nimbus's bed. "Tell her that, would you?"

Birdie nods, then pauses. "Actually, you can help me with something. Do you know exactly how many people are in the house?"

"Do you think there's anyone you haven't already met?" River narrows her eyes.

Birdie tries not to look crestfallen. Another silly *maybe*, tormenting her. Maybe Magpie is still here, somehow, hidden in the back where Birdie hasn't been allowed. There's got to be enough space there for more than one person.

Birdie shrugs and turns it into a curtsy. "Just trying to learn the house so I can best serve everyone here."

Birdie steps into the hall, leaving River and Nimbus. Her stomach hurts, and her heart aches. She misses her secret friend.

Sitting outside their door, telling them stories. The hiss of a drawing being slid through to her. Feeling a little less alone in the world. She left her poor friend locked away on the empty third floor of the minister's country manor, and for what?

Half in tears, Birdie rushes to the greenhouse, needing a few moments alone to gather herself. Besides, if Rabbit can be drunk and Minnow can run off to do nothing upstairs, Birdie can sit during the day. She weaves through the reaching plants, ducking under branches and fronds, and then—

Forest is on the bench. Her impulse is to hide and avoid disturbing him. But he shifts, making it clear he's aware of her. Now she has to pretend she was in here for an approved, necessary purpose. As she walks past Forest like she's on her way to do something important at the far end of the greenhouse, he holds out a tin full of crystallized-honey treats.

Birdie pauses, dragging her gaze off the floor to his face. Large, deep-set, remarkable eyes over a nose she can describe only as innocent. It's at odds with his decidedly manly cheekbones and jawline. And full lips. Very full lips.

Oh *no*. She doesn't know what Forest's ability is, either. "Can you read my mind?" Birdie demands.

He shakes his head, holding back a smile.

That's a relief, at least. "Do you ever talk?"

He shakes his head again, smile fading like fog burned away by the sun.

Well, at least if he's lying and he *can* read her mind, he's not going to tell anyone what he finds there.

He scoots, making room for her on the bench. Birdie shouldn't. But she's so sad and lonely and frustrated. She doesn't want to be a maid right now. She just wants to be a girl, sitting on a bench next to a boy, eating something sweet.

Might as well go swimming when it rains, as they say in her quarter. Birdie sits and takes a piece of candy. It feels even more rebellious than breaking into the minister's office and stealing confidential letters from his desk. The burst of sweetness on her tongue is a simple, pure delight the likes of which she hasn't had since she lost Magpie.

Birdie tries not to smile at how stupid she's being, but every time she glances at Forest, he's glancing at her. Like they really are just a boy and a girl, sitting on a bench, eating candy. Like it doesn't threaten Birdie's entire world.

The door to the greenhouse bursts open. Birdie jolts up at the noise, terrified of being caught.

"Birdie! Are you in here?" It's River.

"What is it?" Birdie calls, rushing to the door.

River gestures to the hallway. "Something's wrong with Nimbus."

Chapter Thirteen

A Message Released

Words are scrawled onto a piece of paper as thin as onion skin.
Sky Forest River Dawn Nimbus Lake Cook (?) House Wife (?) Maids no one else

Thin paper into thin tube, tied onto thin pigeon leg. With a kiss on a feathered head for luck, the message is released from the tower window, off in a clatter of wings. At least one thing is escaping the House of Quiet today.

CHAPTER FOURTEEN

A River Diverted

River's pacing in front of the door to the stairs, waiting. Minnow looks surprised to see her when she finally unlocks the stairway and steps out. It's baffling how maids assume no one is ever watching them. The maids were the same at her house, getting up to more mischief than anyone, all under the guise of being invisible. She always envied them that. River's been watched her entire life, but made to know it.

"It's Nimbus," River says, even though Minnow didn't ask anything. "He started hyperventilating, like something was upsetting him. He was so sad and scared, and there was nothing I could do. I couldn't help him." River angrily wipes away the tears threatening to spill. It's not fair, being powerless. She's seen how Birdie looks at her, how Minnow responds to her. She knows they think that privilege is the same as power. But for girls in families like hers, it never is. "I could really use that walk outside right now. I have to get out of this house."

"Sorry," Minnow says. "I have to scrub the bathtubs."

River narrows her eyes. She and Minnow are the same height,

but she tilts her chin up so it gives the impression that she's looking down on the other girl.

She might not like people from her station in life, but she knows how to be one. "Scrub them until they're *golden*?"

Minnow freezes. River watches as a cascade of emotions flow over the other girl's face upon hearing her own casual usage of northern slang thrown back at her. But after a heartbeat, Minnow raises a single eyebrow, just as imperious as River. "You're not using 'golden' correctly."

River cracks. She likes Minnow so much. She knows Minnow is a liar and is vaguely afraid of her, but she can't help it. The fact that Minnow's eyes want to swallow her whole and Minnow's lips look as soft as a lie-in on cold mornings, well. River has never claimed to be immune to beautiful girls. And she's never met someone like Minnow, who sparked something deep inside her from the moment they first spoke. "You'll have to teach me the proper usage, then. On our walk. Outside."

River stomps ahead of Minnow to make it clear she'll brook no argument, but steps quietly once they get closer to the kitchen. "If we're lucky," she whispers, "we won't even have to ask permission."

Sure enough, in the kitchen they're greeted with snores. Cook is passed out at the table. Just as River was hoping. Cook was already hitting a bottle during breakfast. River knows the scents of all the main spirits, thanks to her father and his friends. Cook's spirit of choice is both cheap and potent.

"Keys," Minnow whispers, pointing to Cook's apron. Apparently Minnow isn't opposed to going outside after all.

River beams at her, shakes her head, and walks into the pantry. At the far end of the pantry, where it's too dim to see much of anything, there's a narrow wall with bare shelves. River reaches beneath one, then another, searching with her fingers.

THE HOUSE OF QUIET

"Yes!" she hisses as the pantry wall swings open into the dirty cotton fog outside.

Minnow follows her, carefully checking the latch and the other side of the door to make certain they won't be locked out. Clever girl. "How did you know that door was there?" she asks.

"If you haven't noticed, there's absolutely nothing for me to do in this wretched house. I've had to make my own entertainment. My first day here, I wanted to steal eggs."

Minnow frowns. "Why? Weren't they feeding you yet?"

"They were for hiding in Sky's room. So they'd rot and make him miserable with the stench. I knew him before. He was bad; now he's worse. Be careful. Don't ever be in a room alone with him."

"I can handle myself," Minnow says with such casual confidence that River knows it's true. Intriguing.

"Anyhow, there I was, lurking, waiting for Cook to go into her bedroom. She stayed in the pantry so long I worried she'd died. When I peeked in to check, though, it was empty. Thus, there had to be a door."

River walks briskly around the side of the house. The wet, heavy air is cold and refreshing. She doesn't mind the peat bog scent. It's better out here where it belongs than trapped and burning inside.

"In your boredom," Minnow says, hands clasped behind her back, tone absurdly innocent, "have you discovered a second staircase in the house?"

River shakes her head. "I haven't even made it onto the stairs you use. Not for lack of trying. Why?"

"Birdie says sometimes big houses have secret staircases. It sounded exciting."

Minnow's lying. It's thrilling, not understanding who Minnow is, why she says the things she does, what she's here for. Everything about her is diverting and distracting and delicious. "Mm," River says with her most dazzling smile, the smile that could fool any leering older man into thinking she believed everything he said. "An exciting staircase! I'll let you know if I stumble upon one."

"You did already find a secret door," Minnow points out, and River feels a rush of triumph for having impressed Minnow.

"I did." River tips her head back and lifts her face, searching for the sun. It's a doomed attempt. Full light rarely breaks free of the oppressive gray shroud clinging to the earth here. She steps toward the landscape, wanting to take a proper walk for the first time in what feels like forever.

"Careful!" Minnow snaps. "Peat bogs are dangerous. Plants and even trees grow on top of the water. You'll fall right through what looks like solid ground. Stuck at best, drowned at worst."

River eyes the ground around them with new suspicion. The house is like her station in life. A beautiful trap. "How can you tell what's bog and what's not?"

"With practice. And even then, not always. But judging from the smell, we're completely surrounded."

"It's nice, though, I think. The smell." River breathes in as deeply as she can. "It's living, if that makes sense."

"It's mostly decay," Minnow says with a contrary frown.

"Exactly. Life is mostly decay. But with little spots of beauty on the way to the grave making it all worthwhile." River bends down and plucks a tiny purple flower, twirling it between her fingers.

"Are all rich girls like you?" Minnow asks, exasperated.

"According to my mother, I'm the single worst daughter ever to curse a womb, which I think means I'm exceptional."

Minnow snorts a laugh, and River feels another rush of triumph. She wants to break through Minnow's playacting as a maid and get to know the real girl. But Minnow is distracted. She's stomping on the ground with a frown on her face, then taking a few steps and stomping again.

"New dance?" River asks.

"Someone found the one solid foundation in the middle of this infinite slog and built a house on it."

"Impossible to get to, impossible to leave. Did they drug you on the way here, too?"

Minnow's alarmed expression makes it clear they did, but she wasn't expecting it to have happened to River, too. River knows sleep. She's an expert at sleeping. And she knows when her sleep isn't natural.

Minnow changes the subject. "How do you know northern slang?"

River perches on one of the pieces of jutting rock in front of the house. Her slippers are soggy, and the hem of her jewel-green dressing robe is dark with moisture, but she doesn't mind. "That's an interesting story. I was in the process of being courted by the minister of defense."

Minnow tenses. Because she knows him, or because she hates the idea of River being married? River hopes the latter.

"He is," River says, "a man with all the charm and allure of a particularly aggressive foot fungus."

Minnow chokes on another laugh.

River continues her story in an airy tone to belie the horror of it all. "On one of my father's stays at the minister's estate, I was dragged along to remind the minister how beautiful and desirably young I am—men like the minister simply abhor a woman with experience or wisdom, as both are too close to power for their tastes. I was bored. A constant theme in my life. While exploring, I discovered several northerners."

"Don't you mean boggers?" Minnow asks, an edge to her voice

as she uses the slur thrown at northerners. Is the edge because Minnow hates the term, or because she hates northerners? River hopes the former; otherwise she's disappointed.

"I don't use that word. Anyhow, they were being held in a hidden outbuilding on the grounds. I visited whenever I could slip away and talk with them. But toward the end of my stay, one of the guards died in his sleep. The prisoners all escaped. I was shocked—*shocked!*—to hear of it. A minister of defense who couldn't even defend his own estate. I informed my father that I could never marry someone so incompetent at their job."

River looks up at the house to hide her feelings. She saw what happened on that estate. Torture. Death. And River, powerless. Until she wasn't.

"What's interesting to me, though," River says, "is Minnow is a southern coastal name. So how do you know northern slang?" She means to push more, but they've come around the side of the house to the front at last. River never got a good look at it, drugged as she was.

She freezes in horror.

The house is grand and beautiful, designed to look more like a house of worship than one of healing. The imposing front door, the decorative windows, the towers.

But that's not what River can't look away from.

Stone angels stand sentry beneath the top floor, looking not up but down. Their wings draw closed, as though to shield themselves from what they see. And in the dead center, guarded by those terrible angels with black water stains weeping from their eyes, there's an enormous red window. It's perfectly round, like the sun seen through a bloody haze.

River knows that window. A pit forms in her stomach, and

she's falling. Into the dread, into the window, into that burning red circle.

Minnow points upward. "Have you been in that room? With the big red window?"

River wipes the cold sweat beading on her forehead. "I told you I haven't made it onto the stairs," she snaps. She turns and looks out at the blank landscape. It's just a window. It's the same as any other window in the house. But having it at her back isn't any better. She feels like it's watching her, waiting. Knowing it's been above her this whole time makes her sick.

Minnow steps around so she's blocking River's line of sight. And so she can watch River's reaction to whatever she's going to say next. "What's your ability?"

River flashes a practiced, coquettish smile. "Why, Minnow. Haven't you figured it out yet?" She takes a step closer. Too close, her face right in front of Minnow's. The alarm on the other girl's face isn't because River's closer than she wants her to be. It's because River's *exactly* as close as Minnow wants her to be.

River smiles and drops her voice to a low whisper. "I can make anyone fall in love with me."

Minnow leans in, their lips a heartbeat apart. River's breath catches; she wants this. She wants this more than she's ever wanted anything.

"Tell me," Minnow whispers, "why you're afraid of that window."

River flinches, then turns and stalks back toward the secret kitchen door. "Better hurry before Cook wakes up and realizes we're gone." But the truth is, she can't tell Minnow why she's so afraid of that window, because she has no idea. All she knows is that she has to do everything possible to avoid wherever that window is. If she doesn't, she's quite certain she'll die.

CHAPTER FIFTEEN

A Bird Conflicted

Nimbus isn't breathing as fast as he was, but he's still wide-eyed, fingers clenched so tightly Birdie's worried he'll hurt himself.

"I'm here; it's okay." Birdie hums softly, sitting shoulder to shoulder next to him on the bed. She wants to hold him like a child, but he never liked hugs before, and she doesn't know if he wants to be touched now. She *can't* know.

Was this what Magpie was like? Did anyone try to comfort her?

There's a soft knock on the half-open door. Birdie stands quickly, not wanting to get in trouble for being too familiar with a resident. "Yes? What do you need?"

Forest leans inside. He shakes his head. She's not sure if he means he doesn't need anything, or just communicating that she shouldn't worry. There's a gentle reassurance in his expression, though. He's not asking her for anything. He's here to help.

He steps inside, trailed by Dawn. Forest points to the girl, then points to Nimbus.

Of course! Birdie would never dare ask anything of someone of Dawn's station, but Forest did. Or, at least, he brought Dawn here so that Birdie could explain things. She nods gratefully at him. Relief softens the sharp line of his shoulders. He offers a small smile of such genuine hope and happiness it almost hurts her to see.

What has his life been like, that being able to do a little good is this important to him?

A deep confusion settles over her. She turns her attention to Dawn, the source of the feeling.

"Oh, Dawn." Birdie rushes to her and puts an arm around her shoulders. Dawn, she's noticed, very much likes physical contact. Her attempt at a braid is even worse today. Birdie swiftly undoes it and plaits it in a neat trail down Dawn's back.

Dawn runs her fingers down it, beaming. "Thank you," she says, the words a little rusty and shy like they haven't been used often.

"You're welcome. I'll teach you how to do it yourself, if you'd like."

Dawn nods eagerly, and Birdie keeps talking. "I'm so glad you're here. You're exactly who we need."

"Really?" Dawn asks.

Birdie suspects she's never been "needed" in her entire life. According to River's chatter earlier, Dawn's the sixth daughter in a wealthy family. The very definition of superfluous. She's probably been made to feel like a burdensome afterthought her whole life. Worse than a burden, after she was infected with an ability.

But now there's a growing sense of excitement in the room. Happiness, even.

"Nimbus needs help," Birdie says.

Silent tears stream down Nimbus's face, his breath coming in panicked, shallow gasps. Like his body is doing it without any conscious thought. It reminds Birdie of an injured mouse they found once. Magpie sat and cried for hours. But Nimbus isn't dying, and this time there's something they can do to help.

"What's wrong with him?" Dawn's mood begins to shift away from happiness and into fear. She's barely thirteen. Still a child. Birdie doesn't blame her for being scared.

"He can't tell us. But you can still help. Can you think of things that make you happy? So you can share those feelings with Nimbus?"

Dawn looks uncertain. She glances back at Forest. He nods encouragingly. She tips her chin up with firm determination. "Yes. I can do that. Oh! I know! Have you ever eaten bread pudding?"

Birdie laughs. "I haven't."

Dawn sits on the bed next to Nimbus. She hesitates, then takes his hand and starts talking, detailing the exact perfect temperature and texture for a bread pudding. The mood in the room lifts once more. Within moments, Nimbus's breathing calms. The tears stop. He might not be with them mentally, but his body is reacting physically to Dawn's mood.

Dawn notices the change, which makes her even happier, which makes everyone *else* feel even happier. "My second-favorite thing," she says, ducking her head bashfully, "is telling stories."

"What kind of stories?" Birdie prompts.

"They're all about the daring adventures of Princess Solstice. She's smart and kind and good, but she's trapped in a castle with five wicked witches who don't want anyone to notice her." She launches into an extensive description of Princess Solstice, who sounds suspiciously like Dawn herself, but with florid details and, inexplicably, an extra set of eyes on the back of her head, which she uses to do magic.

Once she's finished describing the exact cut and style of the princess's dress, Dawn lets out a happy sigh. "I've got ever so many stories about Princess Solstice. I've been dying for someone to share them with. Do you think—do you think Nimbus would like me to tell him my stories?"

Birdie nods. "Nimbus loved—" She catches herself talking about him in the past tense. He's still here. He's going to get his treatment and get better. "He loves stories. He used to sneak books into his room every night and get candle wax on the pages, trying to read after dark."

As Dawn waves away Birdie's offer to stay and says that she's going to take care of Nimbus on her own, it strikes Birdie that this was perhaps even more of a kindness to Dawn than to Nimbus. Dawn needs a friend. She needs to feel wanted and useful. And this way, Birdie can worry a little less about Nimbus.

She shouldn't be worrying about any of them. She should only be looking for ways to get into the House Wife's records.

Frustrated with herself but unable to regret this small success for two lost children, Birdie steps into the hallway. She means to thank Forest for his help, but Lake is there, standing in Forest's way. Her hands are on her hips, a fierce scowl on her cherubic face.

"When you scream," she says, "it makes my ears bleed. Also, tell your father to stop shouting. He's very unpleasant." She turns her head, tracking something's progress down the hall toward the entrance. Then she looks at Forest again, closing one eye. "How are you there *and* here?" She stomps a foot, furious. "Everyone should only be in one place. I hate this. Here." She holds out a sheet of paper toward Birdie, then stomps away as soon as Birdie takes it.

There's a bold red circle with what might be a girl in the center of it. Birdie stares after her, puzzled.

"Any idea what that was about?" She looks up at Forest, but his smile is gone, replaced by an expression of genuine fear. Before she can ask what's wrong, he strides away, long legs taking him around the corner in a few short steps.

Birdie's more disappointed than she likes. After their stolen moment on the bench and then his help here, she thought—

Well. She thought nothing useful or appropriate or helpful. She needs to put the barriers between herself and all of them back up, for her own safety.

The rest of the day passes in a tedium of work. The windows in the greenhouse are in desperate need of cleaning, so she sets to it. Part of her can't help but hope Forest comes in again. Whenever her thoughts stray, they land on him. What got him sent here? Why doesn't he talk? What was he like before?

"Focus," she mutters to herself. She can't afford to care about any of this. Only Magpie matters. How to get through that door and access the House Wife's records is the only question she should have.

It's hard to gauge the time of day with the sun so muffled by fog and clouds, but Birdie's stomach lets her know when suppertime is near. She missed lunch entirely. With a longing glance toward the House Wife's still-closed door, Birdie hurries into the kitchen to help set the table.

She's going to tell Cook about Rabbit's drinking. Birdie hates herself for it. But she has to be the one to help the House Wife. Otherwise this has all been for nothing.

Cook isn't in the kitchen, though. Everything is in disarray— piles of dishes on the counter, an abandoned pot of something congealing on the table, the remains of lunch shoved to the side.

Birdie knocks on Cook's bedroom door.

"Go away," Cook slurs.

Cook isn't coming out again today. Birdie's on her own. But she's only ever trained to clean a kitchen, not use one. What can she possibly throw together for everyone?

Minnow emerges from the pantry with her arms full. "Oh, there you are. I saw you were busy with the greenhouse, so I cleaned the bathrooms."

"With help!" chirps a voice behind her as River appears, arms equally full.

Minnow barely suppresses an eye roll. "Yes, with help."

What is Minnow up to? And why is she so close with River? Cook specifically warned them about River, since no one knows what River's ability is.

If Minnow isn't really a maid, what if River is also more than she's letting on? Dr. Bramble has been trying to sneak someone into the House of Quiet for years. It makes sense that he wants to understand the treatments, since he helps run the procedure. He probably feels guilty for the ones it hurts. But maybe he isn't the only one trying to learn how it all works.

Rumors of northern spies have circulated in Sootcity for years. What if they've decided to infiltrate the House of Quiet as well? But which one would it be: the maid who doesn't know how to be a maid, or the chatty, overly friendly rich girl who claims to know everyone but won't say what got her sent here?

Maybe Birdie's paranoid after six months spent skulking and spying at the minister of finance's country estate. But one of the letters she stole was about the minister of defense and several northern spies who escaped from detention there. No one knows where the spies went.

River gestures at the kitchen, unaware of Birdie's growing suspicions. "Cook is indisposed, so we're making supper. Hope you like stew, because it's too late to start anything else!" She lifts the lid on a large pot simmering on the stove. The room fills with aromatic steam.

"Hope you like stew with the *wrong seasoning*," Minnow grumbles.

"You're going to love it." River brandishes her spoon menacingly.

"Do you know how to make bread pudding?" Birdie asks River. A small test, since bread pudding has been popular among the wealthy for the past year. "It would make Dawn so happy. She's really been sweet with Nimbus today."

River's eyes light up. "If Dawn's happy, everyone's happy. I've helped make dozens of bread puddings, because my family's cook is the only tolerable person in the whole house." River grabs Minnow's arm, drags her to the stove, and shoves the spoon into her hands. "Stir. And don't you *dare* mess with the seasonings." She disappears back into the pantry.

"I don't work for you," Minnow grumbles.

For the first time in as long as she can remember, Birdie's useless. The only thing left to clean is the pile of dishes, but she can't do those without getting in River's way.

"Why do you look so nervous?" Minnow asks. She drops her voice to a whisper. "The stew *is* good. I can't admit it after telling her she was doing it wrong, though."

Birdie leans against the counter and peers into the bubbling pot. "I don't have anything to do." It's such an unfamiliar sensation. Though she's always depended on her fellow maids, there was never a moment there wasn't too much work for all of them. But today, between Minnow actually helping and a shocking amount of labor and aid from the rich residents, Birdie can . . . rest?

"Speaking of nothing for you to do," Minnow says, "I cleaned the top floor. We won't need to do it again for at least a couple of weeks, since no one goes up there anyway. One less thing to worry about."

Maybe Birdie's been wrong about Minnow. But she won't let her guard down. About either Minnow or River.

River hurries past them, checking the temperature of the oven and muttering to herself that it needs to be hotter. Or colder. She can't seem to make up her mind. Birdie loses a little faith in the prospect of bread pudding.

"I cleaned the second floor, too," Minnow continues. "Have you noticed our rooms were converted from closet space?"

That explains their strange proportions. She hates her narrow room. Birdie doesn't want to be that confined and alone until she's dead. "Why didn't they just put us in the empty bedrooms?" She wishes she were sharing a room with Minnow and Rabbit. It's so hard to sleep in silence. Plus, every maid knows it's safest to never be alone.

Birdie shudders, remembering the House Wife looming over her in the darkness, watching her sleep.

"Empty bedrooms?" Minnow echoes.

Stupid! Birdie scrambles to cover up how she knows what's behind the locked doors. "One of them was open. Just a room with a narrow bed."

Minnow puts the lid back on the stew. "Strange. I could have sworn all those doors were locked when I checked them yesterday."

Before Birdie can think of a reply, Rabbit appears. She bounces off the doorframe, not quite making it into the kitchen. She giggles, then stumbles in and sits with a *whump* at the table.

Minnow shoots Birdie an alarmed look. Birdie shares the sentiment. It's one thing for Cook to drink, since she's clearly worked here forever, but Rabbit should know better. With her lack of experience, she'll never be paid more than she is right now, and her family spent everything they had on her procedure.

Birdie's plan to have Rabbit removed curdles in her stomach. Looking at the pathetic maid now, all Birdie feels is compassion. She'll find Magpie, but she won't destroy another young woman to do it. And she won't betray who she is and where she came from. They help where they can, and Birdie can help here.

"I'm getting her to bed before anyone sees," Birdie says. Minnow nods, mouth pursed tightly. Not in judgment, but in shared worry.

Birdie guides Rabbit down the hall toward the stairs. Rabbit stumbles and weaves, her weight nearly all on Birdie. They hit the wall together. Rabbit slides down to the floor. She sits with her legs splayed in front of her, skirts in disarray.

Birdie's aghast. "What did you do today?"

Maybe the House Wife is the one who let Rabbit drink. It's an explanation, but not one that makes any sense. Nimbus's neighbor, the minister of justice, had a nasty reputation for luring girls from the lower quarters to his home with the promise of good food and fun. The House Wife doesn't seem like that type of person. And how is she treating Sky, if she's busy drinking with Rabbit or taking advantage of her? Is it possible there's someone else back there Birdie hasn't met yet? An actual doctor?

It's baffling how little Birdie knows about what's happening in this house. How little anyone knows. Not even Dr. Bramble, who works on the procedure, could tell her how the house works or who is here. Why keep them separate? It makes sense to combine procedure and treatment.

Rabbit's giggle fades. Her eyes fill with tears. "I helped the house. I'm too tired. I'm too tired to go upstairs, Birdie. I'm sorry."

Birdie's at a loss. She can't get Rabbit up the stairs on her own. Maybe she can get Rabbit back to the kitchen so they can prop her up in a chair. Maybe no one will notice.

There Birdie goes again with the maybes.

As though summoned by her anxiety, Forest appears at the end of the hall. Birdie is ready with excuses on Rabbit's behalf. She might hate Rabbit for having the procedure wasted on her, might resent her for getting in the way of Birdie's work here, might despise her for risking her entire family's future by messing up so badly, but she won't let another maid be ruined. Not if she can help it.

Forest leans down and gently picks Rabbit up. He looks at Birdie, waiting.

Birdie scurries ahead. She unlocks the stairs, then leads him up to their hallway. He carries the insensible maid like she weighs as much as a stack of clean sheets. When Birdie points out Rabbit's room, Forest lowers the girl onto her bed, then backs out so Birdie can get into the narrow space. She removes Rabbit's scuffed black boots and tucks her in.

"Get some rest," Birdie says. "We'll talk tomorrow."

Birdie will protect Rabbit while she sobers up, and then they'll have a serious discussion about Rabbit's responsibilities. But Rabbit will be in no condition to function early tomorrow. Birdie still wins. She'll get the spot helping the House Wife, and she didn't have to destroy an innocent girl for it. She knows she's not helping Magpie as viciously as she could, but she thinks Magpie would approve. She hopes so, at least.

She closes Rabbit's door. Forest is waiting in the hallway, eyebrows raised. This must be the first time he's been upstairs. None of the residents are allowed up here, and the stairs are always locked.

Forest gestures at Birdie's own room. She left the door open, and she fights the urge to be embarrassed now that he's seen she's essentially living in a closet.

"Not quite as nice as downstairs," Birdie says. Her room is ruthlessly tidy. The only evidence that she's staying in it is her friend's last drawing, propped up on the table behind the washbasin.

I'm sorry, she said against the wood separating them right before she went to the minister with her demands for a placement in the House of Quiet. *I'm leaving to find my sister. Will you come?*

This was the response. It's a forest, the sharp lines of ink rendering everything menacing. Soaring above it is a single tiny bird. Something in the way the bird cuts through the sky fills her with hope. But the bird is alone. Her friend stayed behind that door, and Birdie left them behind forever.

It's a reminder. Both of what she came here to do, and what it cost her.

"But that's all right," Birdie continues, filling in the silence. "I don't mind small spaces. It's just too quiet up here. Like this whole house. And some people in it," she teases. Then her stomach drops in horror. She's gone too far. She can't tease him.

Instead of anger, Forest's full lips twitch in a smile. He puts a single finger over his lips. She wants it to be her finger instead. She takes a step backward. She needs to remember who she is. Who he is. Why she's here. This whole day has been confusing, starting with the House Wife creeping into her room and ending with Birdie getting help from so many unexpected sources.

"We should—" she starts, but stops.

There's a pattering of footsteps above them. Light, like someone dancing across the floor. But who would be up in that unused space right now?

Seized with sudden, inexplicable hope, Birdie sprints down the hall and up the stairs. But when she reaches the top, the echoing space is empty. No one dancing. No sisters twirling until they get so dizzy they both fall down, splitting open the younger sister's eyebrow.

It's empty. So whose footsteps did she hear?

CHAPTER SIXTEEN

A Dreamer Revealed

There's a single flickering point of light, drawing hopeful little moths tired of being in the dark. Birdie's candle sputters, about to go out. The night presses in around them, relentless and ravenous. But Birdie walks resolutely forward. She walks past Lake, and Dawn. She walks past a woman with two scarves, past children ragged and hollowed out with hunger. She walks past a man and a woman who look like her, each holding out a silent hand, their eyes averted. She walks past Forest, then Nimbus, then a door standing alone in the darkness. Tears stream down her face.

The candle dips lower. Birdie will be alone in the dark forever. Her shoulders stoop.

"It's okay," she whispers. "I don't matter. I can't matter. I have to find her."

There's nothing to be done. Whomever Birdie's looking for, it will consume her.

Another dream pulls harder. It's an undertow, slipping beneath the surface of all the dreams, tugging everyone toward it eventually. The darkness is gone, and so is Birdie.

The red circle is the only thing left, brilliant and burning, getting closer and closer. There is no mind behind that circle. The dream exists without a dreamer, like it was always there, waiting.

No. No no no no no.

The sheer animal urgency of forcing eyes to close against that red circle is at last enough to disrupt the dream.

River backs up so fast she loses her balance and falls, jarring her eyes open.

Eyes. She has eyes. She has a self. This almost never happens. She exists in the dreams, but only as an awareness. Always an observer, never a participant. Though sometimes she tries to influence things—like with poor Rabbit's first kitten dream—more often than not she just tries to get out.

Always sleeping without rest, claimed by others' minds as soon as her own body succumbs to exhaustion. River hates it, but she can't stop it. And at least this is something new. The heavy scents of salt and blood welcome her back to the beach. Though on a normal night that might be alarming, tonight it's a relief. The red circle won't find her here.

Freed from existential terror, River picks her way over the beach rocks, each perfectly uniform, to where Minnow is sitting. She's on her boulder, staring out at the gray waves. They come with startling precision, evenly spaced. A clockwork ocean. Beneath her rock is the puddle with the house far beneath the surface. River doesn't want to look at it, either, so she climbs up next to Minnow.

"Minnow?" River asks.

The other girl looks at her, beach-rock-round eyes narrowing. "That's not my name."

Interesting. Also interesting that this is twice now River's been able to speak to her in a dream. And this time she's *herself.* Except, not quite. It's like she's put on a ball-gown version of River.

Her limbs feel more elegant, and her skin glows like she has her own private light source.

River gathers her wits. Though this isn't the same existential dread as the red circle, this is clearly Minnow's idea of her, and she can't be subsumed by it, no matter how flattering and intoxicating it is. She has to hold on to herself.

"What's your name?" she asks.

"Doesn't matter."

"Whose blood is that?" River points to Minnow's hands and skirts.

Minnow's sigh is so weary it breaks River's heart. "They still haven't told me. There was no blood when my mother died. But this is hers, in a way. It's for her."

River should leave. There's only one thing she can do in a dream that changes the waking world, and she definitely doesn't want to do that to Minnow. This feels like she's cheating. She wants Minnow to tell her things in their waking life. She doesn't want to spy and steal information like she did at home.

But she doesn't want Minnow here alone in this cold, gray place, covered in blood.

And River doesn't want to be alone, either. She feels safe with Minnow, gore notwithstanding. Somewhere out there the red circle is waiting for a dreamer, and River can't, *won't*, be that dreamer.

She nudges the other girl with her shoulder. "We have all this water right here. Let's get you cleaned up. No sense in keeping blood on your hands. But let's use the ocean, not that puddle." River doesn't want Minnow going anywhere near the house under the bog. Not after her story.

Minnow frowns, like the idea never occurred to her. "I don't have to have blood on my hands," she says, slowly. Just like that, the blood is gone. It's a start. And it's a start that River gave her. Before Rabbit, she'd only ever tried to nudge things toward nightmares to torment her awful parents and the wretched minister of defense. To say nothing of what else she did at the minister's estate.

"Much better," River says. "While we're changing things, we could find someplace warmer to meet. This is beautiful, but so cold."

River turns to see if she's managed to get a smile out of Minnow, but more than the blood has changed. Before, Minnow was distracted, like River was part of the landscape. Now Minnow's fully present, aware of herself . . . and of River.

Minnow leans close. "*You're* so beautiful," she whispers. "I want to swallow you whole."

The air around them is charged, like the atmosphere before a storm. River feels the space between them. There are threads woven there, drawing tighter and tighter, pulling them together.

River's accidentally visited this type of dream before, but she's never been the subject of one. She knows it isn't real, she *knows*, but the electric thrill dancing along her skin is undeniable. A warning of lightning about to strike. River wants this white-hot intensity to burn away everything else.

"You should kiss me," River whispers.

The threads between them snap taut. They crash into each other like waves hitting the shore, but there's nothing orderly about their frantic movements. They kiss like there's nothing in the world outside their bodies and the points where they meet. And, because it's a dream, it's true. There *is* nothing outside what they're doing and feeling.

For once, River doesn't resist. She lets the dream do exactly what Minnow said she wanted: swallow her whole.

Lips aren't enough. River leans back, frantic and aching. She pulls Minnow with her. But instead of the boulder beneath them, there's a soft surface. The surprise of it shocks River right out of the dream.

"No, no, I want to go back," River demands, the feelings inside her so urgent and overwhelming she might burst if she doesn't find her way to Minnow again. But the lingering thrill scurries away from her like insects exposed to the light.

The red circle found her again. River's trapped in it. She can't get out because she can't find the dreamer, and if she can't find the dreamer, she can't disconnect from them. *Who* is dreaming this? Why?

River tries to squeeze her eyes shut, but she doesn't have eyes. She doesn't have a body. She's nothing. There's only the red circle.

Wake up, wake up, wake up, River whimpers. She'll be free when the dreamer wakes up, but . . . what if there is no dreamer? What if everything else was the dream, and now, at last, reality has claimed her once more?

CHAPTER SEVENTEEN

A Bird in the Night

The sound of footsteps pulls Birdie out of her fretful sleep.

She sits up in bed, suddenly alert. The footsteps weren't part of any dream; she's certain of it. But were they in her room, the hallway outside, or upstairs?

Birdie creeps from bed and peers out her door, expecting the House Wife to be standing there, watching her. Birdie doesn't see her, but that doesn't mean she's not here. The far end of the hallway is shrouded black so deep anything could be standing there.

Anyone, Birdie corrects herself. The House Wife is a person. She just doesn't act like one.

Rabbit's door is closed, as is Minnow's. Birdie hurries to the stairs and feels her way up to the third floor. She pauses every step, listening, wondering if she'll be able to hear anyone else on the stairs with her over the pounding of her own heart. The higher she goes, the more certain she is that someone is here with her. That a hand is about to reach out and grab her ankle, throwing her down.

Fear paralyzes her. She wants to get to the top—needs to see who or what is up there—but she's not alone. She knows she isn't.

"Hello?" she whispers, her voice small and quivering. As soon as she says it, she wishes she hadn't. Because which would be worse: no answer . . . or a voice right next to her?

Birdie flings herself upward, all attempts at stealth abandoned as she rushes the last few steps and trips out onto the top floor. She's never been more grateful for moonlight. The low, round windows let in just enough to see that no one is up here. Again.

So what did Birdie hear? In a house this quiet, whose footsteps tugged her out of sleep?

Birdie shivers. She's in only her night shift, not even shoes on her feet. She turns back to the stairs and then freezes again. The darkness is waiting, and in it, she's certain she won't be alone. She imagines the House Wife lurking three steps down, that placid, empty smile on her face. She imagines Cook with a knife, taking care of the problem in the house. The minister of finance, here at last to settle the score.

And then, worse, that poem whispers through her thoughts. *I pray for death before I wake.* What happened to the child who wrote it? What if—one way or another—they never left the house?

Whether it's a ghost or person stalking her, Birdie can't stay up here forever. She holds her breath, taking the stairs one at a time, pressing her feet down as silently as she can. She clings to the wall. Maybe there's no one else here. Maybe if she's very quiet and very small, they won't notice her. Maybe they don't want to hurt her, they're just unquiet, too, in a house that's so relentlessly silent.

Maybe, maybe, maybe, she thinks as she descends with agonizing care. The steps seem to stretch into infinity in the blackness. How had she not noticed before how many stairs there were? It feels like too many. Everything about this house is unsettling, like it was designed to keep her off-balance.

There's a shuffling noise beneath her. Birdie freezes.

"Hello?" a small voice whispers, the echo of her own tentative question earlier. For a moment she thinks it's exactly that. Her fear, lingering, trapped here forever.

But it's not her voice. "Minnow?" Birdie asks. "Is that you? What are you doing?"

"What are *you* doing? Why were you upstairs?"

"I thought I heard a noise. But it must have been a dream." Or a maid who isn't a maid, creeping along the hallway.

"I'm headed downstairs. Can't sleep. And there's still some bread pudding left over."

It's a sensible excuse. But Minnow barely touched the bread pudding at supper. Birdie doesn't believe for a second that she's stumbling around in the dark to get an extra helping. "Did you hear anything? Or see anyone creeping about?"

Minnow lets out a small laugh. "Only you."

"Let's go down together, then." Birdie moves past Minnow, accidentally stepping on her foot. "Sorry! Why can't we have a lamp, or at the very least candles?"

"Bogs burn. Forever, if the conditions are right." The way Minnow says it, she sounds very small and very far away.

"Can't very well light the bog on fire if we're always locked in," Birdie grumbles. She unlocks the door at the bottom of the stairs and steps out into the hallway. It's dim, but after the pitch-black stairs it feels positively radiant. "Speaking of bogs," she says, wrinkling her nose, "is it just me or is the stink even stronger?"

The air feels cold and thick, like someone left a door or window open.

"The windows don't open," Minnow says, apparently having

the same thought. "They've all been nailed shut." Minnow turns to Birdie with a puzzled look on her face.

Something's wrong. Birdie's known it since she woke up. She was just wrong about which floor something was wrong on. She rushes down the hallway toward the foyer and turns to face the front door.

It's wide open. And standing there, framed by the hungry night, is Nimbus. His hands are on his head, squeezing, as though trying to hold something in. Birdie rushes forward and pulls him all the way inside. Her heart is racing. He could have gotten out. He almost did.

How did the door get open? And how did Nimbus get out of his room in the first place? Minnow is standing, staring out at the night. Birdie thought she caught Minnow going down the stairs. Maybe she caught her coming back up them, though.

Minnow shuts the door and turns around. Her face is drained of color, round eyes so wide Birdie can see the whites all around her gray irises.

"We never would have found him," she whispers.

Birdie doesn't think even Minnow can fake this reaction. She's horrified. So maybe Minnow was up to mischief, but Nimbus wasn't supposed to be the victim.

"Nimbus?" Birdie prods, hoping for a reaction. Silent tears trace down the boy's face. The thought of him out there, alone and cold and lost, makes her feel physically sick.

Minnow gently guides his hands away from his head. "Come on. Let's get you back to bed."

Birdie walks ahead of them. Nimbus's door is open. There's no sign of anyone else. Wild conspiracies run through Birdie's head. Someone else broke into the house. This is a trick, designed to catch her being up and about when she's not supposed to be. The house is haunted by the child who scratched that poem into the wall.

Then the most likely explanation occurs to her: Cook is drunk and neglected her nightly door-locking rounds. She really *does* need to lock the doors for everyone's safety. This house might be too quiet, it might hold vicious mysteries scrawled onto walls, it might echo with mysterious footsteps, but it's still safer than what's all around them.

Nimbus climbs onto his bed, silent but obedient. Birdie can't shake the thought of him sinking, his halo of tight curls floating around him. She stays by his open door, hands over her stomach, finding it hard to breathe.

Minnow is doing Birdie's job. She leans down and tucks Nimbus in, then lingers, stroking his forehead.

"Don't leave alone," Minnow whispers. "If you want to get out of this house, you need a guide. Take me with you, and I promise I'll get you to safety."

Birdie frowns. She doesn't know if Minnow realized Birdie could hear her. What kind of promise is that? And how can Minnow make it? None of them can get through the bog. Not without the driver and his well-practiced horses.

Minnow begins humming a song. Nimbus closes his eyes.

"What is that melody?" Birdie asks.

Minnow doesn't look at her, keeping her gaze on the boy they saved. "My mother used to sing it to calm down scared patients."

"She was a doctor?"

Minnow nods. "A surgeon, when she had to be." She picks the song back up and it finishes, trailing off on a sweetly melancholic note.

The song works. Nimbus's breathing becomes even and regular.

Someone leans in the doorway next to Birdie. She turns and sees River, her eyes shadowed and hollow. River is staring at Minnow.

"I couldn't find you again," River says.

Minnow hurries to them and Birdie closes Nimbus's door. She can't lock him in, because then River and Minnow would know how adept she is with lock-picking tools. Besides which, her tools are upstairs, along with her dress and her shoes.

"Can't go back to bed tonight," Birdie says. "I'll stand sentinel and make sure he doesn't wander."

"What do you mean you couldn't find me?" Minnow asks River. "Did you try to go upstairs? Seems like that's the only door in the whole house that's still locked."

River shakes her head, eyelids heavy. "That's not where I was trying to find you."

Birdie gives Minnow a puzzled look. Minnow shrugs, then tries to make her voice sound annoyed and teasing. "Did you need me to sing you to sleep, too?"

River's eyes can't seem to focus on anything as she stares at the ceiling above them. "I don't want to sleep again."

Minnow looks at Birdie. This time it's Birdie's turn to shrug. She doesn't know what to do with River, either. They can't really force her back to bed if she doesn't want to go.

"No sleep it is, then," Minnow says. "I'll make bread. You can both sit in the kitchen with me. And Birdie, you'll be able to see down the hallway if Nimbus wanders again."

Birdie nods. It's as good a solution as any. Birdie takes a seat on the bench against the window so she can keep sentry while Minnow prepares the dough. River sits at the table, resting her head on her arms, face turned to watch Minnow.

"Do you make bread often?" she asks.

Minnow smiles, but it's a sad, faraway smile. "My father died going out for bread. After that, my mother never wanted me to visit the bakery. As though it was the bread's fault. So I had to start baking."

Birdie's learned two things about Minnow. Her father is dead, and her mother was a doctor. And possibly also dead, given the past tense. Then again, both of those could be lies. But there's something raw about Minnow tonight, something vulnerable that Birdie hasn't seen yet. Maybe it was the fear of what could have happened to Nimbus. Birdie took it so personally because she cares about Nimbus; why was Minnow so shaken up?

If Birdie had known she'd be up all night, she would have left herself some dishes to do. It feels wasteful, sitting here, doing nothing. Once the dough is rising, Minnow joins her on the bench. River immediately moves to sit next to her, resting her head on Minnow's shoulder.

Birdie tries not to feel jealous that the two of them seem capable of defying rules and decorum to find comfort in touching.

"Don't let me sleep," River whispers.

"We won't," Minnow promises.

There's movement in the hallway. Birdie stands, ready to rush out. But instead of Nimbus wandering and lost, Forest walks into the kitchen. He's wearing his customary button-down white shirt and dark gray trousers even now, though he has a soft-looking blue robe over them. Birdie feels her cheeks burn, being seen in nothing but her night shift.

"Door unlocked?" Minnow asks.

Forest nods. He sits at the table, facing them. For the briefest moment, Birdie wishes she were sitting alone on the bench to see whether or not he would have sat next to her like River is sitting beside Minnow.

The silent, beautiful boy pulls out a pack of cards and begins shuffling.

Minnow perks up. "Do you know Soldier-Run-Knife?"

River's voice is so deliberate that Birdie feels like she's missed something. "I think you mean Draw-Pass-Stab."

"That's right. I always forget the name." Minnow gives Birdie a bland smile. The deception is back in place. What is Minnow hiding? River clearly knows something about it.

Forest deals the cards. Birdie sits across from him with the hallway in full view, just in case. River and Minnow join them. Only two rounds in, though, River's head droops.

"Wake me if I start screaming." She puts her head down. Birdie gives Minnow a questioning look, but Minnow just stares back. If she knows what River's worried about, she isn't saying. But she sits protectively close, where she'll be able to wake the other girl at a moment's notice.

Maybe the deception Birdie's picking up on is something innocent. River and Minnow are in love. It's the simplest, sweetest answer.

Maybe, her mother echoes in her head.

They play hand after hand, the games blurring together. Forest smiles every time Birdie lays down a winning set. They're so careful not to touch each other's fingers, they might as well be holding hands. It's almost like a game within a game. Getting as close as they can without ever actually brushing against each other. Birdie wonders if the game is one-sided, but that secret smile keeps tugging at Forest's lips.

When Birdie starts shivering, Forest takes off his robe and drapes it across her shoulders. She would have said no if he'd offered, but he didn't. He just gave it to her. She's never felt something so soft; it's her favorite color, and it still holds his warmth.

Maybe Minnow isn't the only fool putting herself in harm's way with an impossible flirtation. But Birdie's the only fool who risks losing her sister forever if she messes up here.

Despite that, and despite knowing how brutal the next day will be with so little sleep, it's a pleasant night. Birdie hasn't felt this way in so long, it takes her a while to settle on what *this* is. When she finally realizes, it makes her want to cry.

Young. She feels young.

She never got to be young. As a child, she took care of Magpie, and then as soon as she turned ten she was sent out to work to earn money for Magpie's procedure. Judging by the way Minnow is quietly but determinedly trying her best to cheat and hissing as Forest's insurmountable lead continues to grow, Minnow, too, needed a night to feel like just a young woman among friends.

Because they are her friends, Birdie realizes. She's down here in her nightgown and Forest's robe, and she knows she's not going to get in trouble.

Just as Forest deals the last hand of the game, River speaks. Her voice is soft and garbled, her eyes still closed.

"They're in the red circle now. It's coming for us, too."

CHAPTER EIGHTEEN

Past and Future in the House of Quiet

Someone is scratching on the door. Little fingernails, dragged down the wood, over and over. It takes the House Wife a long time to notice because there's so much noise, but eventually she hears it.

It takes her even longer to realize she's still standing in the middle of the room. Sometimes she forgets things, like how to tell her legs to move when she needs them to. It's hard, having a body. "Open the door," she says to herself.

It works. She walks over and unlocks it. One of the noisiest children, a young girl with red curls and full cheeks, is waiting in the dim hallway.

"Mouse?" the little girl asks.

The name is like a splinter jammed under her fingernails. The House Wife shudders, shaking out her hands. There's a tugging inside her chest, but the thread is too frayed. It snaps before it can pull anything free. "Mouse?" she whispers back.

"Are you in there?"

The House Wife considers the question. It's hard to keep her mind on questions, to listen to anything other than the heart of the house, desperately beating beneath all this noise. But she does her best. At last, she shakes her head. "Not anymore, I don't think."

The House Wife has made the little girl sad. Then the girl shrugs, her frown disappearing. "But you're not in the bog with the others yet."

"Not yet. Would you like to come in? I'm supposed to be careful and only take one of you at a time, but no one is watching right now."

"No. That's not how I die." The little girl states it as fact, and the House Wife believes her. She nods and closes the door once more. They were never allowed to tell her no before. The House Wife closes her eyes and whispers a promise to herself and to the heart of the house.

"They'll all be quiet soon."

Everyone is quiet in the end.

CHAPTER NINETEEN

A Bird Behind Glass

Five days in the House of Quiet, and Birdie's no closer to getting into the House Wife's room.

No matter what Birdie does, Rabbit is the only one the House Wife ever takes. Birdie can't understand why, either. That night when Rabbit seemed drunk and Birdie, Minnow, and Forest went out of their way to protect her? That's just Rabbit's demeanor. The bright-eyed, eager attitude when they first met was a performance. The real Rabbit is withdrawn and lethargic. She sleepwalks through meals, barely says or eats anything, and does no work for the rest of the house.

Maybe the House Wife's demands are so strenuous that it's all Rabbit can do to stumble to bed afterward, but Rabbit won't say anything about what she does in there. She always pretends to be too tired to remember. Birdie knows bone-deep exhaustion. She's worked until her fingers cramped and wouldn't move. She's scrubbed on hands and knees on floors so cold she couldn't walk after and had to crawl to bed. She's still never been too tired to remember what she did that day.

Birdie regrets protecting Rabbit, and now she's lost her chance because the House Wife doesn't seem to care how incompetent Rabbit is. The House Wife herself is so strange, she probably doesn't even notice. And if she's slipped into Birdie's room in the middle of the night again and found Birdie absent, well, she doesn't seem to care about that, either.

Other than Rabbit, Sky's the only person who gets through the House Wife's door. Birdie wouldn't have asked him questions about his treatment regardless, but he gives her the same wide berth he has since that second morning. Nimbus had a science lesson once with magnets. No matter how hard he tried, he couldn't get two of the ends to stick. They repelled each other with too much force. It's like Birdie is that opposite magnet for Sky.

She knows *opposite magnet* isn't the right term. Hawthorn would correct her with a single raised eyebrow. But he's not here. If only Birdie could write to Dr. Bramble and tell him about the opening for a tutor. Doubtless Hawthorn could get Sky to tell him all about the treatment.

Then again, maybe not. Because Sky's different in general. Birdie watched this morning as Minnow *accidentally* touched Sky's arm. He barely flinched, and he didn't yell at her at all. He doesn't seem exhausted so much as drained. Whatever the treatment is, it isn't easy on him.

If Birdie could just see the treatment, maybe she'd have some answers. About what was wrong with Magpie when she came here, about what was done to fix it, about where Magpie went afterward. But whomever the House Wife treats after Sky will be someone who likes Birdie. Someone who will gladly answer her questions. She's made sure of it.

She pauses sweeping to peer in on Nimbus and Dawn. Dawn spends most of her time with him, happily reading aloud or drawing or telling her endless stories. Birdie can't tell if it's helping, but it's not hurting. Nimbus hasn't scared them again since that last time, and he hasn't been wandering around at night.

Dawn notices Birdie and waves.

"Thank you for keeping an eye on him," Birdie says. "And please save a story for this afternoon when I'm cleaning in here. I want to know what happens to Princess Solstice's flying horse after her evil sister Hurricane used her terrible mind-control powers to convince the horse to be hers instead."

"You won't believe it!" Dawn promises.

Spurred by the girl's borrowed happiness, Birdie sneaks into the greenhouse for the best part of her day. Other than Sky and Rabbit, they've all become a strange sort of society in just a few days. Dawn has taken Nimbus under her wing. Everyone watches out for Lake and helps her when she does things like walk into walls and then angrily shout that there isn't a wall there at all. River took over the kitchen—Cook is always drunk now—and the older teens sneak out every night for companionship and card games.

That isn't the only sneaking, though. Every day around this same time, River and Minnow steal outside for walks. They think no one notices, because *they* don't know that every day around this time, Birdie meets Forest on their bench in the greenhouse.

He holds out the candy tin as she sits next to him.

"Did I miss them?" she asks.

He shakes his head.

"Oh, good." Soon, the mist swirls, announcing the arrival of their friends. River dances in circles around Minnow in contrast to Minnow's utilitarian march.

Birdie shifts into her Minnow voice, low and impatient. "Please don't interrupt me; I need to concentrate on walking."

Then she switches into her lilting, musical River voice. "But you look so pretty when you're cross! And you're *always* cross, so you're *always* pretty, which is why I simply must *always* look at you."

Back to Minnow's voice. "If you insist on being in love with me, the least you could do is make it worth my while by cleaning the toilets."

This earns a surprised laugh from Forest. It fills Birdie more than Dawn's contagious emotions. That's her real goal here. Not making up conversations between River and Minnow, but trying to get Forest to laugh. He still hasn't said a word, but his laugh is enough.

Minnow and River are past them now, her game won for the day. Birdie leans back with a sigh.

"So," she says, continuing her one-sided conversation from the day before. That's part of what makes being with Forest so easy—he doesn't talk, so she doesn't have to be reminded that she's treating him like a friend instead of someone far above her station. "I can't get a coherent answer from Lake, but I know Nimbus's mother employed a lady's maid with abilities. I never met his childhood nanny, and I know his tutor has no abilities." She holds back a scowl. She should be grateful to Hawthorn for introducing her to Dr. Bramble, but he was there when she was preparing to be picked up by the carriage. His condescending tone informing her of what she was to do and look for—as if she didn't already know—still makes her angry. People like Hawthorn are too often cruel. They can't stand to look at someone like Birdie without remembering they're closer in station to her than they are to the wealthy they imitate.

But Birdie might still need Hawthorn once she finds out

where Magpie is. If she ever sees him again, she'll curtsy and act as though he really is better than she is, because that's what he needs to believe.

Birdie clears her throat and moves on. "Then there's River. She said there were two employees with abilities in her household. Both worked exclusively for her father. She had minimal contact with them. I haven't talked to Sky—have you noticed he always has to be on the opposite side of the kitchen from me? But we can assume his circumstances were similar. And your household had people with abilities, but not your nanny or a nurse when you were younger, or your tutor when you were older, correct?"

Forest nods.

Birdie toys with the stair key in her apron pocket, frowning at the greenery around them. "That's why Minnow's theory doesn't make sense to me. Why would *you* catch something? Surely if it were that contagious, family members living with people who had the procedure would develop abilities. Unless they're hiding their abilities, which doesn't make sense. Once you're on the Ministry's registry, you get placed in jobs. Why avoid that?" Birdie sighs, shifting to face Forest. "But I have no other theories. Unless you somehow forgot visiting the city and undergoing the procedure in the enormous Ministry building belching black smoke into the sky like a dragon?" Birdie heard once that half the coal coming into Sootcity went into the machine for the procedure. She always wondered how much of the soot coating her clothes at the end of the day meant that some new child had the means to provide for their family.

The cost of progress, her father always said. Smoke that got into lungs and suffocated weak babies and frail elders. It wasn't the only source, but it was by far the worst. And still Birdie was happy taking in lungfuls of it, imagining that someday the smoke she breathed would be the smoke that meant Magpie was extraordinary.

Forest squinches his face in a pantomime of being deep in thought, then relents and shakes his head.

"Any theories you care to share?" Birdie teases, nudging his shoulder with hers.

Forest frowns, then abruptly stands and walks out of the greenhouse.

Panic squeezes Birdie's chest. She hasn't touched him like that before. It was inappropriate. And teasing him was cruel of her. It's inexcusable how comfortable she's let herself get. What was she thinking, crossing these lines? Treating him like a friend? Maybe *more* than a friend. But he's not her friend. He never could be.

And she can't afford to spend her time like this. Sitting with Forest makes her happy, and she doesn't deserve to be happy, because it doesn't bring her any closer to finding Magpie.

Her worst fear is that Magpie really did come here, and she really did get the treatment, and she really did get better. But because Birdie never stopped at home to talk to her parents, because she hates them so much for what they did, she missed the news that Magpie was home. They could have passed on the road, Birdie coming in and Magpie going out.

The image of Magpie sitting at home, eating supper with their parents, all of them wondering where Birdie is makes Birdie both want to laugh and scream. She has no way of getting word, either. All her hope and striving and deception and risk, and she's still nothing but a maid without a sister. Maybe not even a maid, if she keeps forgetting her place.

Birdie hangs her head, defeated. A shadow looms over her. Birdie looks up to see Forest holding a thick book.

"You want to read?" she asks. That's why he left?

He shakes his head and sits next to her. Her relief is immediate and nearly overwhelming. He's not mad at her. She hasn't ruined the best part of her life here.

Forest opens the book, searching. Then he points emphatically at the page number.

"Fourteen?" Birdie asks.

He's watching her carefully, like he's waiting for some extreme reaction or change. When none comes, he nods and moves on, looking for more words and pointing to them. Eventually, he's built a whole sentence.

Fourteen very ill just before change

"Are you saying you got sick first? Before your ability appeared?"

He nods, relieved that she understands.

"Maybe there's something there. Thank you for telling me. But . . . you can't just write this out?" Birdie had actually assumed that Forest never learned to read or write. It would be surprising for someone from his background, but not unheard of. Most everyone in the lower quarters never learns.

Then the more likely explanation washes over her with a surprising burst of humiliation and sharp regret. He probably assumed *she* couldn't read or write. And she's just given away the fact that she can.

Forest shakes his head in answer to her question.

"Why not?" Birdie asks, tired and sad and frustrated with herself and the house and the entire world.

He looks in the book again, until at last he finds the word he needs. He taps it three times.

Dangerous.

CHAPTER TWENTY

A River Rejected

River wakes after sunrise, head aching and stomach twisted. It's the first time since she got here that she's slept through the night.

And she doesn't remember any of her dreams. Not even the ones with Minnow. River's had feelings for other girls before, but never like this. Never so intense and persistent. If it weren't for that terrifying red circle, River would actually love sleeping just for the opportunities to spend time with Minnow when Minnow at last has her guard down.

Not that River isn't trying to get that guard down during the day, too. She's been a relentless flirt. Minnow doesn't seem to mind, but she never fully reciprocates. Minnow's waiting for something, River's sure of it. She always seems alert. She pays too much attention to the others in the house, while paying very little attention to the types of things Birdie does. For example, Rabbit's constant inebriation doesn't bother Minnow at all. She never complains that Rabbit isn't doing her share of the work. Minnow helps keep the house running, but she doesn't care about the work the way Birdie so obviously, desperately does.

Then again, Minnow isn't fixated on the House Wife and her locked door the way Birdie pretends not to be. It could simply be that Birdie's got more ambition than Minnow, but River knows that's not it. Minnow isn't lazy like a dog lying in the sun. She's *ready*, like a cat perched on a ledge.

But sleeping through the night means River missed their midnight kitchen time. She hurries to her door, expecting it to be locked for once and is disappointed to find it open.

Did they leave her out? It stings. Not just because she doesn't like imagining Birdie and Forest getting smiles from Minnow when those smiles are River's to win, but because no one else seems to understand that this house and at least two people in it want them dead. How can she keep them safe if they don't include her?

She's tried to check on Sky's dreams again to see if he's still happily stalking and slaughtering them, but she can't find him. It's like he's gone quiet. Which she supposes is the point of the house, but why would it take away his dreams? She hasn't tried too hard, though. She always finds her way to Minnow, sooner rather than later, and stays there as long as she can.

Minnow, unfortunately, is still on her list of people in the house who might be deadly. But who is she to judge a little light murder?

River stumbles into the hall and nearly runs into Birdie. Who, judging by her sleep-red eyes and dazed expression, is also just getting up for the day. Something is wrong.

"You slept in, too?" River asks.

Birdie nods, clearly troubled. Minnow bursts out of the stairwell behind her, frantically tying back her still-wet hair. "Why didn't anyone wake me up?" she demands.

"We all slept," River says. Curious.

"Come on," Birdie says. "We're behind schedule." She snags Minnow, and River retreats to the kitchen, surly and alone.

There's something else off, too, but she can't put her finger on it. It nags at her all morning as she prepares breakfast. Minnow comes in to help, but she's distracted and no fun at all.

Minnow looks up in a start as a burst of flour explodes against her apron.

River goes back to kneading the bread dough. "*Someone* hasn't heard a word I've said for the last ten minutes."

"Something's strange," Minnow says.

River smiles, because she's figured it out. But she wants to tease Minnow for a little longer. "I know what it is."

"Oh, really?" Minnow leans close, and then she frowns. "How does sleeping all night leave you more exhausted than barely sleeping at all?" She traces a thumb around the crescent of the shadows beneath River's eyes. River freezes, holding her breath, afraid to break this moment. Remembering everything they've done in Minnow's dreams.

Minnow must remember it, too, because she looks down at River's lips and keeps her thumb on River's cheek.

"The stove," River breathes.

"Yes, it's nice and warm."

"And it smells like . . ." River prods with a smile, her own eyes drifting to Minnow's lips. She knows what those lips feel like in their dreams. She wants to taste them while they're both awake.

"Like woodsmoke. Not peat," Minnow says. But rather than congratulating River on figuring out what is different, or leaning in and rewarding River's cleverness with a longed-for kiss, Minnow looks like she swallowed a rock. She takes a step back and stares at the stove, unmoving, unblinking. Then she turns and walks into the pantry with all the grace of a wooden puppet.

River scowls. She expected Minnow to be more curious, to puzzle over this mystery with her. Because River knows for a fact that last night there was no wood left. Dawn wanted to roast nuts, and Minnow teased her that without wood to burn, the nuts would end up tasting like dried peat. Then she offered to go out into the bog and get Dawn some fresh peat to nibble. Dawn pretended to be horrified but was actually delighted by the attention, which meant everyone in the kitchen was delighted, too. It was a good evening. Even Cook came out and took over supper.

Birdie comes into the kitchen with Forest. He's River's baking assistant, when he's not skulking in the greenhouse waiting for Birdie to meet him. They think no one knows, but they're not that good at being sneaky.

Forest is gentle and kind and spews poison in his dreams. River has no doubt he's capable of terrible things and has maybe already done them. He's on her list, too.

"Did you sleep last night?" River asks, keeping one eye on the pantry.

He nods. They both look rough. Birdie's hand keeps drifting to her forehead like it's aching, and Forest slouches his broad-shouldered self at the table instead of getting to work helping River.

None of the other residents have come in yet. They're almost always on time for meals, which are the most entertaining thing in the house. River frowns, puzzling it out. Last night, Cook didn't let River prepare the meal *or* the aromatic tea she gave everyone as a treat afterward. It was the first meal in days that River hadn't been in charge of. Is it possible Cook did something to them to make sure everyone would sleep through the night?

Why drug them now? They've been sneaking around every single night. Surely if Cook knew, she would have reprimanded the maids.

The wood. It's new. Someone brought in supplies last night.

Did Cook think they might try to leave on the carriage? They've all been sent here by their families; they have nowhere else to go. And it's not as though seeing supplies being delivered would disturb them. If anything, it would have been the highlight of the week.

Which makes River suspect that whoever came in the dead of night was bringing something else. Something none of them were meant to see. But what?

River scans the kitchen, trying to take stock of what else has changed. There! A sprig of flowers in a teacup by the window. River knows every flower that grows within safe walking distance of the house, because she's picked them all to tuck into Minnow's hair while Minnow grumbled but let her do it. Those flowers were brought from somewhere else, for Cook.

If the driver is sweet on Cook, that's interesting gossip. River hurries into the pantry. Minnow is staring at a container of flour like she's seen a ghost in it. Or maybe she's still dazed from being drugged.

"I've figured something else out," River says.

Minnow turns to her, a dull look of resignation in her eyes. This isn't the aftereffects of the tea. This is something else. Somehow, between coming into the kitchen and walking into the pantry, Minnow's become a different person. There's a distance between them, a cold flat sheen to Minnow's gaze.

"What changed?" River asks. She tries to demand, but her voice comes out tight and afraid.

"The smoke. You said so yourself." Minnow tries to move past her, but River throws out an arm to block her.

"No, something else happened. What happened, Minnow?"

Minnow lifts a hand and presses it softly against River's cheek. River leans her head against it, the weight of Minnow's eyes roving her face nearly physical. At last, Minnow smiles. It's a gallows smile, though. A smile of endings.

"It isn't you," Minnow says. "It was never you."

And then Minnow steps around her and leaves as River's heart shatters.

CHAPTER TWENTY-ONE

A Bird at Play

Everything feels off this morning. Not just because they're all bleary-eyed and tired and there's strange, angry tension from River and disconnected apathy from Minnow, but because something in the atmosphere is pressing down. Birdie's head is packed full of cotton.

She can't stop watching Minnow. Minnow claimed not to have been up early, but she's different today. Birdie had started to trust her, but maybe she was wrong to. Because if there's a spy in the House of Quiet other than Birdie, who's to say that spy hasn't been more successful?

Maybe Birdie's been too focused on the House Wife's room. Maybe she needs to get into Minnow's first.

"Storm coming." Minnow looks out the window as everyone finishes the toast and eggs River slammed in front of them. "Guess we can't play outside today."

Lake bursts into a peal of laughter. It's so shocking to have her mentally here with them for once that everyone else laughs, too. Even dull-eyed Sky in the corner cracks a distracted smile.

"We *should* play today," Birdie says, putting her hands on her hips. Cook's not awake, and the House Wife hasn't made her usual breakfast appearance. Who can get mad at them?

Besides, Lake, Nimbus, and Dawn are practically still children. And the rest of them—well, they aren't much older, are they? They deserve a day off. Even working in the big houses, they managed to cobble together times to let loose. There's nothing to do in the House of Quiet but wait around for their turn at treatment. Of course everyone is exhausted and worn thin.

Plus, a little disruption might be exactly what Birdie needs. She's been playing her part too well, and it's gotten her nowhere. If the House Wife hates noise, they'll just have to make more and see if she doesn't come out of her room.

"But we don't have any toys," Dawn says. She sits up straighter, trying to pitch her voice lower to sound more serious. "I mean, we have no paddleball sets, or darts, or even a lawn."

Birdie takes Dawn's hands and pulls her up from the table. "I grew up without any of those things. No one can make better games out of nothing than kids from my quarter."

Birdie gathers a length of twine used for tying meat, a packet of stale crackers, and a tin of sugared fruit rinds. How had she not noticed that before?

"Is there something to mark the floor?" she asks. "Not permanently, though." Birdie will have to clean whatever messes they make.

Forest puts a hand on her shoulder. She knows it's him instinctively because of the jolt it sends through her. It's the first time he's touched her deliberately. She glances down at his long, elegant fingers, his hand engulfing her shoulder. Her breath catches.

She looks up at him. He points toward the hallway and walks out. He's taking care of her request. It's amazing how quickly they've come to understand each other.

"Well, come on," Birdie says to the others, trying to sound like she isn't crumbling inside with how badly she wants Forest to touch her again. "We aren't playing in the kitchen."

"The study?" Minnow asks. Everyone is excited by this idea except her. Which is odd, because she's so competitive during their card games. Maybe Minnow and River had a falling out. River certainly seems upset. But Minnow doesn't.

"Top floor." It's perfect. A wide, open space. Birdie's annoyed she didn't think of it sooner. But then again, she's a maid, not a nanny. She's never been in charge of entertaining before. Just making it appear that the house and everything in it cleans itself.

Minnow scowls. "We can't."

"Why not?"

"We're not allowed up there."

"No one said that."

"The stairs being locked says *they* aren't." Minnow juts her chin out toward the residents filing out of the kitchen. "Besides, the House Wife will need help. And Rabbit's not down here yet."

Birdie tries to hide her alarm. This is the first time Minnow has implied she wants the role of the House Wife's maid. If Minnow stays down here and the House Wife comes out, she'll get into that room before Birdie does. Is that what Minnow's shift in demeanor is about?

"Come or don't; it's up to you." Birdie feigns indifference, but it's not lost on her that Minnow hesitates in the foyer. She *is* trying to take the spot. Come to think of it, Minnow has always made sure to be in the kitchen or the hallway when the House Wife appears. Available and ready.

Birdie has to figure out what Minnow is really doing here, and she has to figure it out today.

With various sounds of excitement and grumbling acceptance,

Lake, Dawn, River, Minnow, and even Sky wait as Birdie unlocks the stairway door. Sky seems barely awake, though he still stays as far away from her as possible.

"Dawn, will you fetch Nimbus?" Birdie asks. "We don't want to leave him out."

Forest appears from the direction of the study with a handful of chalk and charcoal. Birdie would never have risked taking supplies, but Forest is allowed. He holds them out for approval.

"Perfect. Much better than the old bricks we used to mark up the street," Birdie says. It *is* better. But the memories send a pang of longing through Birdie. Magpie was still so small when Birdie left to start working. What games did Magpie play without her? What adventures and intrigues and childhood triumphs and heartbreaks did she have? Birdie hates that she missed those things, hates that she's missed everything, hates that she's still missing the one person she has to find.

She wants Forest to meet Magpie. She's sure they'd get along.

Is she sure, though? She doesn't know Magpie anymore. And outside this strange bubble of existence, would Forest even be her friend? Or is this the only place in the whole country where a rainy-day activity like this could happen?

Dawn guides Nimbus out, chattering happily to her unresponsive companion. It warms Birdie's heart—unavoidably, thanks to Dawn's ability. This outing isn't necessary, but it feels right. *Do what good you can, where you can.*

"Up!" Birdie declares, unlocking the door to the stairs. Dawn's eyes are wide, like she's engaging in a transgressive act. River helps her with Nimbus, each of them taking one of his hands. Lake seems to not know where she is again, so Forest steps in. Birdie brings up the rear with Sky. He has to press his whole body against the wall to maintain a distance between them, but it's automatic, like he doesn't even know he's doing it.

"Where are we going?" he murmurs, blinking in the dim light.

"To play some games."

To Birdie's relief, Minnow darts into the stairwell after them. She still looks nervous, though.

"Do you want to get Rabbit, or do you want me to?" Birdie asks.

"Leave her where she is," Minnow says.

River glares back down at Minnow before peeling off down the hallway toward the maids' rooms. "I'll get her."

Interesting. Something *is* wrong between them. A breakup, or a conflict between conspirators?

"What?" Minnow snaps.

Birdie tears her eyes away from where they've fixed on her adversary. "Nothing."

At the top of the stairs, Forest has already gotten to work drawing a series of numbers on the floor. The small round windows let in enough light for them to function, but it's gloomy. Or maybe that's just Birdie's mood despite Dawn's effect.

River joins them. "Rabbit's not there," she says. "The House Wife must have needed her early. No treatment for Sky today, I suppose." She juts her chin out toward where Sky sits, charcoal in hand, mindlessly rubbing it back and forth on one of the boards.

Birdie tries not to look upset, but she is. Yet another chance to jump in to help the House Wife ruined. The one morning she doesn't get up early and Rabbit somehow does.

"Sky, are you done with treatment?" River asks.

Sky doesn't respond.

"It's got to be soon." River says it lightly, but Birdie despairs hearing it. That's probably the tension between River and Minnow. River's going to claim the next treatment spot, and they're worried about it. All this time Birdie spent building trust with the residents, and the one that mattered most was never going to help her. She should have known better than to relax, better than to enjoy herself, laughing and chatting and playing card games.

"What's the twine for?" Dawn calls. Her braid this morning is her best yet after Birdie tried to teach her and then Minnow grumblingly took over.

Birdie sets aside her worries and frustrations to focus on the task at hand. The better she is at pretending nothing is wrong, the easier it will be to catch Minnow and River in whatever act they're trying to commit.

"For fun," Birdie declares.

They play three-foot monster, sightless search, hop-top. Dawn draws everyone's portraits on the walls—she's not technically accurate but captures the *feel* of each of them, down to Sky's sleepy sneer—and Lake shocks them by beating everyone in foot races. Birdie suspects Forest threw it, though. There's no way with his lanky stride he couldn't win. When she catches his eye after, he doesn't so much as betray a smile, but he does wink at her. She looks down to hide her own warm rush of a smile.

Sky doesn't participate, but he seems content. And Nimbus is as relaxed as she's seen him so far. His eyes track less, and there are a few times when she could swear he briefly makes eye contact. Maybe all of them being together like this is good for him.

The most likely answer, though, is that they've managed to make Dawn so genuinely happy they have no choice but to be the same. Even Minnow laughs, the sound echoing loudly around them as River tries to teach them all a formal dance. Minnow can't manage the moves to save her life.

"No, *I* lead," River says.

"I don't want you to lead," Minnow responds, deliberately trying to trip River. Dawn watches, clapping the beat no one is moving to.

"The birds are all gone," Lake says, staring sadly upward. She starts drifting toward the far tower. "No more messages. All alone."

"No!" Minnow drops River's hands. She sprints across the space and roughly grabs Lake's arm, pulling her back toward the group. When Birdie catches her eye, Minnow looks away.

"It's not safe," she says. "The tower stairs are missing steps. If any of them get hurt, it'll be our necks."

It's true. But Minnow managed to panic despite Dawn's contagious happiness. Which means she has incredibly strong feelings about no one going in that tower. And she also knows that there are stairs and some of them are missing. Which means she's explored this space more thoroughly than Birdie ever did.

As though to diffuse any lingering attention, Minnow takes charge, directing new games. The rain slashes against the windows, making the cavernous room feel almost cozy. The hours tick by. Minnow plays like she has nothing to hide, all while keeping everyone focused on their activities.

"I'm sorry, my doves," River says at last, "but I insist we break for lunch. Otherwise, I'll get too hungry, and I'll have to eat whoever is youngest and plumpest and prettiest."

Dawn squeaks in mock fear as River growls and chases her toward the stairs. The others follow, Minnow eagerly shepherding them.

Birdie stops on the stairs at the maids' hallway. "I'll see if Rabbit's back and wants to eat," she calls, waiting until she hears the stair door at the bottom open and then close.

Birdie goes back up. She hops over Forest's squares and

numbers, careful not to smudge them. The stairs at the far tower await. Stairs that are in perfect working condition, with not a single board missing. Which Minnow already knew, because she's the one who "cleaned" this room.

Birdie should have explored better. She should know better than anyone that just because something appears empty and plain doesn't mean there isn't something going on inside.

At the top of the stairs is a trapdoor. It's dark, but she feels around until she finds a latch. She catches the swinging door just before it bangs against the wall. Gray, rain-streaked light filters down from the tower windows, illuminating a cage holding pigeons. On the floor next to the cage is a small leather pouch. Birdie undoes the tie and peers inside. Oil pencils and tiny slips of paper.

Someone's sending messages. And it isn't Cook or the House Wife, because they have no reason to hide it.

When Birdie climbs down and turns around, she almost isn't surprised to find Minnow waiting, knife in hand.

"I wish you hadn't gone up there," Minnow says.

CHAPTER TWENTY-TWO

An Arrow Nocked

"Who are you?" Birdie asks. She doesn't look afraid, or angry. Arrow wants her to be angry. Wants Birdie to attack her, to lunge at her. To make what happens next self-defense and not murder.

Arrow came here to become a murderer, but not like this. Not Birdie. No matter what the maid is hiding, Arrow doesn't want to kill her.

But she will.

"It doesn't matter who I am. I know who you are."

Birdie surprises Arrow again. She *laughs*. "Who am I, then?"

Arrow feels oddly defensive. Like Birdie's the one in control. Like Arrow should be embarrassed to be holding a knife. She adjusts her grip. This is why she's here. This is why she abandoned her home, her people, her life.

Not that she has much left of any of those, anyway.

Arrow should just kill Birdie. Slit her throat and be done with it. She knows where to aim, what moves of a blade can do quick but irreparable damage. The whole journey here, she imagined elaborate methods of killing the southern operative. But now that she knows it's Birdie, Arrow doesn't want to do any of them. She just wants to get it over with.

So why hasn't she moved yet?

"You're a plant," Arrow says. "Recruiting for the military. Here to find those with the most devastating abilities to send them north so they can hurt my people. Don't pretend you don't know."

Birdie has the audacity to frown. "*You're* from the north. I wondered. But who told you I was working for the military?" She tilts her head, much like her namesake might while considering a meal.

Arrow wishes they had given her the name a week ago, before she liked Birdie. Before she'd seen Birdie be kind and helpful to everyone here, including Arrow. When she sent Iron the names of those in the house, she didn't even list Birdie's. So how did Iron know who Birdie was, if Birdie isn't their target?

No. Iron wouldn't get this wrong. They had risked too much to get Arrow into this house.

"Just tell me what wasn't real," Arrow says, needing something to spur her on to this final terrible act. "Tell me what you were lying about. Tell me where you're really from, what your name really is."

Birdie still doesn't look angry or scared, but she does look a little sad. "My name is Birdie. I'm from the lower east quarter of Sootcity. We call it the light quarter, even though it's always dark, because most of it has been taken over by factories making gas lamps. I'm not part of the military. I've worked as a maid since I was ten, and I extorted the minister of finance to get my spot here."

"What?" Arrow wasn't ready for that last bit of information. Why would Birdie need to extort the minister of finance to get here if she's working for the Ministry of Defense?

For a while, Arrow was terrified River was the operative, with her connection to the minister of defense. She was devastated to find Birdie's name buried in a newly delivered sack of sugar, but at least it wasn't River's. That's her only consolation.

"My sister came here," Birdie says. "A little over six months ago. I think. No one can access the records, so I'm not sure. I was hoping I'd find her, but I'm not a lucky person." Birdie gestures toward the knife as evidence of that truth. "Are you going to stab me or not?"

Arrow scowls. This keeps going worse. Iron wouldn't have hesitated; she would have already taken care of Birdie. But Iron wouldn't have needed a knife to do it. Arrow's useless. She needs to keep Birdie talking while she figures out what to do. Or how to do what she already knows needs to be done.

"I'm not going to stab you here," Arrow says. "We're going out into the bog. I'll say you ran away. No blood, no body, no way to prove me right or wrong."

"Well, that's a relief. I was worried you were a liar *and* stupid."

Arrow laughs. She can't help it. Birdie's funny when she's not pretending to be the meekest maid to ever live.

"You said your dad died going to get bread," Birdie says. "Was that a lie?"

Arrow's throat is tight and painful. "The miners were picketing. One of the soldiers with abilities made everyone panic. In the chaos, my father was trampled to death. He wasn't even there for the demonstration; he was just trying to get across the street to the shops."

Birdie's expression goes soft. "Oh. And your mother?"

"Doctor and surgeon, for whoever needed it. Which more often than not were termites."

"Termites?"

"You'd call them bogger insurgents. Terrorists. Freedom fighters."

"Them? Not us?"

Arrow scowls. "My mother wouldn't let me join. She saw the cost, day in and day out, on the kitchen table she used to operate. And then one day I came home and she was dead. Lying on that same table."

As always, Arrow wonders: Did the soldiers bash her mother's head in when she fought back? Did her mother do it to herself before they could burrow into her thoughts? Or did the termites kill her before she could give them away?

It doesn't matter. Gone is gone. That's what they tell themselves, in her village. *Gone is gone*, they said, when the soldiers lit their bordering peat bog on fire so they'd lose their fuel source and more men would have to go work in the mines, extracting coal for the south's industry. *Gone is gone*, they said, when Arrow's favorite little neighbor wandered into that burning peat bog, looking for his missing cousin, and never came back. *Gone is gone*, they said, when kids were taken from yards, from homes, and then from schools, whole groups of children just vanished. Carted south, never to be heard from again.

Gone is gone.

Arrow's never been able to accept that. She knows her mother is gone, but it does matter. It has to matter. And besides, not everyone who goes stays gone. Iron is proof of that.

When Arrow was little and even more of a rot-brained fool than she is now, she told her friend Iron that she wanted to go to the south and get the procedure so she could see in the dark.

"That's not an ability!" Iron had laughed, jabbing her meanly in the side.

Despite her name, Iron was as buttery and golden as a perfect summer day, the kind they got once, maybe twice a year up north. But, just like those days, Iron's loveliness was a deception. Because behind the sun is always a knife of coldness waiting to cut them back down and remind them they don't get beautiful, gentle things.

Iron wasn't kind as a child. And when she came back from the dead to offer Arrow a chance to help the north, she was even worse. But she was also the *only* stolen child who escaped. A miracle. The north never got miracles. Who was Arrow to deny her request?

Arrow never asked who the real Minnow was or what happened to her. She doesn't want to think about it. Just like she doesn't want to think about what has to come next. Because no matter what she thinks of Birdie, the north has to come first. She has to fight for it, because so few others can.

"It's all just luck, isn't it?" Arrow asks. "Luck that my mother traveled to the north, fell in love with my father, and decided to stay. Luck my father died, trampled to death in a crowd. Luck I grew early and didn't look twelve anymore that night all my friends disappeared. Luck that my mother was able to do what she did for as long as she could. Luck that she got caught. Good luck, bad luck, it's all the same: random and uncontrollable." Arrow looks down at the knife. So little has ever been within her control, but this still is.

"Wait," Birdie says. "Your friends disappeared when they were twelve?"

Arrow scowls. "Don't pretend you don't know what happens."

"Please, tell me." Birdie leans closer. She should be leaning away, trying to escape.

"You take them. The children. You snatch them up and send them south to work in the factories or on the farms or who knows where. We never see them again." Except for Iron, who made it back. But she didn't make it back whole. She made it back . . . different.

"Stone. Hammer. Obsidian. Silver."

Arrow flinches. "I had a cousin named Obsidian."

Birdie's voice is calm but insistent. "I'm not an agent of the south. I don't know who told you that or why. I'm only here to find my sister. But I think I know what's happening to the children taken from the north. Those were names scratched into the floor of one of the cells. I think they were here."

"Why would they be sent here?" Arrow asks, and then it all falls into place. Iron never told Arrow how she got her terrible power, or what happened to the children who were taken alongside her. "They're putting them through the procedure," Arrow whispers. "But *why*? Why would they do that? Why would they want potential enemies to have abilities?"

"I don't know," Birdie says, and Arrow finally believes her. She's played enough card games with Birdie to know that Birdie has a tell when she's trying to be deceptive: she makes full eye contact. And right now, Birdie's not doing that. She's being herself, looking down more than up. The way she's always been trained to, because Birdie is, in fact, a maid.

Iron was wrong. That's the only explanation. Birdie's death wouldn't do a thing to help the north. So who *is* here that Arrow actually needs to kill? Or was Iron's intel completely off from the start?

"We both need the same thing," Birdie says. "Information. We have to get through the House Wife's door."

Arrow lowers the knife. She's not going to kill Birdie. It might be a mistake, but it's a mistake she can live with.

"Have you managed to get onto the hidden third floor yet?" she asks.

"What?" Birdie looks aghast. "There's a hidden third floor? *That's* why you were asking about secret staircases!"

Arrow sighs. "Maybe I don't want to be partners if you didn't notice how many extra steps it takes to get from the second floor to this one. I figured that out the very first night."

"I haven't been coming up here every day to play with my pet homing pigeons."

Arrow folds her arms, feeling prickly. "I wasn't going to let them starve. And I've been doing a good job being a maid."

Birdie gives her a flat look.

"Fine, a passable job."

A single eyebrow rises and Arrow regrets her decision not to murder Birdie. "How are we getting into the House Wife's room, then?" she asks. "That's got to be where the stairs are. I've checked every wall panel and looked for hidden spaces on the first, second, and fourth floors. Nothing."

Birdie bites her lip. "I can pick locks, but the House Wife is always inside her room. We need to lure her out long enough for one of us to take a look."

"I could set a fire," Arrow says. "As distraction. The House Wife runs out, we run in."

"Unless we get through that door and immediately find every single answer we're looking for, we need to be able to stay in the house until we have a ride out through the impassable bog."

"Do you have any better ideas?" Arrow demands. She came up the stairs thinking she was finished here, for better or worse. Mostly worse. Entirely worse, if she's being honest. She would have had Birdie's blood on her conscience forever, *and* left River behind with no explanation.

Birdie holds up her hands in a placating gesture. "A distraction *is* a good idea. I had limited options because I thought I was on my own in this. But if we're partners . . ." She trails off, waiting for confirmation.

Arrow knows what Iron would tell her to do. Even if Birdie isn't the right target, she knows too much now and is a liability. The fact that Birdie isn't already dead is evidence that Arrow's mother was right. Arrow isn't cut out to be a termite.

Do you know why I named you Arrow? Mama asked, the night before she died, after yet another fight between them. *Arrows fly straight and true once loosed, so be careful where you aim.*

Killing Birdie is the only way to keep her secrets safe. But Arrow isn't Iron, even if she did come here with terrible vengeance in her heart. She can't just eliminate Birdie the way Iron got rid of whoever the original Minnow was. Besides, Birdie's trying to save someone.

Just one person, Iron whispers in Arrow's head. *Against your entire country.*

If the termites valued individual lives a little more, though, they would have taken better care of her mother. Arrow wouldn't be alone. And she's so tired of being alone. She wants an ally. A partner. A friend.

It doesn't mean she's giving up her knife. If she finds a person whose death will actually help the north, she won't hesitate.

She hopes.

"You do know I'm an enemy to the entire south, right?" Arrow asks. "Everything you know about the north is wrong. We were peaceful, and solitary, and happy, until the south discovered our coal stores and decided to 'take care of us' by grinding us into submission. If I help you, it will be to find out where the kids from the north were sent and get them back so we can take down the Ministry."

Birdie nods. "I don't blame you. And honestly, I don't care about anything as long as I get Magpie back."

"Then we understand each other." Arrow holds out her hand. "My name's Arrow, by the way." It feels good to say it out loud, but also strangely traitorous. She should have told River first. She *wanted* to tell River first.

"Nice to meet you, Arrow. My first act as your partner is to inform you that Forest is right behind you and has been this whole time."

Arrow whirls around. Sure enough, Forest looms, staring down at her with his upsettingly blue eyes.

"How are you that big *and* that stealthy?" she demands.

He shrugs.

She wants to punch him, just to get a reaction. "How can we trust him, though? He's one of *them*."

"Who is he going to tell? He won't even write things down," Birdie says. Then she addresses Forest. Her voice is tentative once more. "I wanted to talk to you about Magpie, so many times. But I was scared. We can trust you, though, can't we?"

Forest nods.

Arrow fights panic. This is spinning out of her control. But maybe that's a good thing. Birdie has no love for her country, and Forest seems to care only about Birdie. So as long as Arrow fits in with Birdie's needs, Birdie will protect her. And when what they need diverges . . .

Well, Arrow will do what she has to.

"Come on," Arrow says. "The others will miss us soon. Be thinking of a distraction. I'll do the same. And you—" she says, pointing to Forest. "Next time you sneak up on me, I *will* stab you."

Arrow walks down the stairs. Birdie and Forest follow. She

feels another strange pang of longing, wishing it had been River up there, backing her up and knowing her truth. But too many people know already. And no matter what River says or thinks, she's not a revolutionary. She's a rich girl with bad luck. And Arrow's the worst thing that's ever happened to her.

Everything Arrow loves dies. She won't do that to River. Let her die, or love her.

CHAPTER TWENTY-THREE

A Bird Spotted

"Wait." Minnow—*Arrow*, Birdie reminds herself for what feels like the fortieth time that day—holds out an arm to block Birdie from leaving the kitchen. As usual, they crept down in the middle of the night, unable to sleep. But tonight they talked alone, debating various plans. Now it's time to unlock Forest and bring him up to speed.

Arrow argued against involving Forest further. "It's not like he can contribute much," she said. But Birdie feels better when he's around. She doesn't let herself think about what will happen when she knows where to look for Magpie next. If she'll have to leave him behind and break her heart again, just like when she had to leave her friend forever locked behind that door in the minister's house. But what else can she do? Ask Forest to come with her?

"What is it?" Birdie whispers, trying to peer past Arrow's outstretched arm.

"Air's different. The front door's been opened."

Birdie didn't notice. Arrow is more in tune with this landscape than the rest of them. Birdie burns with a flush of shame, thinking of the term they use for northerners. Boggers. A hateful name, thrown around without care. She knows nothing about the north, other than that it provides coal and other resources and requires a constant military presence. She had no idea how bad things were. But even Nimbus never had a geography or history lesson that covered what's been done to their neighbors.

"Someone's here?" Birdie asks.

"Or someone got out." Arrow rushes forward, Birdie hot on her heels. If Nimbus is out there alone . . .

Raised voices pull them up short. One of the voices is new. But the other is all too familiar.

"Who is that?" Arrow whispers.

"The minister of finance." All Birdie's hopes at last drain away. He's here. He must have recovered the letters she stole for leverage. It was selfish and stupid of her to leave them hidden in the neighborhood junk pile. Birdie will never forgive herself if he hurt Mare, who never had food or coin long because she always passed it to whatever child needed it most. But Birdie will never have the chance for forgiveness anyway, because now he has no reason not to make her disappear forever.

The other man sounds upset. "When you told me you had a way to fix him, I thought you meant restore him to who he used to be!"

"Your son screamed every time someone touched him. He collapsed into fits at the slightest contact. And don't pretend he wasn't a horrid little cretin before that. We all remember what he did to that girl at the minister of reform's ball. He's a perfect heir now. Pliable and placid and, most importantly, quiet. Isn't that right, Sky?"

"Yes, sir." Sky's voice drifts down the hallway, so soft they barely hear it.

"But he's—they—they changed him. I'm going to the council; they'll hear about this. They'll hear about *everything*."

The minister's voice remains calm and cold. "How long have we been friends? Decades, isn't it? I know exactly how many times you've visited this house. And you're still benefiting from it, with your son healed. Improved, even. But by all means, tell the council. Explain why Sky was in the House of Quiet. See if the stain ever washes off, if anyone ever considers him a worthy match. He is your only heir, is he not?"

"Think of your own son! How would you feel if our positions were reversed?"

At this, the minister's voice finally shifts. He sounds confused and angry. "My son? Now you're speaking nonsense. If you're unhappy with my discreet solution to your embarrassing problem, perhaps you'd like to observe as Sky receives one last *treatment*."

"No! No, you're right. This is better. I was just surprised, is all. I'm happy. My boy's happy. Aren't you, son?"

Sky doesn't answer.

"Good," says the minister. "Beetle, fetch the maid."

Birdie grasps Arrow's hand and drags her back to the kitchen. "Please," she whispers. "Please, promise me you'll find my sister."

"What?"

"Swear it! Swear you'll find Magpie. Tell her I tried."

Arrow looks terrified, but she nods. "I swear."

Birdie takes a deep breath, then steps free of the kitchen to meet her fate. She doesn't want Arrow tainted by association. The minister is visible now, waiting in the foyer. The last time she saw him, he was sitting at his desk, staring impassively as she revealed her treachery and made her demands. He'd smiled and said the House of Quiet seemed like a good place for her.

She understands now. He knew she'd be stuck until he had everything in place to come and get her. She never actually tricked him into anything. He always had the power. He even *looks* more powerful. Younger. Stronger. His face less lined, his skin flushed with health.

He glances over at her movement, eyes flicking across her and then away.

"Here," a new voice says. It's the driver from the carriage. Birdie should run. She should hide. But she's rooted to the spot. Because Beetle—the driver—isn't looking for her. He's got another maid in his arms. Rabbit is completely limp, her skin a dull, lifeless color. Even her copper curls seem tarnished. And . . . she's not breathing.

The change from the bubbly, nervous, kind Rabbit she met in the carriage to the maid they all knew here was drastic, but Birdie was so focused on finding her sister that she thought of Rabbit only as an obstacle. Rabbit needed her help, and Birdie failed her.

"Dump her in the bog with the rest of them," the minister says, as matter-of-factly as if he were informing his butler to plan for guests. Then he turns away from Beetle and talks to someone else. "It's long past time to streamline this entire operation. Moving to the coastal facility will make everything easier, especially with the shipments from the north. I can still count on you to push the plans forward, right?"

"Yes, of course," the other man says. "Come along, Sky. We'll wait in the coach." An older man in a pristine suit more expensive than the procedure Birdie's entire family spent a lifetime saving for escorts Sky out. They don't even glance at Rabbit's body.

Birdie wants to scream. To attack the minister. To hit him until he tells her what happened to Rabbit, what he meant by *the rest of them,* what happened to Magpie. But she's frozen with fear. He wanted her to see Rabbit's body and know what's coming.

The House Wife's singsong voice floats through the hallways. "Hurry," she calls. "There's so much noise, and we need to quiet it. If we can't quiet the noise . . ."

"You weren't supposed to kill the maid," the minister says in a mildly irritated tone, as though the House Wife has misplaced his slippers. "She was for practice."

"We need more," the House Wife says. "It used to be easier."

"Well, you've got that other one to tide you over now. And *try* to be subtler with the rest of them than you were with Sky. The four of them have parents who will be vital to your continuing survival. Do you understand?"

"We understand everything," the House Wife says.

"Doubtful," the minister mutters. "I'll be back soon." He turns on his heel and steps out of Birdie's line of sight. The door opens. It closes. He's gone.

He saw Birdie. She's sure he did. But maybe this was what he wanted her to understand. He can come and go as he pleases; she's only leaving here the same way Rabbit did.

Oh, Rabbit. Birdie's heart aches, and her eyes burn with tears. Rabbit needed her help, and Birdie never saw it. She was too fixated on finding her sister. Who is the House Wife? What is she doing back there? And did it happen—

Did it happen to Magpie?

Arrow puts a hand on Birdie's shoulder. They dart down the hallway to the safety of the dark stairs. Once they get to their stairwell, Birdie's shaking so hard she has to sit down. Arrow sits next to her.

"Is Rabbit—"

Birdie nods, unable to speak.

Arrow puts her arm around Birdie, holding her close. Her voice is fierce and assured when she talks again, like she's trying to be certain enough for both of them. "Magpie's not dead."

"How do you know?"

"Because he said Rabbit wasn't supposed to die. Which means that's not how it usually goes. It was an accident. She was supposed to practice on Rabbit. They must be doing something new. With the residents, or to prepare for this move to the coast, and it went wrong."

Birdie wants to believe Arrow. She wants to believe that she'd know if Magpie was dead. She pretends that's the truth. Both because she needs to, and because she knows Arrow also needs to believe that there aren't dozens, if not hundreds, of northern children's bodies out there in the bog.

"*Five*," Arrow says, snapping her fingers. "There are five residents left."

"What do you mean?" Birdie asks.

"I mean there are five residents. He said that *four* of them have parents who matter. Which means one of them . . ."

"One of them isn't a real resident. One of them isn't here for treatment at all."

One of them is a traitor.

After a few agonizing minutes, Arrow squeezes Birdie's hand. "I'm going back to the kitchen, in case there's anything else to hear. You go up to the top floor and send out one of my pigeons. You aren't the threat, which means we still have to figure out who is. Write *minister of finance* and *Beetle*. Then hide on the tower stairs. The minister might not really be gone."

Birdie does as she's told, like a coward. She scribbles the names, releases the pigeon, and then sits in the dark, terrified, certain at any moment the driver will appear and drag her to join Rabbit in the bog. But no one comes. After what feels like an eternity but was probably only an hour, she goes to her room. She'll wash the tears off her face, and then she'll go through Rabbit's things. She needs to find something to lead her to Rabbit's family. She owes them the truth of what happened to Rabbit. She owes them so much more than that.

When Birdie walks into her room, there's a drawing on the floor, as if someone slipped it beneath the door. A bird, hiding beneath a branch, peering out. But the bird is on high alert. The danger hasn't passed. The bird still needs to stay hidden.

Birdie sets it next to the drawing on her washstand. It's a companion piece, done in the exact same style. A style she'd know anywhere, because she has a whole satchel of drawings just like it. Which means not only was the minister here, but her friend was, too.

That . . . or her friend has been here the whole time.

CHAPTER TWENTY-FOUR

A Bird Plotting

As morning approaches, Birdie paces the kitchen. She can't stop staring at the empty chair by the door. The one where Rabbit would slump after a day of *helping* the House Wife. She tries not to remember how chipper Rabbit was when they met. How excited to be contributing to her family's future. Rabbit is gone, as is the ghost who took her place.

Arrow sits on the window bench, staring out at the dark night. If anyone comes, they'll have a lantern and she'll be able to see them.

Birdie wrings her hands. "We need to figure out who isn't really here for treatment. They must be spying for the minister, since he's trying to change things. Which is another wrinkle. We might not have much time before they board up this house and move the entire thing to the coast. I doubt we'll be taken along."

"It's not Nimbus," Arrow says. "No one could fake what he's going through, and he's in his room most of the time."

Birdie nods, relieved they're in agreement. "It's not him. It's got to be someone the minister already knows and trusts; Nimbus

THE HOUSE OF QUIET

never crossed paths with him. I worked in both their houses. I would have known."

"Not Dawn, either," Arrow says. "We'd feel her emotions about it. She literally can't be sneaky. Maybe Lake? She pops up in strange places all the time. She could be eavesdropping. And she might not be as young as she looks."

Birdie sits at the table. "The day before yesterday I found her in the linen closet having a heated conversation with no one. She'd been in there so long she'd soiled herself."

"Oh," Arrow says softly.

Birdie shares Arrow's disappointment. Lake, like Nimbus, is truly incapacitated by her ability. Unlike two others. Two others who have never said what their abilities are, or proved they even have one. Two others who have made themselves central to the household activities, who are always in a position to observe, who are old enough to know the minister and work with him. "It's Forest, or . . . River."

Arrow shakes her head, round eyes narrowing. Then something in her seems to settle, leaving her gaze heavy. "River's constantly prodding for information. And she set herself up in the kitchen, which seems out of character for someone with her upbringing. It puts her in the middle of everything—making it easy to keep tabs on Cook, the House Wife, and the rest of us. She also claims to know almost everyone, including Sky. Which means she knows his family. And she's connected to the minister of defense."

"That's who the minister of finance was working against. I stole letters to that effect."

"And," Arrow says, her voice slowing with reluctance, "she knows I'm from the north."

Birdie raises her eyebrows. "You didn't think you should tell your partner that someone else in the house knows that?"

"She doesn't *know* know. Only suspects. I haven't told her any-thing. But she's not the only one who's made an effort to get close to us. Forest followed me upstairs when I confronted you."

"Because you had a knife!"

"He didn't know I had a knife. He was just following me. And that night we found Nimbus wandering, Forest came into the kitchen after us. It was like he knew we were awake. Like he was watching, or waiting. And since then he's made sure we're never up in the middle of the night without him."

"River's done the same!" Birdie protests.

Arrow holds up a finger to shush her. "I know. Which is why I brought her up before Forest. But we can't ignore Forest just because you get lost in those upsettingly blue eyes."

Birdie wrinkles her nose, then sighs. Arrow's right. And she's being more than fair in considering the person she has feelings for, too. "Fine. Yes. Forest is suspicious."

"He could be anyone. He could be reading our minds, or put-ting thoughts in. Or he could be doing nothing at all. No abilities. Just a spy making certain everything at the House of Quiet is run-ning how they want it to now that important children are here, or gathering evidence for the minister's argument that they should start a new facility."

"If that's the case," Birdie says, "why didn't he turn us in when the minister was here? He knows neither of us is who we say we are."

"The same reason River didn't come out, if she's the spy. Be-cause they weren't expecting the minister."

"How do you figure?" Birdie leans forward, curious.

"Remember yesterday morning? Cook knew the coach was coming in, and she didn't want anyone seeing whatever—or whoever—it was bringing, so she drugged us."

"The tea," Birdie says.

Arrow nods. "The tea is the signal that Cook knows the coach is coming."

"That's how you knew your message was here, too," Birdie says.

Arrow shifts uncomfortably on the bench, as though pained by remembering what she was trying to do mere hours ago. "Not the tea. It was the wood. I realized supplies had come in. My contact said she'd send me messages in the sugar bags."

Birdie taps her fingers against the table. She never can sit perfectly still. "If Forest or River is at all clever, which we know they are, they've figured that out. Without the tea, they had no reason to suspect any visitors."

"So it could still be either of them."

Birdie doesn't want it to be Forest. She's already trying desperately to ignore the very real possibility that Magpie, her Magpie, her heart out there in the world, is actually not out there but lying still and cold forever in the bog. The idea of facing Forest's betrayal on top of that threatens to overwhelm her.

She shrugs, trying not to show how upset she is. She has a job to do, and she'll do it. That's what Birdie's good at. Pushing down her own feelings and getting to work. She doesn't matter. She never has. "Either way, between the spy and the minister trying to shut down this house, we're running out of time. We'll do the distraction in the afternoon. And I figured out how."

Arrow frowns. "When did you figure it out?"

"When you were scared because the door was open and Nimbus might have gotten out. It's nearly happened before, so no one will suspect us if it actually happens."

"You want to send Nimbus outside?" Arrow looks genuinely horrified.

"No!" Birdie holds her hands up. "No, I would never put him

in harm's way. We'll bring him upstairs to the maids' hall. We can put him in one of the empty rooms. No one will think to look there, since the stairs are always locked and those rooms are locked, too. Dawn will be the one to discover he isn't in his room when she visits him for story time after lunch. And then we just have to make certain the secret pantry door is cracked open. Someone will notice it eventually during the search and think he went outside. That will bring the House Wife out of her room. I know it will."

Arrow shakes her head. "But if we make everyone think Nimbus got outside, they'll go into the bog to look for him. That's too dangerous. Someone will end up dead."

Someone else. Rabbit's already out there. Birdie thinks of her, floating frozen just beneath the surface, glowing pale and freckled and alone. She won't let that happen to anyone else.

"Not if you're with them," Birdie says. "Can you safely lead them around for an hour?"

Arrow hesitates, conflicted feelings warring across her face.

Birdie puts a hand on Arrow's. "I promise I won't just look for where Magpie is. I'll look for them all."

Arrow swallows, then nods, reluctant but resigned. "It's a good plan. I think it will work."

"It means you'll lose access to the pantry exit, though. Doubtless it will be locked and barred afterward. No more walks with River."

Arrow raises an eyebrow in surprise, and Birdie almost smiles at the innocence of Arrow's shock at being caught.

"The greenhouse is all windows," Birdie says.

"Ah. Well, it's for the best anyway."

"What's for the best?" River asks, leaning in the doorway.

CHAPTER TWENTY-FIVE

An Arrow Alone

"How'd you get out?" Arrow asks, alarmed.

River folds her arms. "I wasn't aware you were my new jailor. My door wasn't locked."

Arrow doesn't know whether that's true or not. It's impossible to say, thanks to Cook's lack of dependability. She and Birdie share a quick glance. River could have gotten out while the minister was here, then.

"Rabbit's gone," Birdie says lightly, watching River for a reaction.

"Gone where?" Either River is genuinely confused, or she's a phenomenal actress. But by River's own admission, she's good at getting people to believe her.

Arrow shrugs. "Her room was cleared out." A lie, but the only way to say what they know without admitting how they know it. "We're waiting to ask Cook about it. Sky's gone, too."

"Oh." Something falls in River's face, and then it hardens. "He must be finished. Has the House Wife come in yet? I want to speak with her about starting my treatments next."

Arrow's head fills with rushing, a terrible wind sweeping through and whipping her thoughts right out. She grabs River's hand and drags her through the pantry and outside. River stumbles after her, confused. As soon as they get around the corner of the house where no one can see or hear them, Arrow stops.

"Don't get the treatment," she says.

River takes a step back, her face as cold as the blanket of fog sealing the land around them. "What do you care?"

"What do I care? I don't want to see you emptied out like Sky! You think the treatments improved him?"

River raises an eyebrow. "Actually . . ."

"Okay, fine, yes. Sky was wretched. But at least he was *himself* and wretched. Do you really want to change like that?"

River puts on her smile. The one Arrow hates. The one that renders her face more art than human. "I know you're leaving me out. I saw the looks between you and Birdie and Forest at supper, and you didn't come get me in the middle of the night. You think I can't understand or help with whatever it is you're all secretly plotting."

Arrow stumbles back. River knows. Of course she knows.

"It's all right. Everyone always thinks I'm useless, until it's too late. I hoped you'd really see me. But you said it yourself in the pantry. It's not me. It was never me. It never is. I'm tired. I'm so tired, and I'm tired of being tired. I used to think what happened to me, terrible as it is, was a gift. The escape I'd longed for. But now—now, it just hurts. Seeing what I could never have in the real world." She turns her head and looks out at the wall of blank white hiding the treachery of the land around them. She takes a half step toward it.

Arrow reaches out and grips her arm.

There's a dreamy, faraway quality to River's voice when she

talks, eyes still on the fog instead of on Arrow. "Don't trust Forest. He spews noxious black poison out of his mouth. There's something wrong with him. Birdie, too. She's always in the dark. She can't find her way out. Whatever she's looking for, she isn't going to find it. Don't let her destroy you, too."

"What are you talking about?" Arrow demands.

"And you." River at last turns toward her, lifting a hand and holding it in the air just shy of Arrow's cheek. Arrow has the sudden devastating desire to tilt her head, to feel River's hand against her cheek. To kiss her like she has so many times in her thoughts and dreams, to hold her, to tell her it doesn't matter *why* she's here, that Arrow's just glad she is. To tell River the truth: Arrow wasn't rejecting her yesterday in the pantry. Arrow was consoling herself that if she had to kill someone, at least it wasn't the girl of her dreams.

"What about me?" Arrow whispers.

"Why are you always covered in blood?"

Arrow takes a step back. "What do you mean?"

"When you sit by that infinitely lonely expanse of ocean every night. What are you doing there? What are you waiting for?"

Arrow's heart picks up. She can't catch her breath. How does River know about the ocean? After Arrow's mother died, Arrow walked to the coast and sat for hours, trying to decide whether to walk into the ocean and keep going until the heavy weight of the water claimed her. That was when Iron found her and gave her a different target for her despair and rage.

But no. River said *every night* Arrow sits there.

Oh *no*. Arrow dreams that so often. But lately her dreams have changed. And River knows. She knows all the things they've done in her dreams. The way Arrow feels about River, the way she's held her and tasted her and been so desperate to devour her. River's known this whole time, because she's not only infiltrated Arrow's heart and mind, but she's also invaded her dreams.

River holds out a hand. "No, listen. Don't look at me like that. I don't do it on purpose. I can't—"

Arrow turns and runs into the fog. The ground is spongy and dew-slick beneath her feet. She sinks down to it, feeling the give, wondering if the plants are hiding the bodies of countless children. She could get swallowed, too, and she doesn't even care. Because she's ruined everything. River knows her heart, knows her secrets, knows *her*. Arrow can't be known. Not ever. That's the one tenet of the termites she understands completely. Being known means death.

But she's sure about one thing now: River has an ability. She's here because her parents sent her. Which means Forest is the traitor.

At least Arrow won't be alone anymore. Birdie's heart is going to be broken, too.

CHAPTER TWENTY-SIX

A Girl Outside Time

Lake stands in a hallway. Or outside. Or in smoldering ashes. She sees so many versions of this place, and most of the time she can't tell which one she's actually in.

"Are you really here?" she asks her companion. He keeps flickering from child to man, so she can't tell what he actually looks like. Only the blue, blue eyes remain the same. "I suppose it doesn't matter, though. You are now or you have been or you will be."

"Which of us are going to die?" he whispers.

Lake laughs. "Everyone." She holds out her hands and spins, encompassing the whole world. "*Everyone* dies, you silly thing."

There's a pause. She thinks he's gone, because she's back in the hallway. It smells fresh and new. Someone is crying nearby. She wants to help them, but a hand appears out of nowhere, holding her arm. Anchoring her.

"Who is going to die in this house?"

"I told you. Everyone. All my friends. Everyone I've met here is dead. Dead or lost. It's the same."

The voice is patient and soft, but compelling. "Tell me: Are any of the people in the house *right now* going to die here?"

Lake stomps her foot. She hates this conversation. It's confusing, and she doesn't like being confused. But she can't help answering. "There's no such thing as now! Not anymore. I don't understand what you mean by that. Oh. Maybe I do." She spins in a slow circle, closing her eyes, thinking. The pretty one, River, she's been young, but she's also been old. And empty. Dawn, too, she's seen that way, and Nimbus: taller, and empty. "Birdie doesn't get older," she says. "That's right. She goes down the stairs, and she doesn't come back up. I never see her again after that. Arrow doesn't get older, either, but I don't know why. And you." She leans closer, taking a deep breath. "You smell like smoke and death. *You're* why I don't get older. I answered your question, so I don't have to talk about this anymore."

Lake skips down the hall—down the empty rock surrounded by bog—through the charred remains of the house—down the hall.

CHAPTER TWENTY-SEVEN

A Bird in a New Room

Birdie can't calm down. The terror of the minister's visit clings to her like the fog clinging to the world outside. Ephemeral but inescapable. He's going to come back, and he's going to move the House of Quiet, taking away Birdie's chance to find information. Worse than those future worries is the new fear that Magpie might have left the house, but not the bog. Magpie is both dead and alive at the same time, in the house, in the bog, out in the world. But nowhere Birdie can reach her right now.

And the only person Birdie knows for sure she can trust is the one person in the house who has tried to kill her. Arrow hasn't come back in from her conversation with River yet, so Birdie does the only thing she knows how to: She gets to work cleaning.

The tasks help calm her body so her mind can function again. She scrubs a bathroom floor and picks a mystery that doesn't feel as dire as the mystery of Magpie's fate.

How did the drawing get into her room?

Birdie doesn't take a lot of time to examine her own feelings. They've never mattered in the past. But that drawing feels personal in a way few things ever have. Maybe because her collection of her friend's art is her only real possession. She has no evidence of Magpie except her own memories. At least with her friend, left behind forever, she had something to keep.

It doesn't make sense that the minister would bring his third-floor resident along on a journey. In the entire six months Birdie was at the house, her friend never left that locked room.

And Birdie is certain it wasn't the minister himself who left her the drawing. It was a warning, not a threat. So if it wasn't the minister, and the odds are very slim that he brought her friend along, that means somehow, impossibly . . . *her friend has been here the whole time.*

It's not Nimbus. Sky is obviously eliminated as well. River knew others in the house, which means she's been out and about the past few years. Or at least, she *said* she knew them. Did any of the others ever confirm it? Regardless, there's nothing about River that screams "locked in the empty third floor of a grand country manor for months on end, if not longer."

She could easily imagine Dawn's or Lake's families locking them up to keep them out of sight. But she would have felt Dawn through the door, no matter how thick it was.

So either her mysterious friend is Lake, who did give Birdie a drawing the other day, even if it wasn't in the same style . . . or Forest. One of their only suspects for the traitor in the house. Maybe it makes sense. After she left the minister, he unlocked that door and sent his secret weapon ahead. But why would her friend agree to it? Why would Forest?

She pauses. The floor is scoured as clean as it's ever been. Birdie moves on to the tub. Scrubbing circles with her hands, chasing circles in her mind. Warning or threat, wherever it came from, the drawing is a reminder of what it cost her to be here. She abandoned her only friend in the world, and for what?

For what?

Birdie wipes her eyes against her shoulder. They're burning, from tears or from fumes; it doesn't matter.

Arrow rushes through the door, mud clinging to the hem of her soaked skirt.

"Get out!" Birdie snaps. All her hard work in here, undone. Whatever else they're up to, they still have to be maids, even if Arrow can't seem to remember it.

But Arrow doesn't move. "Have you seen Lake? She didn't come to breakfast. I went to find her, but I can't. She's nowhere."

Birdie drops her cleaning supplies and rushes out into the hallway. "Lake?" she calls. "Lake!"

"I already checked her bedroom, the study, and the greenhouse."

"Check all the bedrooms and closets. She might have wandered into the wrong one." Birdie splits from Arrow and does a frantic search of every space the small girl could possibly fit into. When they meet back in the hallway, Arrow shakes her head.

"Is the door in the pantry unlocked?" Birdie asks.

The blood drains from Arrow's face. "Lake could have slipped by while I was still outside. Oh no, Birdie, what if she's out there alone?" Gone is the girl holding a knife and pretending she could ever use it. Arrow's devastated, as desperate and afraid as Birdie.

Birdie sprints into the kitchen. River, Forest, and Dawn are sitting at the table, all giving her a curious look. Birdie pounds on Cook's bedroom door. They need everyone. It opens at last to reveal a disheveled Cook.

"What is it?" Cook asks.

"Lake's missing. We can't find her anywhere."

The others stand as Cook rushes past them and into the pantry, then reappears, walking like she's been struck in the head and is about to collapse. "Unlocked," she says. "I always forget to lock that one."

"We'll divide into pairs," Arrow says from the kitchen entrance, keeping watch on the hallway as though Lake might wander by. "I'll show you how to walk out there. You have to make sure every single step you take is safe before you move. And we have to go quickly. The longer she's out there, the less likely . . ." Arrow can't finish the sentence.

"No," Cook says. "The House Wife can find her."

"How?" Birdie demands. The House Wife seems about as useful as the decorative vases in the foyer.

Cook bustles past without answering.

"I'll check on Nimbus," Dawn says, running out. Forest follows. Birdie doesn't know what he's going to do, but she knows it will be helpful.

No, she thinks with a sinking heart. She doesn't know that. Not for certain.

Arrow waves a hand to get Birdie's attention. Birdie frowns. Arrow widens her eyes. And then Birdie realizes what Arrow's communicating. She nods tightly. This wasn't the plan, but . . . it's the same thing. They might not get another opportunity. It feels awful using Lake's actual peril for their advantage, but what choice do they have?

"*What?*" River demands. "I know you two are plotting something." But she doesn't sound angry. She sounds sad.

"We need to find Lake," Arrow says. "Will you go out with me? I promise I'll keep you safe." She seems tentative and unsure.

What happened between them earlier? Hopefully Arrow didn't give away any information she shouldn't have.

River's eyes pool with emotion, but then she cuts it off. "Of course I'll help," she snaps. "And maybe *I'm* the one who will keep *you* safe. You don't know."

Before they can go outside, the House Wife drifts into the kitchen, blocking the doorway. She takes them in with a sweep of her eyes, and then turns toward the rest of the house. "The others are too noisy."

"What?" Birdie asks. There's no noise at all.

"They're too noisy," the House Wife says again. "They need to gather where I can hear them all in the same place. Then I can find the lost one."

"I'm going to look outside," Arrow says.

The House Wife holds up a hand. Her voice is sharp for once. "Get them all together so I can hear the one who's missing."

Arrow and Birdie share one last glance. "Right. Come on, Birdie. Let's gather everyone while the House Wife waits in here. It might take a few minutes. We're not sure where Forest went."

As soon as they hit the hallway, Birdie sprints, turning at the foyer and going straight back to the House Wife's room. The door isn't even locked. At last, at last.

Birdie takes it all in with a panicked glance. It's a bedroom decorated entirely in red, not as richly furnished as the others, but it's too pristine. It looks like the bed hasn't been slept in at all. Birdie touches the quilt there and finds a layer of dust. The whole space is chilly, too. No fire in the fireplace and no evidence that any has been lit in ages. There are some papers on a desk. Birdie grabs them and shoves them into the bodice of her dress. She'll look at them later.

There's a door on the side of the room. None of the other bedrooms have closets. She doubts this one does, either. Could it be the mysterious missing staircase? Birdie holds her breath as she rushes over, turns the doorknob, and—

Birdie's in the hall. She blinks, confused. The House Wife is standing in front of her, staring.

She must have heard the House Wife coming back and made it into the hallway just in time. But. No. That's not right, because—

"Why are you here?" the House Wife asks.

"I was looking . . . I was looking for . . ."

"For Lake," Arrow interrupts, rushing toward them. "We found her. She was on the third floor, halfway up the tower stairs. She was playing a game of find-me-quick. By herself. Without telling anyone. My fault. I must not have locked the stair doors. I won't make the mistake again, so sorry. But now that everyone's safe, we should get back to work."

Arrow clumsily curtsies to the House Wife, then grabs Birdie's arm and drags her down the hall. Birdie trips over her own feet while her thoughts trip over themselves.

Arrow pulls her into Sky's now empty room. "Well?" she demands. "What did you find? And why were you standing frozen in the hallway?"

"I don't—I can't—I don't know what I found."

"You mean you don't understand what you found?"

"No, I mean I don't know. I was in her room and then I was in the hallway, and—" Birdie puts a hand to her racing heart. Something crinkles. The papers! She pulls them out of her bodice and hands them to Arrow.

"This is it? Everything? You were in there for several minutes." Arrow frowns down at the papers.

"What?" Birdie's heart starts racing. "No, that's not right. That can't be right. I remember going into the room and finding those sheets, and then I was in the hallway. There's nothing in between." Birdie turns, eyes narrowed. She tries to take a step toward the door to go back to the House Wife's room, but she *can't*. It's like an invisible figure is standing in her way. As soon as she gives up on getting back to that room, though, she can move again.

"Someone did something to me," Birdie whispers.

"The House Wife?" Arrow suggests. "She was with me the whole time. She's the one who found Lake. But it was just the two of us looking. Everyone else was in the kitchen." Arrow bites her lip. "Any of them could have left, though. We wouldn't have seen them. So I don't know for certain where River was, or . . ."

"Or Forest," Birdie finishes for her.

CHAPTER TWENTY-EIGHT

A Storied Dawn

Dawn wants to have secrets.

She watches the older ones run around—handsome and mysterious Forest, beautiful and funny River, gruff but kind Minnow, lovely and delicate Birdie. She loves Birdie like she's never loved anyone. Minnow, too. They're the first people to ever look at her and think she could be useful for something. And she's been *so* useful. No one else could help Nimbus. Every morning Dawn wakes up and remembers that she has a job to do. A purpose. It fills her with pride, which makes it easy to be happy.

After the excitement this morning with Lake disappearing and then being found, Dawn was too worked up to sit in a bedroom, so she brought Nimbus to the study to draw with her. He sits while she draws, but it's nice. She likes it, and she thinks he does, too. Sometimes he hums—so quiet it's hard to hear—but she thinks it's because he's happy. Not just happy because she is, but really, actually happy to have a friend. To have someone to sit with.

It's how she feels, at least. She hopes he does, too.

"What do you think of Forest?" she whispers conspiratorially. "He's the handsomest man in the whole world. I know what you're thinking; you think I have a crush on him. Maybe I do." But Dawn feels that way about *all* of them—Forest and Birdie and River and Minnow. It isn't that she wants any of them to hold her hand or kiss her. It's that she wants to be older and lovely and full of intrigue like them.

Dawn sighs, resting her chin on her hand. "Do you know why Forest doesn't talk? He had a terrible curse laid on him by a witch. She took one look at his eyes and fell madly in love with him, but his heart already belonged to a princess. The witch declared that if she couldn't have him, no one would. She took the princess's memory and sent her away to be a maid. And then she told Forest the only way his love would ever remember him was if he could tell her his name . . . but then the witch took away his voice! And the only way *his* curse is broken is if his love kisses him. He wandered the whole world searching for his lost love, and at last he found her. But she doesn't remember him, so she won't kiss him and break his curse, and he can't tell her who he is and break her curse. Trapped in the terrible chains of their curses, he stays near her, longing and hoping that it will be enough. That one day she'll look up and see who he really is, and both their curses will be broken. Oh, it's so dreamy and romantic and sad, isn't it?"

There's a noise by the door. Dawn looks up with a start to see Forest leaning there. She blushes, but he's smiling. He likes her story. She's *very* good at telling stories.

Forest beckons to her. Dawn feels a thrill of excitement. At last, she's being included! She practically skips over to him, catching herself at the last moment and walking somberly so he'll know she's mature enough to help.

Forest leans down and Dawn leans in, heart racing, waiting to hear at last what he sounds like.

CHAPTER TWENTY-NINE

A Bird Betrayed

An unfamiliar calm descends on Birdie. They actually accomplished something today. Cook is aware of what's going on for once, as is the House Wife, so Birdie rushed the stolen papers to Rabbit's room upstairs without looking at them. That way she can't be caught with them, and tonight, when she and Arrow can be alone, they'll look at them together. And they'll try to figure out what happened to Birdie in the House Wife's room.

Birdie's fine, though. They may not have found everything they needed, but they found *something*, and they got away with it. Overall, it feels like a huge win. Especially since Lake is safe and sound. And with Cook awake, they don't have to worry about making all the meals today. They can just relax for once.

All her friends are safe, and she's safe, here, with them. She hasn't had real friends since she was a child. She forgot how nice it could be.

The afternoon claims them, sleepy and pleasant. Birdie joins the others in the study, where they're doing practically nothing at all. Dawn reads aloud to them. Arrow's on the sofa. River lies down with her head on Arrow's lap, and Arrow strokes the soft curls along River's hairline.

Birdie knows they're suspicious of River, but it doesn't feel urgent. Nothing does.

"I can sleep now, because no one's sleeping," River murmurs.

Birdie looks around the room, happy. Nimbus sits beside Dawn, who puts down her book and begins working on a portrait of the sweet boy. Lake's lying on her back on the floor, tracing her fingers through the air like she's writing secret messages. Birdie's absent-mindedly tidying because even if she's relaxed, she's still not lazy. Never that. Arrow catches her and smiles, sticking out her tongue.

Birdie turns to find Forest's eyes, wanting to see if he's laughing at her, too, but he's not in here.

Forest. *Forest.*

The calm persists. But calm has never been Birdie's default state. Even with it washing over her in waves—*Dawn, it's Dawn making them feel this way!*—she still has hold of her natural fear of being caught relaxing and losing her job. She's been shaped by that dread since she was ten. Magpie's future—and hers, too—depended on her working as hard as she could at all times. That training goes deeper than any invading feelings.

Birdie gestures to Arrow. If she doesn't leave the room right now, she's going to forget why she's so determined to.

Arrow looks confused, and then she frowns. If Birdie's default is fear, Arrow's default must be suspicion. Birdie watches as it jars her out of Dawn's influence. Arrow stands, placing a pillow beneath River's head, and then follows Birdie out into the hallway.

Birdie hurries them around the corner, trying to put as much distance between them and Dawn as she can. They turn just in time to see the door to the stairs close.

Birdie checks her apron pocket. Her key is still there. Arrow holds hers up, too. But they didn't account for Rabbit's.

Someone is going upstairs.

"The papers," Arrow hisses. They've got enough of a buffer from Dawn now that the artificially mellow mood is fading.

Birdie feels like she's about to be sick, but she keeps pace with Arrow. They enter the stairwell, going up as quietly as only a maid and a spy could. Arrow stops Birdie on the landing to their floor, then pulls her up a few more steps into the darkness.

"Better to ambush him," she whispers.

Arrow assumes it's Forest, too, then. It could still be someone else. Cook, or the House Wife, or an unknown person who stayed in the house last night without them noticing. But Birdie knows who it's going to be. She's never had luck, after all. And she pushed it too far, thinking she could find love with anyone, much less someone like Forest. Thinking she could ever have something that was just for herself.

After a few minutes, her heartbreak is complete. Forest appears with their papers in hand. He doesn't look in their direction, stepping down toward the main floor.

Arrow jumps on his back. "Get the papers!" she shouts, wrapping her arms around his neck and her legs around his waist, trying to pin him.

Birdie darts around Forest, grabs their precious evidence, and then leaps down the stairs three at a time. She knows Arrow can handle herself, but neither of them is strong enough to fight Forest on their own. She expects Arrow to be thrown down after her, the terrible sound of a body bouncing on hard steps, but there are no sounds, no bodies, by the time Birdie bursts through the door at the bottom of the stairs.

And realizes she has nowhere to go.

The front door is locked. The secret pantry exit is locked now, too, thanks to Lake. None of the windows open. Birdie could throw a chair through one or break a greenhouse window, but Arrow's made it clear no one will survive venturing into the bog.

Birdie turns in to the greenhouse and finds her bench. Forest will come for her and the papers. She might not be able to escape, but she can know why he worked so hard to keep these from her.

Birdie reads and doesn't understand what she's seeing, until she does. She leans back, hollowed by devastation. All this time, all her work, all her plans.

She never stood a chance.

CHAPTER THIRTY

A River in Control

River wakes up alone. Where did Minnow go? Things felt okay between them again. Better than okay. River sits up. Dawn, Lake, and Nimbus are all still happily lounging, but Forest, Birdie, and Minnow are gone.

River refuses to be cut out, no matter how pleasant the afternoon is. Everyone always underestimates her, and it hurts that Minnow does, too. It hurts that they all assume she'll stay in here, comfortable and cozy, while they do something stupid without her. She wants to do stupid things, too. She's better at it than any of them. Just ask the minister of defense and his ruined reputation.

River stalks out of the room, letting Dawn's happy lethargy slough off her like shedding a skin. She checks the kitchen first, but it's empty. She comes out into the long hallway to see Forest exiting the stairs on the far end of the house. He shouldn't be on those stairs. And why is he alone? Where are Birdie and Minnow?

"Stop," River says. Forest freezes, then waits as she crosses the distance to him. River stands close, too close, and stares up at him. He looks profoundly guilty. He did something.

"Where's Minnow?" River asks.

Forest points to the stairs.

"And where's Birdie?"

Forest shrugs, then points to the greenhouse.

River nods, then leans close. "Hurt either of them and I'll kill you where you can't fight back."

There's a hint of a smile as Forest nods. Like the prospect of someone willing to kill for Minnow and Birdie is one he finds pleasant, rather than threatening.

"As long as we understand each other." River turns and goes up the stairs. On the second story landing she finds Minnow sitting, rigid and miserable. "What are you doing here?"

Minnow's face twitches, and then her spine slumps. "I can't move."

"You can't move?"

"That's what I said," Minnow snaps. "Forest told me to sit on this step until he comes and gets me or until it's nighttime, whichever comes first."

"Why did he do that?"

"Because I was trying to strangle him."

"Why were you doing that?"

"None of your business. Did he find Birdie?"

"Birdie can take care of herself." River sits beside Minnow. The black sludge pouring from Forest's mouth in his dreams was maybe not a threat, so much as a representation of his own private torment. "Oh, *that's* why Forest doesn't talk. Because when he tells you to do something, you do it. I suppose we're all very lucky he's careful."

"Ask me how lucky I feel right now."

River laughs. Grumpy Minnow might be her favorite Minnow. And Minnow stuck on the stairs, unable to run away from her and this conversation? The very best one of all.

"He won," Minnow says. "But he's trying not to hurt us, and I don't understand why. He could have thrown me down the stairs, or slammed me into the wall, or told me to cut my own throat."

"Hmm." River leans back, shoulder to shoulder and knee to knee with Minnow. They sit there in silence, River waiting patiently.

At last, Minnow lets out an exasperated huff. "Fine! You were right. I can trust you. I think I always knew, but nothing in my life is as terrifying as trusting someone. I'm sorry about what we did in my dreams when we—" Her voice breaks, and River can feel the blush even if it's too dim to see it. "It's just that in there, it was uncomplicated. And out here it's so much more complicated than I can ever explain. You have to understand that."

"I do."

Minnow nods. And then, tentatively, like she's reaching for River's hand, she says, "My name's Arrow."

River nods. "It suits you. You were never a Minnow." Then she turns and leans in until her lips are a breath away from Arrow's, letting Arrow make the final choice. Hoping, hoping, hoping that Arrow chooses her.

Arrow does. And it's even better than in the dreams, because it's real. At last there are no lies or space between their lips.

CHAPTER THIRTY-ONE

A Bird Uncaged

Forest approaches slowly, then stands a few feet away, hands clasped in front of himself. Waiting.

Birdie sets the papers down. "This is a list of the new incoming residents and descriptions of their abilities, as well as how much their families are paying for secret treatments. You aren't on it. Because you aren't supposed to be here. And no one knows you are, do they?" Birdie can't think of a single time Cook or the House Wife interacted with Forest. That first morning, Cook didn't even introduce him. It was River. And whenever Cook has set the table, she's been one place setting short. Birdie chalked it up to her drinking, but it's more than that.

Forest did something to Cook and the House Wife. They don't realize Forest is here. They can't see him at all.

"Who are you?" Birdie whispers.

Forest reaches into his vest pocket and retrieves a folded piece of paper. He holds it out like an offering. Birdie's fingers tremble as she unfolds it. It's a drawing. Not a bird, this time, but Birdie herself. Rendered with loving, precise detail.

Her friend. *Forest.* She didn't leave him behind after all.

"I told you where I was going, that last night," she says, trying not to let tears fall onto the portrait. She sets it carefully onto the bench next to the other papers. "Did you come here for me?"

Forest nods. Birdie tries to get her breathing under control, but her body is in rebellion. No. She'll get it under control. She's good at never showing what she feels. It's part of her job. "To help me? Or to stop me?"

He just purses his lips. Maybe he thinks helping her and stopping her are the same thing.

The mystery of her friend on the third floor is solved. It was Forest, being kept secret because of his ability. Birdie can see it now that she's made the connection. He has the same set to his eyes, the same strong jawline as the minister of finance. But the minister's lips are thin and harsh, his nose aggressive, his eyes dark. He's only one-half of the equation of Forest. But Birdie's seen the other half countless times. The portrait of his dead mother always watched her as she worked to break into the minister's study. She had the most remarkably blue eyes and the same full lips.

"Does your father know you're here?"

Forest shakes his head.

Birdie never once saw the minister go up to Forest's room. *Forest's room.* She trips over that new information, reordering all her memories. It was Forest behind that door, all those long lonely months. Him she talked to. Him she poured her heart out to. Him she left behind.

But he followed her. And it's going to destroy him. "It's not safe for you, Forest. You need to leave."

He lifts a single, wry eyebrow.

"I mean it. You didn't see Sky at the end. And Rabbit, she—she killed Rabbit. You need to get out of here. You *all* do."

Forest shakes his head. Birdie wants to strangle him. Though

Arrow already tried, and apparently that didn't go well. Oh, no, *Arrow*.

"Arrow?" she asks, halfway to standing before Forest holds up a hand.

Safe, he mouths.

She doubts Arrow is happy, but she doesn't doubt that Arrow is safe. Not now that she knows Forest is her friend. But it's not enough. She needs more information. "Please," she says. "You have to talk to me. You have to tell me what's going on. Did you stop me, in the House Wife's room?"

Forest reaches into his pocket and pulls out another paper. This one has been elaborately pasted together from words sliced out of books. It must have taken him ages.

If I say it, you have to do it. Sometimes people get hurt. If I could, I'd talk to you all day, every day. Only you.

Birdie can't look up at him. It's too much. "You stopped me, though. It took me so long to get through that door, and you stopped me. You had no right. I know you're trying to protect me. But that's not what I want. I don't want to be protected. I want to find my sister, and I want—"

Birdie's mouth stops short. She doesn't know what else she wants. Her only friend, her truest, dearest friend, is here, and he's Forest. Even before she knew that, when she looked at him, she wanted more than she can ever allow herself to.

A lifetime of doing things only for others, of shaping herself into the perfect daughter, the perfect sister, the perfect maid, has bound her to her tasks so tightly that wanting anything for herself is unthinkable. Her task is finding Magpie again. Nothing else can matter.

She loves Forest. It's as simple as that, now that she has the full picture of who he is to her. But he's going to get hurt if he stays, and he's already gotten in the way. She has to know whether Magpie is still out there somewhere. Even if it means breaking her heart, and Forest's, too. Why wouldn't Forest want her to know?

Lake's words from the kitchen their very first morning come back to her. If Birdie goes down the stairs, she dies. That's why Forest stopped her. She might be willing to risk everything to know what happened to Magpie, but he's not.

"I don't know what to do," Birdie says, trying to hold back tears. She always has a task, and she always has a way to accomplish that task. But now she's torn.

Forest kneels in front of her, reaching out and taking her hands. His elegantly engulf hers. They're so soft and warm and familiar that she's overwhelmed. But Birdie isn't afraid when Forest opens his mouth.

"You should do what *you* want," he whispers.

An iron band—around her chest for so long she stopped noticing it years ago—shatters. Birdie draws the first full breath in a lifetime of holding herself back, of making herself small and invisible, of never knowing what she wants because she can't afford to think in those terms.

It's not like after the House Wife's room, with the confusion and the sensation that something was physically blocking her. It's the opposite of that. Forest's words have done what nothing else could have:

Birdie's *free*.

And she knows exactly what she wants to do in this moment. She throws herself forward, pressing her mouth to his, eagerly, hungrily. He nearly loses his balance but recovers, wrapping his arms around her waist. She puts a hand against his cheek, finding the curves of his lips with her own, reveling in them. He answers her kiss, tentative, painfully sweet and hopeful in his caution.

There is no caution in Birdie. Not anymore. She hitches her skirts up, unable to bear any distance between her and Forest. With her legs around his waist, she holds him tighter, kissing him harder, fiercer. If she and Forest can somehow be together when everything in the world should have kept them apart, she can find Magpie again. If Birdie can be free, Magpie can still be alive.

After a few breathless minutes, her lips stinging in the most delicious way, her hands desperate for further exploration that will have to wait, Birdie pulls back. Forest looks at her like he's just woken from a nightmare into a dream. He smiles, and Birdie knows what that smile tastes like.

There are no more barred doors. No more years of conditioning binding her to one life and him to another. Anything and everything are possible now.

"Let's go get Arrow," Birdie says. "And then let's find my sister. Together."

CHAPTER THIRTY-TWO

A Bird Conspiring

Birdie paces in the greenhouse, regretting her decision to let Arrow be the spy tonight. She knows it made the most sense—Arrow has no connection to the minister of finance, unlike Birdie or even Forest. But it's agonizing, waiting in here for Arrow to report back. Worrying that maybe she won't be able to report back.

When the tea showed up at dinner tonight, they were all taken by surprise. Another delivery, this soon? Or the minister, coming back already? They faked drinking it, and as soon as Cook retired to her room after locking the residents in, Birdie picked those locks to free River and Forest.

They sit on the bench in the dark, waiting with her.

"I could go out," River whispers. "Pretend to be walking in my sleep or something."

"We can't draw attention." Birdie's wrestling with her own impulses, though. Before, making decisions was easier. She always defaulted to her training. But now she's at war with herself. Because she wants to be in here with Forest—she always wants to be with Forest—*and* she wants to go out and help Arrow.

She understands why Forest said what he did, and she's

grateful, but supper tonight was the first time she realized just how dangerous it makes things. Because when Cook told her to pass out the tea, Birdie almost said no.

She can't say no to things like that. Not if she wants to keep her job here. And she does want that. For now.

Forest reaches out as Birdie stalks past, brushing his hand against her apron. She grasps the tips of his fingers and squeezes them to reassure him, or herself, or both of them. But she can't stop pacing.

At last the door opens and shuts as quietly as Arrow can manage.

"Well?" Birdie hisses.

Arrow hurries over to them, crossly slapping away errant plant fronds. "It was just one person in the coach. Looks a little older than us. His clothes were nice, though, and his hair was very—" She gestures around her head, movements that could be interpreted as indicating his hair had a lot of body and lift, or it was on fire.

Birdie assumes the former. The style in Sootcity right now among the wealthy families is for men to have their hair straightened and then curled, so piles of ringlets sit atop their heads like pampered pets. She's glad Forest isn't stylish, because she's never been able to take anyone with that hair seriously.

"Another resident," River sighs, disappointed. She grabs Arrow's hand and pulls her to sitting so they're practically on top of each other. River wraps her arms around Arrow's waist, and Arrow tips her head against River's shoulder.

It makes Birdie happy. They deserve that connection. And she's so glad she's not alone in this anymore. She's been alone for so long. They all have. No wonder they bonded so firmly, so quickly, even with all the secrets putting up walls between them.

When the whole world tells you you'll never matter, people who truly see you are family, regardless of where you all started.

"Cook and the driver had a conversation, but it was hard to hear. There's another delivery in a week, but I think they're plotting something. She's upset. She doesn't want the house to shut down and get moved."

"Of course she's upset," Birdie says. "She'll lose an easy job where no one watches or cares what she's doing."

Arrow shakes her head. "It felt like more than that. She was crying so hard she could barely breathe."

Interesting. "She didn't care that Rabbit died. What would break her like that?"

"The driver's name is Beetle, right?" River asks. "What does he look like?"

"A stupid old man," Arrow says grouchily.

"Could you be more specific?"

With a sigh, Arrow ticks off a few traits. "Skinny arms and legs, round stomach, heavy jawline, receding hair, pale skin, murky blue eyes."

"I've seen him!" River says, so excited she stands, nearly dumping Arrow onto the floor.

"When?" Birdie asks.

"In Cook's dreams. She's always dreaming about picnicking in a field with him and a little girl. I think they're married."

"That explains the flowers in the kitchen," Arrow says.

"Exactly!" River claps her hands together once. "So if the house closes, they both lose their jobs."

It's an explanation, but Birdie's certain they're still missing something. It doesn't matter, though. She doesn't care a bit about the fate of Cook or Beetle, knowing how callous they were about

Rabbit's death. Knowing it wasn't the first body they'd deposited into the bog.

"So what's our next move?" Birdie asks.

"We all know what our next move is," Arrow says, her voice bladed.

"No," Birdie snaps. She reaches for Forest's hand once more and holds it, letting him know she's on his side, no matter what.

River turns up one of the gas lamps on the wall, giving them a soft glow. "No one will notice it unless they come around to this side of the house. We need to see each other clearly for this conversation."

Arrow's still focused on Birdie. When did Birdie become the person in charge? It's so absurd she could laugh, but nothing feels funny right now.

Arrow jabs a finger toward Forest. "All he has to say is 'Let them in' or 'Stay out here' or even 'Tell us all the secrets of the House of Quiet,' and the House Wife won't be able to stop herself."

"You don't know that." Birdie understands Arrow's frustration. She also knows firsthand how unexpected the results of Forest's commands can be. This afternoon she didn't clean a single bathroom, because she didn't want to. Which, for one day, is fine. But the long-term consequences of being a maid who does only what she wants are dire. They need to move fast. Both because the clock is ticking on the minister's return, but also because Birdie doesn't know how much longer she'll be able to keep up the ruse of who she used to be.

It's not Forest's fault. His intentions were good. But intentions don't matter when it comes to power like his.

Unfortunately, the nuances of Forest's ability don't matter to Arrow. She folds her arms and narrows her eyes. "Yes, well, unless

Forest can give me a compelling reason why it won't work, I say that's our best plan."

Forest stares at Arrow, and Birdie wonders how she can be unmoved by the incredible sorrow in his bright blue eyes. He reaches into his pocket—as always, he's wearing soft wool trousers and a crisp button-down shirt, because he can't be ready to help Birdie at a moment's notice if he's in something as vulnerable as nightclothes—and pulls out a drawing pad. He quickly sketches something and then holds it out.

"Lake?" Arrow asks. "Why do we need Lake? She can barely walk through doorways; I don't think she'll be much help. And we can't pull the 'Lake is missing' trick again. Cook will get wise to us."

Forest shakes his head and points again to his drawing of Lake.

River takes over before Arrow loses all patience. "She told you something, didn't she? Something she saw?"

Forest nods. He turns to a clean page and quickly sketches. This drawing is rougher, the hurried lines harsh and upsetting. A skull.

River sits on the bench next to Arrow. "Someone dies."

Forest cuts his eyes toward Birdie, then looks back at Arrow, desperate pleading in his gaze. Birdie sighs. She wasn't going to tell Arrow this part, but apparently Forest wants them all on the same side. Or at least, he wants Arrow and River on *his* side.

River slaps her head in understanding. "*That's* why you didn't let Birdie finish searching the House Wife's room. Because Lake told you Birdie dies in there."

"I wasn't aware you were fluent in Forest," Arrow grumbles. "But here's the good news. I'm not Birdie. Forest does his voice thing on the House Wife, *I* go in, all our problems are solved."

"We have to be cautious," Birdie says. The words are like

pulling teeth, and once again that sense of the whole world being tipped onto its side comes back. Because being cautious has always been her default, and now she has to force herself to care. "I know you're impatient—I am, too—but once our cover is blown, we're never getting back in."

"We have time." River's voice is soft. She leans against Arrow, taking her hand. "There aren't any children from the north here right now. Not upstairs, and not hidden back there somewhere. I know all the dreams in this house, so I know all the dreamers."

"No children? No others at all?" Birdie lets go of her last remaining hope, that somehow Magpie was back there, behind that door. That maybe there was still an easy reunion to be had. She knows it's irrational, but it's what she wants. And she's entirely made of want now. Birdie drops to a crouch, presses her face against her knees, and screams.

Forest's hand comes down gently onto her back, and he leaves it there until she comes back up for air.

River shifts uncomfortably, alarmed at Birdie's demonstration of rage, but Birdie doesn't care.

"I'm certain there aren't groups of hidden children," River says. "But I can't quite account for every single dream. There's one—I don't—I don't like it." She shudders. "It's a red circle, like the window outside. Usually I see the dreamer in the dream, or at least have a sense of them, but in that one, it's like—it's like the dream exists without a dreamer."

Arrow offers the most likely explanation. "It's the House Wife. Nothing about her is normal."

"It's probably the House Wife," River agrees with a sorry expression. "Oh. Oh! When I fell asleep on the sofa. I thought it would be peaceful because everyone was awake. But I still dreamed of the red window. I can't imagine the House Wife was asleep then."

"There's still a chance someone else is here," Birdie says, hand in a fist over her heart like she can calm it that way.

Arrow points to Forest, seizing her opportunity. "Which means we go back to my plan. He tells the House Wife to let me find the third floor."

Forest looks pained. Birdie shakes her head. "It's dangerous. He—"

"Do you want to find your sister or not?"

"Of course I do," Birdie snaps. "But if she's here, she's not going anywhere. We can afford to be careful."

"We can't afford anything! You saw what happened to Rabbit. There's no time to waste. And this is so much bigger than your sister, anyway. This is connected to the suffering of my entire country. I'm sorry if I can't be *patient*."

River puts a hand on her arm, but not even River can keep her here. Arrow storms out.

Birdie's always been opposed to harming others. But thinking of the House Wife, of Rabbit's lifeless body, of the names and the poem carved into the wall upstairs, that changes at last. She doesn't care what the consequences might be to the House Wife's mind.

Birdie can't look at Forest, because she doesn't want to see the hurt in his eyes, and, thanks to him, she does what she wants now. "If we don't come up with something else by tomorrow night, we do Arrow's plan."

CHAPTER THIRTY-THREE

A Bird Reunited

Birdie notices there are enough places set at the table this morning. Which means they do, in fact, have a new resident, because Cook would never set a place for Forest. She can't perceive his existence.

Birdie sets the extra place for Forest. She wants to, so it isn't difficult. She lets her eyes drink him in as he sits, shoulders broad, back straight. His simple white shirt, unbuttoned at the top, seems to only emphasize how beautiful his features are. A canvas for the art of his face. He feels like a dream. Like a miracle in a lifetime of relentless reality.

He meets her gaze, full lips twitching up at the corners. Before yesterday, she would have immediately looked away. But she doesn't want to. And she can always do what she wants now.

He'd rather do anything than use his ability on the House Wife again. Birdie understands. Maybe some of the House Wife's strangeness is because of whatever he did to her brain. Maybe Cook didn't drink before that. Maybe their minds have been screaming at them this whole time that something's wrong, but because they can't understand it, they're coping. Poorly.

But Birdie has no pity in her heart for either of them. Only for those they've hurt and will hurt. She won't let Forest be on that list. She has time to come up with another plan. She'll think of something before tonight; she's sure of it.

Cook grumbles. "Where is he?" She's awake this morning, but the bags under her bloodshot eyes are swollen and she keeps looking toward her bedroom, where she hides whatever spirits she's drinking. "I have to do everything around here," she mutters, which makes Arrow laugh out loud. Cook glares at her before stomping out of the kitchen to retrieve the new resident.

"Who do you think it is?" River asks.

"Who who is?" Dawn asks, pausing midway in spooning breakfast into Nimbus's mouth.

Arrow gives River an exasperated look. They aren't supposed to know someone arrived last night.

River shrugs. "There's an extra plate at the table. I think someone new is in Sky's room." An easy enough explanation. River is better at this than the rest of them.

"Oh, how exciting!" Dawn's interest spikes, so everyone looks at the door, rapt, waiting.

Birdie's less influenced than usual. A new resident is a complication, not an exciting change. They'll have to be more careful around whoever he is. The spoon misses Nimbus's mouth, so Birdie fetches a clean napkin and doesn't see the moment the new arrival appears.

"Good morning," a familiar voice says.

Birdie whirls around, her stomach dropping as she takes in those bronze curls over his forehead. His suit, slightly wrinkled from the journey. And his hazel eyes, coolly appraising as he glances over the residents. His mouth curls just a little in distaste, and Birdie follows his gaze to where Nimbus stares blankly ahead.

"*Hawthorn?*" Birdie asks.

Nimbus's old tutor startles, whipping his head around to look at her. He clears his throat and then scowls. "Why are you addressing me so informally?"

Birdie dips a quick curtsy to cover her own confusion. "Apologies."

"Yes, well, see that it doesn't happen again, maid," Hawthorn says, reverting to his cool, clipped tones.

Dr. Bramble must have been trying to get Hawthorn into the house, too. The tutor! River said one was coming. Of course the doctor didn't pass up the opportunity. This is going to complicate things so much.

And not just in terms of Birdie's goals. She didn't tell the others about her sponsor. All she told them was of her search for Magpie. Now she'll have to admit that she's supposed to pass information along to one of the architects of the procedure. Someone who actually *is* in a position of some power in the south. How will Arrow feel about that?

Hawthorn clears his throat and looks back at the table. Once again his eyes barely glance over Nimbus. Why isn't he upset to see his old charge here in this state? He was Nimbus's tutor for years.

The answer is so obvious Birdie could laugh if she weren't so sad and angry. Hawthorn already knew what happened to Nimbus. *That* was how Dr. Bramble was aware that things had changed in the House of Quiet and wealthy children were being sent here now. In fact, Dr. Bramble might have had something to do with the letters that went out to the families, informing them of their children's mandatory treatments.

Did he set this entire thing in motion from the very start just to create enough chaos within the House of Quiet to slip in not one but two informants?

Birdie seethes that they didn't see fit to share any of this information with her. She's not their partner; she's their maid.

"Good morning! What's your ability?" Dawn asks.

Hawthorn's eyebrows pinch in alarm and disapproval. "That is an impertinent question to ask of anyone. One should always introduce themselves in a manner befitting their station, and wait an appropriate time before inquiring into any personal matters."

Dawn rolls her eyes. "So your ability is being annoying. You really are the new Sky."

"Young lady, I am your *tutor*. My name is Hawthorn, but you may all address me as 'teacher' or 'sir.'"

"Who is that?" asks Lake, but she's not looking at Hawthorn as she points frantically at the wall.

"I'm your tutor," Hawthorn repeats, slower this time. "You," he says, jutting his chin toward Birdie. "Show me to the schoolroom."

Birdie walks ahead of him. She wants answers. And maybe—*maybe*, always that maybe, some things never change—it will be good to have Hawthorn here. He can help them get through the door so they don't have to use Forest at all.

But first they need to have an honest conversation, which will be difficult. There's a barrier between them. It's clear in the way he closes the door behind himself and turns toward her, his demeanor instantly changing from stiff and formal to familiar. But not familiar in the way of one friend to another. Familiar in the way of an employer to a servant.

"Hello, Birdie," he says. "I trust your time here has been productive?"

Birdie laughs, and Hawthorn once again looks shocked. Though not as shocked as he looked when he first saw her in the kitchen.

"In some ways, yes," Birdie says. "In what we were actually

THE HOUSE OF QUIET 203

hoping to find, not so much. But why did you act so surprised to see me in the kitchen?"

Hawthorn clears his throat and adjusts his tie. He's wearing his usual suit, with pressed trousers, a vest, and a tie over a white shirt. He could almost pass for a junior minister, but he's missing gold cuff links and buttons and the beard only wealthy men are allowed to grow. The lower classes have to spend time and energy shaving every day or risk fines. It's an archaic rule that everyone gossips is going to change, but it never does.

"Well, I saw Nimbus, so I assumed someone here would spoil our connection to each other. I figured it was best if I do it myself." That can't be it. He's going to keep withholding information. Fine. So is she.

"I can tell you who the rest of the residents are," she offers.

Hawthorn waves dismissively. "I already know who's here."

Birdie holds back a glare. If the doctor and Hawthorn already knew who was here, they would have known that Magpie wasn't in treatment anymore. And they still let Birdie come, full of hope.

She tucks that information away and continues as though she isn't now wary of everything that comes out of Hawthorn's mouth. "Sky's father retrieved him already. He was accompanied by the minister of finance."

"Your old friend," Hawthorn says, raising an eyebrow above his round, copper-rimmed glasses. He's fussily put together, handsome in a bland sort of way with his bronze curls and marble cold skin. She could see wealthy, bored spouses of wealthy, boring people being quite charmed by him.

She thought Hawthorn was on her side because he connected her with Dr. Bramble. But that benefited him, too.

Nimbus left the books out for Birdie to learn from. Hawthorn never did.

"Was the minister's visit a problem?" Hawthorn asks. "Did you tell him about us?"

"We didn't speak."

"Interesting. Doesn't that puzzle you?"

Birdie almost answers that it very much does, but then she realizes the truth. If Forest could make the House Wife and Cook not even realize he's here, couldn't he do the same to his own father? The way the minister's eyes flicked right over her like she didn't exist—it wasn't a game. It was because, to him, she doesn't exist anymore.

Her heart swells with affection and gratitude. She might not like that Forest intervened without her permission when she went into the House Wife's room, but no one has ever worked so hard to protect her.

Come to think of it, no one has ever deemed her worth protecting.

It seems prudent to deny Hawthorn information, the same way he's denied her. She shrugs. "I'm so isolated here. I can't hurt him."

Hawthorn lets out an impassive *hmm*. "What else?"

What else? What else can Birdie tell him that doesn't give away any of her friends' secrets? She tries to want to please him. She can't manage it. If he can help her, fine. Otherwise she has no use for him. "Nothing else matters. We need to get into the House Wife's room to see her records. Magpie isn't here, and I want to know where she went after treatment."

Hawthorn doesn't respond. He clasps his hands behind his back and walks slowly around the room as though studying it. "The minister came at night, correct?"

"Yes," Birdie says.

"Has anyone ever come during the day?"

Birdie shakes her head. "No."

"Is there any discernable schedule?"

"I heard the driver say he'd be back next week. That's all I know." She leaves out that it was Arrow who overheard it, and also omits the detail of the tea warning.

Hawthorn's eyebrow rises once more. "You were spying last night?"

"I do my job," Birdie snaps.

"Good girl." His pronouncement feels like a pat on the head for a pet who's performed a task. Hawthorn pauses, then steps close to her, invading her personal space. The maid he thinks she still is wouldn't stand her ground. She grits her teeth and pretends, taking a step back and lowering her eyes.

"The third maid, Rabbit," Birdie says, her throat tight. "Something the House Wife did killed her. Do you have more information about what happened to Magpie?"

He sighs. "We honestly thought you'd find her immediately. Your connection to her is the only reason we chose you. It's very disappointing. Nothing has gone according to plan."

For the first time, Birdie believes he's telling the whole truth. Instead of reassuring her, it chills her in a way she can't explain. If he didn't even care about his own former pupil's condition, why would he care about a maid's lost sister?

Before she can think better of it, she speaks up. "And the other children, the ones from the north. Do you know why they were sent here for treatment?"

Hawthorn's answer is measured, like he's weighing each word and adjusting so none have more impact than others. "What makes you think northern children were ever here?"

Not an admission that he knew, but it's obvious. If they already had this much information, why send her at all?

"The rooms on the second floor. There was evidence of them left behind."

"That's not good," he says, voice laced with disapproval. Not good that there was evidence, or that children from the north were here?

"Is that what Dr. Bramble wants evidence of? Misuse, so he can close the House of Quiet forever?" Maybe Birdie should tell Hawthorn that the minister of finance is trying to take over and move everything to another facility on the coast.

Hawthorn takes another step back. She realizes his glasses are just glass, serving no purpose. Worn as a costume. There's a flash of naked greed and cunning in his eyes no fake glasses could ever mask. "We don't want to *end* the House of Quiet, Birdie. We want to understand it. That's the important thing. Can we still count on you?"

"Of course." She dips a curtsy so he doesn't see her absolute rage.

That's what this is all about. The doctor and Hawthorn don't want to help anyone. They want to learn the secrets of treatment to use as leverage. The papers she stole listed the staggering amounts of money the wealthy families were charged. Hawthorn doesn't want to destroy the minister of finance; he probably wants to become him. And doubtless Dr. Bramble has his eyes on becoming the minister of health and progress. If he can control both ends of things—the procedure and the treatment for when it goes wrong—who could tell him no?

Birdie withheld the minister of finance's plans, but she would bet anything Dr. Bramble already knows about the upcoming change and the rush to gather information is because of that.

Birdie's been such a fool. Men like Hawthorn and Dr. Bramble are trying to leave Birdie's class behind forever. Of course they'd never care about helping her or anyone like her.

"One more thing," Hawthorn says, picking up a pencil and pushing his finger against the tip. "None of the others know about me, or Dr. Bramble, or your connection to us. Right?"

"Right."

Hawthorn nods. "See that you keep it that way."

She intends to.

CHAPTER THIRTY-FOUR

A Forest Listening

Forest messed up.

He's known Birdie for so long. He's listened to her cry, tell stories, talk about her life and her home and her hopes and her fears. He couldn't touch her there, couldn't even see her, but she was the bright star his entire small, dark world came to revolve around. And then she left.

He knew she didn't want to leave him. She begged him to open the door, but he was too afraid he might hurt her. He should have listened to that fear. He should have respected it.

But if he had, Birdie would be dead. His father set out that same day with plans to have Birdie murdered, and only Forest's intervention stopped it.

So he can't regret it. And here, he got to see her. He got to watch her taking care of everyone. Laughing and smiling and brushing the hair back from where it falls soft and free from her bun. She's the most beautiful girl in the whole world, and even before she knew who he was, she was drawn to him. She trusted him.

And it's that trust he violated. Because he knows Birdie. And he knows that she would never have accepted that they could be together, thanks to how she was trained from childhood on to disappear. To fade into the wallpaper. To never have a need or desire that came before what was asked of her. She was going to keep her head down and her achingly sweet eyes on the ground.

He could see it happening in that moment in the greenhouse. He was going to lose her, and it was so unfair that he spoke. Knowing what he knows. Having seen exactly what he's capable of. It was the single most selfish thing he's ever done, telling Birdie she should do what she wants.

But—

Forest closes his eyes, heart racing so fast he can feel it in his throat. But she chose him, because that's what she wants, now that she's at last allowed to want things for herself. It feels like a miracle.

But he isn't a miracle. He's a curse. And so he's waiting in the hall outside the study, listening in, because what if Birdie does something out of character thanks to him? What if she needs him again?

"You," Arrow snaps. Forest turns to take in the other maid. Not a maid. Arrow's face is a contradiction. Her round eyes always make her look innocent, bordering on confused, and yet she's always angry.

She beckons for him to follow. Seeing his hesitation, she rolls her eyes. "He's a tutor. Birdie will be fine. We need to talk."

Arrow's relentless, so Forest lets her lead him into River's room. He looks around, surprised not to find the other girl.

Arrow launches a furious question at him. "Why are you so selfish?"

He's been wondering the same thing. He hangs his head. She's right. He should never have risked saying something to Birdie.

But Arrow continues. "You never stopped to think that what you can do could solve all of this? Could solve everything? You have *power*, Forest. Maybe that's the problem. You've always had power, so you don't know what it is to have none. You can do more than I ever could, maybe than anyone else in history ever could, and you're doing *nothing*, and I need a reason not to hate you. Make me understand. Make me understand why you can fix this but you won't."

Forest lifts his hands, palms up. Arrow isn't mad about Birdie. He supposes not everyone's thoughts revolve around her, after all. But he can't answer Arrow, for any number of reasons.

With a growl, Arrow grabs a sheet of paper and a pencil off River's nightstand. "Write it down, then."

Forest shakes his head.

"Sink me in a bog and stomp on my head, you infuriating lump. Write something and see if I'm compelled to do it. It can't possibly work through writing, too. I know none of these abilities make sense, but that makes even less sense than usual. I've *never* heard of that. And we pay attention to abilities where I'm from. We understand better than anyone else all the ways they can be used."

Forest looks down at the paper. He thinks and thinks. He took a risk with Arrow on the stairs yesterday, but the parameters were so clear. He needs to make certain they're that clear this time, too.

At last, he writes down a phrase and holds the paper out to her.

Arrow snatches the paper from his hands. *Softly clap your hands together a single time.* She claps her hands . . . then does it several more times. "Ta-da!" she says. "You did it. You wrote a sentence, and now you know that you can't compel us by the power of your pencil alone."

Forest wraps his arms around her in a hug, lifting her off the floor and spinning her in a circle. His silent laughter shakes them both. This isn't just relief. This is sheer, giddy joy.

He can write.

He . . . can write. His elation drains away, realizing what this means. He sets Arrow back down, and she squeezes his arm and smiles at him.

"Yes, fine, you're happy. Let's move on. Wait." She frowns. "Why did you think it would work through writing?"

Forest sits, pencil in hand. He writes as fast as he can, letters rushed but still precise and elegant. He loves drawing, has always preferred to express himself through art, but he's missed words so much.

I wrote a letter to my father when I realized what my ability was. I told him I should be locked in the empty third floor, that no one should ever come speak to me or visit me, only deliver food and leave. And my father obeyed it exactly. He never once visited or tried to communicate with me.

"Oh," Arrow says. "I see." She puts a hand on his shoulder, resting it lightly there. Because he doesn't need to say the rest.

Forest was equal parts afraid that it was compulsion that forced his father to do that . . . and that it *wasn't* compulsion. Because if he ever tried writing again and it wasn't part of his ability, he'd have to admit that his father willingly locked him away and avoided him entirely.

He already knows who his father is. What his father is. But having it confirmed hurts. Maybe Forest didn't need to make his father forget him. He was already doing it without any help.

But now that Forest can communicate, he keeps going. Arrow has to understand.

Before I knew what I could do, I had been sick. A doctor came and broke the fever, but when I woke, everything felt strange and wrong. My mother was fussing over me. In my pain and delirium, I told her to go away. She walked out of the house and into the countryside. No one has seen her since.

I still didn't know what I was doing, or the ability I had.

"How could you have?" Arrow's voice is soft.

My head ached like it was splitting in two. A maid asked me if I needed anything, and I told her to please shut her mouth. I found out later she starved to death. They couldn't even pry open her jaw to save her life. I killed her because I was impatient and careless.

Arrow squeezes his shoulder. There's nothing she can say. Forest has to live with this.

I started to suspect what was wrong. I tried to be cautious. I thought about every word that left my mouth, but still damage was done in the most unexpected ways. A poorly constructed sentence, the wrong word choice, a startled exclamation. Anything that I said was a weapon. My voice was violence. I locked myself up and never let anyone visit or talk to me.

"What made your father decide to send you here, then?"

He didn't. That's why I'm not on the list. Birdie was—

Forest stops, closing his eyes. He grips the pencil like it's a lifeline, then writes the rest. Birdie in his house, the first person to make him feel real in years. Following her here. Protecting her from his father by making him forget them both. Making Cook and the House Wife incapable of noticing him.

Arrow snickers. "That's a neat trick." But after a few moments, she adds, "And a sad and lonely one."

Forest writes more forcefully, the words nearly carving themselves into the paper. *I could just as easily have blinded them by accident, or made them go mad because my instructions weren't precise enough. There's no predicting all the outcomes. I won't risk Birdie's safety. No matter what.*

He leans back and looks at her, an eyebrow raised defiantly. Arrow is a force to be reckoned with, but now she knows how far Forest is willing to go to protect Birdie.

CHAPTER THIRTY-FIVE

An Arrow Scheming

Arrow sighs. "I'm sorry. I assumed you didn't want to help because you can't understand the stakes. That was unfair of me. I have very low opinions of people in the south. But some of you are all right."

I do want to help, Forest writes. *But I'm terrified of what will happen to Birdie if she goes up those stairs.*

"There *are* stairs in there, then!" Arrow punches his shoulder. He flinches, but she doesn't apologize. He deserves it, after using his voice on her yesterday.

"That's our solution," Arrow says. "We leave Birdie out of it entirely. River, too. We take the burden and risk away from them, do it all ourselves. They're still innocent. We aren't. I got my mom killed, too," Arrow says, her throat squeezing so tightly she has to force the words out. She's never said it to anyone. Not even to herself. But the day her mother died, Arrow was gone because she was angry. If Arrow had been there, if she hadn't been asking about termites around the village, drawing attention . . . who knows what might have been different?

Arrows fly straight and true once loosed, so be careful where you aim. But Arrow had been tired of being careful. She wanted to be dangerous. Destructive. Vengeful. And then her mother was gone forever.

Forest frowns, but he doesn't reject her outright. Then he turns and writes, *I don't actually want you to get hurt, either.*

"Sweet of you," she says, "but not your concern. I can take care of myself. Besides, Lake hasn't prophesied my death, has she?"

His face goes blank. Arrow's pulse flutters. It looks like Lake has, in fact, prophesied Arrow's death. And Forest is hiding it from her because he'd rather she dies than Birdie.

Forest surprises her once again. *Lake said you don't get older than you are now. But that was it. Nothing about stairs.*

"If Birdie uses the stairs, she dies, and I don't survive long enough to get wrinkled and gray. Which is too bad. I'd be very striking with gray hair." Arrow doesn't want to die, but she'd rather die than leave this house without helping her people. She has to find out what happened to the stolen children and where they are now.

Her only purpose here was to kill the southern agent. Iron wouldn't approve of this. But Iron was wrong about Birdie, so doesn't it make sense for Arrow to set her sights on something even bigger and more important in the service of their people?

If it means risking her life to get into that hidden staircase and discover what's actually been happening in the House of Quiet, it's worth it.

What might have been isn't; that's all there is to it. Another of their sayings, but she likes this one better than *Gone is gone.* It's just as fatalistic, but it's also peaceful. Whatever futures she might have, if she doesn't get them, she doesn't get them. She's never going to have a future with River, anyway. Only a right now.

"But," Arrow continues, putting a hand out before Forest can write more, "Birdie's not going on the stairs. Which means she's not going to die. Which means everything else Lake saw is in flux, too. We can change it all."

Do you really believe that? Forest looks at her.

"I have to," she says. Because if Arrow really doesn't believe anything can be changed, she would have given up and walked into the ocean that day on the beach. Part of her never left that moment, if her dreams are any indication.

The two of us, then, Forest writes.

"The two of us," Arrow agrees. "I'll delay, say the tutor complicates things and we should see if we can use him before we make any decisions. But tomorrow morning, when Birdie's cleaning: We get past the door and find out what's on the third floor."

Forest nods.

"Then let's get out of here before they catch us and suspect we're conspiring. Or, worse, in love." Arrow shudders in an exaggerated display of disgust. She's rewarded with a smile. She can see what Birdie likes about Forest. He's not her taste, but there's something exhilarating about getting a reaction from someone so stoic.

Arrow heads in the direction of the kitchen, and Forest goes to lurk somewhere in Birdie's vicinity. Arrow can't blame him. All she wants to do is lurk near River.

A door slams ahead of her. Arrow hurries in and finds River at the table, calmly kneading dough. There's a smear of flour on River's cheek. Arrow closes the distance and brushes it off, happy for an excuse to touch River's warm skin.

"What was the slamming door?" Arrow asks.

"Cook told me to go see to my studies, and I told her to go see to her bottle. Then she said this is *her* kitchen, and I told her she was in the way of *my* oven full of biscuits. Then she threw her hands in the air and said she didn't know why she bothered feeling sorry for me when I'm insufferable and entitled. I said I never asked her to feel sorry for me, but could she please fetch the sugar from the pantry if she was going to insist on staying? At which point she retreated to her room. Then a beautiful girl came in and touched my cheek and made me wish she was touching me other places, preferably in a dark, private room."

Arrow chokes on a laugh, shocked at River's boldness. Then she leans in close. "As a maid, I have access to many dark, private rooms."

"And as an insufferable, entitled brat, I demand you take me to one right now, so we can—"

"Hello," Birdie says, breathless and wild-eyed. "Everything all right? I heard a door slam."

"Everything's fine." Arrow narrows her eyes at Birdie. "Everything all right with *you*?"

Forest enters too, trailing Birdie by a few feet, the ever-loyal shadow.

"Just met with the tutor. He's—" Birdie pauses. "He's a complication," she says at last.

Interesting. Birdie's not telling them everything. "A complication?" Arrow prods. Oh no. What if the tutor tried to put his hands on her? Forest would destroy him. Maybe that's why Birdie looks like she's trying desperately *not* to look upset.

Birdie waves a hand. "Just that we have another set of eyes, and this one is more likely to pay attention than the House Wife or Cook. So be careful."

"Maybe we pause for a couple of days," Arrow suggests, frowning like the idea bothers her but also is what's best.

Birdie nods. "I agree. And if the tutor asks any of you questions, brush him off, or feign madness, or whatever. Be like Lake."

"What!" Lake shouts, stomping into the kitchen and glaring at all of them. "Birdie again!" She points accusingly. "You keep dying! But you're here!"

"I'm sorry," Birdie says politely.

Forest shoots an alarmed look at Arrow. Arrow gives him a minute shake of her head. If he's not careful, he's going to clue everyone else in that they have a secret plan in the middle of all the other secret plans.

"It's very selfish of you," Lake says with a huff. "Stay off the stairs!"

"But my bedroom is upstairs."

"Not those stairs! You know what stairs I mean!" Lake whirls on Arrow, redirecting all the anger her little body can hold. "You keep changing things! It's very confusing."

"I'm sorry," Arrow says. "That must be difficult, having confusing information thrown at you."

Lake softens and nods at her, grateful for the acknowledgment and unaware of the underlying sarcasm. "It is. The biscuits are burned," she proclaims, then turns on her heel and walks off.

River rushes to the oven and rescues her biscuits. They're perfect, a golden brown. "She saved them!" River sets the tray on the table to cool.

A burst of hope sparks in Arrow's chest. She and Forest exchange a weighted glance. They changed something by listening to Lake. Maybe, just maybe, they can change everything.

"Why do we think the House Wife hasn't started another treatment yet?" River asks, leaning against the table. "We haven't even seen her since the search for Lake."

Arrow can't be bothered to worry about that right now. Buoyed by her newfound optimism, she grabs River's hand and pulls her into the hallway. "What's going on?" River asks.

Arrow answers by kissing her. It's not frantic and lust-soaked like their dreams, and it's not surprising like their stairwell kiss. Instead, it's something Arrow hasn't had in her entire life: pure sweetness.

"Excuse me!" the tutor exclaims, aghast. "*What* is happening in this house?"

Arrow pulls away from River. Birdie was right: The tutor is extremely inconvenient.

"Get back to work before I have you disciplined," he says. Then he turns his gaze on River. "Miss River, please join me in the study. I'm conducting preliminary tests to determine everyone's individual needs, and—"

River laughs, weaves her fingers through Arrow's, and says a word that sends thrills down Arrow's spine. "No."

She and Arrow run down the hall toward the greenhouse. Maybe Arrow will die on the stairs tomorrow. Maybe she won't. But she has hope, and she has River, and they have today, together.

CHAPTER THIRTY-SIX

A Nimbus Shattered

H e pads down the hallway.
He's sleeping, dreaming. Sleeping, dreaming. Sleeping, dreaming. Sleeping, dreaming. Skimming away from those selves because there are no real thoughts, nothing to keep him there.

He climbs the stairs.

She's standing, waiting, staring at the red circle and ready for more in the morning. It doesn't matter which one she takes, but it will be nice to know them fully. To give them the blessing of quiet. But it *has* to happen in the morning. The one who was delivered when they took Sky and Rabbit is empty now, and they need more if the heart is going to keep beating.

It's hard, when there's no one to put the noise into. She has to hold it all. She never sleeps anyway, but this is a wakefulness that *hurts*. It's a wakefulness that leaves too much room to think about how she knew Rabbit's name. She hasn't known any of their names before. *Is Mouse still in there?* the little girl asked, and she's not, but the House Wife misses her now.

He turns down the hallway. He walks quietly but confidently, box in hand, assured as always that he's doing the right thing. If he's doing it, then it's right. That's the compass he lives his life by, his only true north: himself.

She's half-asleep, leg hanging off the bed, too sad and tired and drunk to lift it. The blood is cut off, and it tingles and burns. Maybe that's why she doesn't move it. She needs sensation, any sensation, anything. She's numb all over and has been for so long.

He stares down at Birdie, still and peaceful in sleep. All they did for her, and this is what they get from it? They only sent her in the hopes she'd find Magpie and be able to handle her. But without Magpie, Birdie is useless. She's a problem, one that he shouldn't have to take care of himself. But he always ends up with all the work, doesn't he? Still, this task is easy enough. A dead bird is a silent one. His hands slip into his box to pull out Birdie's executioner.

None of these bodies are his none of these minds are his none of these hands are his but at last Nimbus finds the right one and for a moment he connects to himself enough to *scream*.

CHAPTER THIRTY-SEVEN

A Bird Broken

Birdie's world explodes.

She's plunged into the sun itself, burning and exploding and whooshing around her, not just light but noise, noise so terrible and bright she can see it, she can feel it through her whole body, and it's too much.

Birdie—the Birdie she was, the Birdie she is, her hopes and thoughts and feelings and memories—disintegrates, lost in the maelstrom of noise with no way back.

CHAPTER THIRTY-EIGHT

An Arrow Powerless

A muffled scream wakes Arrow. Her first instinct is rage—she was with River, and she's still brimming with a flood of unresolved sensations and desires that can't be enjoyed now—but then it's fear. Who's screaming downstairs?

Arrow darts into the hallway. Birdie's door is ajar. Arrow pushes it all the way open to see if Birdie's already gone, but she's still in bed. How did she sleep through that scream?

No. Birdie's not sleeping. She's *convulsing*. Arrow leans into the hall and shouts. "Help us! Up here, come help us!"

But how can anyone? They're all locked in their rooms. They agreed not to meet tonight, just in case Cook didn't lock up the tutor. River's daylight defiance was one thing, but they can't afford to have their midnight freedom revealed.

Stay with Birdie, or go get help? Every second is costing them dearly. "I'll be right back," Arrow gasps, then sprints down the hall. She takes the stairs two, three at a time, tumbling down half of them, popping back up bruised and battered and undeterred.

"Forest!" she screams as she runs past his door. "Tell everyone to wake up!" She doesn't have time to pick these locks.

"Wake up!" Forest shouts from his room.

Even though she's well and truly awake, Arrow's eyes widen and her pulse quickens. No trace of exhaustion or confusion lingers. In the kitchen, she kicks Cook's door open. The startled woman falls out of bed, thumping onto the floor. Arrow doesn't even break stride. She slides to a stop, grabs the keys out of Cook's discarded apron, and turns on her heel. Back through the kitchen, back through the hall, Forest's door first.

She throws it open. "Birdie's hurt," she shouts as he barrels past her to the stairs. She unlocks River's door next, then shoves the keys at her. "Get Dawn. Maybe she can help. And figure out who screamed."

"What's wrong?" River calls, running for Dawn's door.

"I don't know." Back up the stairs, back down the hall. Forest is on the floor, Birdie held in his arms. She's still now, except her wildly rolling eyes. Birdie's jaw is clenched so tightly Arrow can hear teeth grinding and creaking. It's the only sound in the room. It's worse than silence. So much worse.

Forest looks up at her, terrified. Pleading.

"I don't know," Arrow says, sinking to her knees. "I don't know." This isn't fair. All Birdie wanted to do was find an innocent girl. But Birdie's an innocent girl, too. Doesn't she deserve to be saved? Don't they all?

Her mother would know what to do. But if her mother were still alive, Arrow wouldn't be here at all. Arrow wipes away tears. "Please. Forest, do something. You have to do something."

Her heart knows the look of pure despair on his face. It's the same feeling she had when she found her mother lying on the table.

Arrow crawls to Birdie and puts a finger against her neck. She doesn't know how to fix this, but she still learned a lot from her mother. The injuries that kill slowly. The ones that kill immediately. And how to know when death is coming and all that can be done is to sing a comforting song and soften a soul's journey out of this world.

Birdie's pulse is fading faster than it can ever recover from.

Arrow shouldn't have demanded Forest do something. Whatever is breaking in Birdie is beyond even his reach. "I'm sorry. I'm so sorry, Birdie."

Arrow slumps in the hallway to give them some space for their last breaths together. One of the worst things that was done to her people was taking away their right to feel their own emotions. Everything had to be guarded, muted, quieted. Nothing could draw the attention of the soldiers. Even when her mother died, Arrow couldn't grieve the way she needed to.

All the pain she's carried with her for so long wells up, and Arrow sinks to the floor. She lowers her head and weeps for a girl she was supposed to murder.

CHAPTER THIRTY-NINE

A Forest Bereft

Forest knows how carefully he has to choose his words. What damage he can do if he doesn't.

But what damage is left to be done? If Birdie is gone, everything else is, too. Nothing matters to him without her. He leans close, pressing his lips against her ear.

"Come back to me," he whispers. "Please don't leave me again." He pauses. He has to be a better man than his father. He has to be less selfish, if he's ever going to deserve the love Birdie has already given him.

With every part of what's left of his soul resisting, he adds, "Unless it's what you want."

The last tension in Birdie's body disappears. She goes as limp and still as death in his arms.

CHAPTER FORTY

A Searching River

Cook stumbles out of the kitchen, rubbing her hip. "The children have all gone feral!" she shouts, taking in the hallway full of them.

"I don't have time for you!" River snaps. She turns back to Dawn. "Do your best to stay calm. You're the most important one right now; do you understand? You're going to be in charge down here."

The girl nods fiercely, taking deep, even breaths. River hands her the keys to the bedrooms, and Dawn sets off to check on Nimbus.

"Those are my keys," Cook says. "Give them to me!"

River glares at her. "If you're not going to be of any use, go back to bed."

"Use for what?" Cook demands.

"Nimbus is upset." Dawn calls from the far bedroom, peeking out into the hallway from the door. "I think he's the one who screamed."

"Stay there and help him calm down," River says. "Lake, my dove, you're in with them until we know what's happening." She nudges Lake in that direction. Lake manages to walk directly there on her own, which is a relief.

"What's the matter?" Hawthorn opens his door and leans his head out. His hair's disheveled, and his robe peeps open to reveal a stark, pale collarbone, making him look strangely fragile. River didn't unlock his door. Why does he get to have freedom if the rest of them don't?

"None of your business," River snaps. "Go back to bed."

He scowls. "I don't take orders from you, young lady."

"I don't have time for this!" River needs to get upstairs.

"My keys!" Cook demands. "I need to check on the House Wife."

River can't deal with her, and she can't have Cook harassing the young ones and upsetting Dawn. She runs into Nimbus's room and gets the keys, then throws them at Cook.

Lake wanders out after her. River's frantic to find out what's happening with Birdie. She's never heard Arrow that scared.

By the time River has Lake back in Nimbus's room, Cook is in the doorway. She looks almost meek. The House Wife stands next to her, hair wild, eyes wilder. A bruise is forming on her forehead, and her elbow and knee are bleeding, soaking almost black through her red dress.

"The noise," she says, voice cracking. "The noise."

"I know," Cook says, wrapping her arms around the House Wife. "Shh, shh. I know. Can we—can we come in? The calm might help her." Cook looks to River for permission. Maybe it's Dawn's radiating calm, or maybe it's just her own desperate wish to be able to turn things over to an adult down here so she can go to Arrow, but River nods.

"Yes. Dawn, none of you go anywhere until I get back." She won't let the House Wife treat the kids, not after what happened to Rabbit. But the House Wife doesn't seem capable of doing much of anything right now.

Cook leads the dazed House Wife in. River dully realizes that this is the chance they've all been waiting for. The perfect opportunity to get into the House Wife's room and explore without risk of being caught. She's not going to tell Arrow, though. Arrow's brave, but she's also reckless. This isn't a night for taking risks.

River runs up the stairs, dreading what she might find there. As soon as she steps out of the stairwell, Arrow crashes into her with a sob.

"Birdie's dead."

River's heart is in her throat. "How?"

"Convulsions. I've seen them before. If you can't stop them, the brain is starved of breath. We didn't change the future. We didn't save her. I can't save anyone."

River strokes Arrow's hair, holding the other girl tightly for a few shaky breaths.

"No head wound," Arrow says. "Not poison, either. We ate and drank the same things. But she can't—she wouldn't just die. She couldn't. She has too much to do. She has to find her sister." Arrow sounds so young when she says it.

"Let me take care of it." River guides Arrow back to her bed, noting how tiny the maids' rooms are, how spare and lonely, and then peers into Birdie's.

Forest is sitting on the floor, holding Birdie's limp body, whispering. River can't make herself set foot in the room, just in case she hears what he's whispering and it breaks her mind apart even more.

"Forest," River says so he knows she's there. He stops. She steps inside the cramped room and crouches in front of them. "Is Birdie dead?"

He shakes his head, but the way he looks up at her with silent horror implies the rest. *Not yet, but soon.*

"Then she's sleeping. And if she's sleeping, I can get to her. And I'll find out what happened." River walks back to Arrow's room and lies down next to her, their bodies wrapped as tightly as they can be.

River closes her eyes. For the first time in years, she's desperate to dream.

CHAPTER FORTY-ONE

A River of Dreams

"Sorry, my heart. I have to find someone else." River pulls Arrow closer and kisses her, wondering if she'll forever associate the smells of blood and the ocean with the thrill of Arrow's lips and hands.

River twirls, trying to spin herself into another dream. One materializes around her. Dawn's on a makeshift stage in the foyer, performing a dance for the whole household. Everyone is clapping, but Nimbus cheers the loudest for her. It's sad that they're the only group Dawn can imagine herself being supported by.

River closes her eyes and tips backward. She opens them and—

The red circle. No, no, no no no. How is it always waiting for her? But she's already holding on to so much of herself, she isn't sucked in yet. She yanks her mind away as quickly as she can.

"Hello," Lake says. She's setting a table for tea in the middle of a vast field punctuated by tiny purple flowers. "What are you doing here?"

"I'm looking for Birdie," River answers, frustrated.

"Well, don't let me delay you." Lake scowls, but then she pauses thoughtfully. "We're friends," she says.

"I like to think so, yes."

"Then you're not here to kill me?"

"Why would I kill you?" River asks.

"You've done it before, and you'll do it again," Lake says with a sigh.

"Killed you?" River's horrified.

Lake huffs, exasperated. "Not *me*. Others. Well, go on."

More alarmed than she'd like to be, River considers Lake seriously for the first time. Deciding to save this puzzle for later, River walks backward, eyes closed.

When she opens them, everything is dark. She whirls, looking for Birdie's candle, but there's no light in here. Nothing. And even worse, there's a claustrophobic sensation, like the dream is compacting, getting smaller and smaller on its way out of existence. If she stays here long, she'll be crushed.

"Birdie?" River calls. She expects her voice to echo, but it drops flat, strangled by the heavy blackness all around them. "Birdie?" she whispers. "Birdie, if you can hear me—don't go. Please don't go. We still need you. *Magpie* still needs you."

River nearly jumps out of her skin as a hand takes her own. It's cold, but it squeezes hers with surprising strength.

"I can lead you out," River says, though she's not sure that's possible. She's never tried it. She's done far worse things to people in dreams, though, so this should be possible, too, shouldn't it? Why should her ability be only a weapon? Blades can kill when they're swords or knives, but they can also help heal things when they're scalpels.

"He told me to come back to him," Birdie whispers, "but it was so bright and loud and painful. I couldn't stay. I can't stay."

"You can. You have to. Come on." River tugs gently on Birdie's hand. She takes a step, terrified that Birdie will slip out of her grasp, but Birdie moves with her. Another step. Another. It's like walking through tar, the darkness clinging to them. If Birdie were alone, she couldn't have pushed through it. But together, they move with achingly, painfully slow steps. It feels like an eternity before River notices a change. The air is a little less close. There's a hint of expansiveness around them.

"Birdie, do you feel that?" River turns, but she's too excited. She knows better than to move quickly in these spaces. The dream falls around her and re-forms.

It's not Birdie's dream anymore. This one smells like River's father: pipe smoke and leather and alcohol. It smells like all the important men River has ever had to endure.

Hawthorn is standing in the center of a room, hands clasped behind his back as he spins in a slow circle. The walls are deep red, trimmed in gold, and all the furniture seems thrown in as an afterthought—a jumble of leather and velvet pieces, a sofa next to a couch next to a chair next to a desk, on and on, a maze of luxury.

Hawthorn finishes his rotation and sees her. That's surprising—she wouldn't think she'd be a presence in his dream. Usually the person has to know her. But when she looks down, it makes sense. She's wearing bloodred velvet, cut perilously low and hugging all her curves. Jewels drip from her neck and weigh down her hands. She's not herself. She's another expensive decoration in the room. Exactly what her parents always wanted her to be.

River's got to go. Who knows how many dreams she'll have to cycle through before finding Birdie again, if she even can. But something gives her pause.

Birdie wouldn't just die, Arrow said. River knows people die all the time. But the timing of Birdie's mysterious ailment can't be a coincidence. She just doesn't understand why the appearance of a tutor triggered such calamity. Yet.

She tilts her head and smiles at Hawthorn. "Hello," she says.

"Look at this!" Hawthorn gestures at everything around them.

River used to play a game to see how long men would speak without ever asking her a question about herself. All she had to do was smile and nod and make the occasional *oh!* exclamation.

"Oh!" She nods with wide, enraptured eyes.

"Exactly!" Hawthorn laughs. "I never even knew this room was here. Look, look at what I've been living in, while all this was *right here*."

He points toward a door that opens onto a small, plainly furnished room. Tidy and clean, but unremarkable. River nods again in silent encouragement for him to continue talking.

"Do you know what all this is worth?" He slaps the back of a sofa like it's the rump of a horse. She half expects it to gallop away. Unfortunately, Hawthorn's dream is too boring for that. "More than I've ever made in my life. More than I ever could make in my life." He laughs again, a dark, bitter sound. "And it was always right here. I just had to walk through that door."

He seems perfectly content to stand there, marveling at his previously undiscovered wealth. River will need to nudge him along. "How did you get such a very fine room?" she asks.

"The procedure, of course," he says.

Time for her other trick: playing the pretty, empty-headed fool. "What's the procedure?"

Hawthorn laughs again, but this time it's indulgent. "Did you come with the room, I wonder? Have you been in here waiting for me all this time?"

"The procedure?" she prods, not liking the sly, hungry shift in his expression.

"Oh, that." He grabs her by the hand, tugging her forcefully along. "Another room!" he shouts excitedly. Through this door is a near-exact replica of the first, with the same red walls accented with gold, the same ghastly chandelier chiming and twinkling above them, the same stink of power and privilege. But instead of overflowing with furniture, this one has a single pedestal with a small box on top.

River silently curses herself for believing she was going to get anywhere with him. This is just another treasure room for Hawthorn. Doubtless formed by all his years spent coveting the houses he lectured young minds in.

She's wasting her time. If someone hurt Birdie, it was probably one of the same two people who hurt Rabbit: Cook or the House Wife. Or both, working together. There was no explanation for how the House Wife got injured. River's never seen the House Wife's dreams, but she's going to try. And if she can't get to those, she has a new suspicion about Cook. The way Cook led the House Wife didn't feel like an employee helping an employer. It felt tender. Maternal even, and River hasn't seen Cook show maternal tendencies toward any of them.

But in her dreams, there was always a little girl. *Silly River.* Little girls grow up, don't they?

She turns to find Birdie again, but Hawthorn grabs her wrist, roughly spinning her back to face him. "Where are you going?"

"You told me you'd show me the procedure."

"You're an empty-headed little doll, aren't you? I already showed you." He kicks the pedestal, the box jostling on top of it. Before River can move, he leans in for a kiss.

River reaches back, grabs the box, and swings it into his face. With a yelp, he lets go of her. She tips backward. This time the terror of falling doesn't push her into another dream, but jolts her awake.

Disgust and frustration cling to her. Morning is nearly here, and it'll be difficult to fall asleep with the memory of Hawthorn's hand around her wrist, bruising and cruel. She nuzzles closer to Arrow's side. River should get up and check on Forest. See if Birdie's improved, or if . . .

Arrow shifts toward her in her sleep, draping an arm across River's waist. River doesn't want to leave this space. She doesn't want reality right now.

Reality is a broken Birdie that River couldn't save, a house full of secrets and menace, and a world that will never let her stay curled around the girl she loves. For so long River's hated dreams, been plagued by them, tried to escape them. But all she wants now is to live forever in a dream with Arrow.

And she'll destroy anyone who keeps her from that.

CHAPTER FORTY-TWO

A Bird Awake

There's a new sensation.

Like scraping a knee and suddenly being aware of the air moving across it, raw and painful and startling. That sensation—that sense—has always been there; Birdie's just never noticed it. And now she can't notice anything else. But she doesn't have any control of it or even the capacity to understand what she's feeling.

At last her body tugs her mind back to well-understood senses. Birdie's listening to a heartbeat.

She opens her eyes. Forest is asleep upright, leaned against the wall, cradling her. There's a shimmer of light all around his head, dancing and pulsing, and she nearly gets lost staring at it. She blinks, trying to clear her vision.

Forest's not asleep, though. As soon as she shifts, he shifts, too, searching her face with desperate hope.

Birdie doesn't know what happened to her. But she feels with absolute certainty that she was nearly gone. And she also feels with absolute certainty that it was Forest who brought her back. Holding her here, just like he's still holding her. Forest, and a hand in the darkness, helping her through those first, hardest steps when she couldn't have made it alone.

"Thank you," she says.

He closes his eyes and lets out a breath of pure relief, resting his forehead against hers.

"Will you tell me what you said?"

His lips twitch into a smile, and he shakes his head. Fair enough. He can keep the secret of how he stole Birdie back from death with only his words. She's alive, and that's enough for her. Birdie stretches, every part of her as sore as if she's worked the hardest day of her life, over and over, for a week, without resting.

The light through her window is filtered through opaque white fog. Her head doesn't hurt, but it's . . . wrong. Like she aggressively scoured every inch inside her brain and accidentally took off the patina that was protecting it. Maybe that's why her eyes are still doing strange things when she looks at Forest. "Is everyone else all right?"

Forest nods, then squinches his face and shrugs.

"Worried about me?"

He nods.

"We should go down, then." Birdie doesn't want to scare them. Forest has to help her—he practically carries her down the stairs, she puts so much weight on him—but they make it to the main floor. A burst of pure happiness fills Birdie.

"Birdie!" Dawn yells. "Everyone, Birdie's down. She's feeling better!" Dawn skips across the hall to her, throwing her arms around Birdie. Birdie hugs her back, pressing a kiss to the top of the girl's shiny, shiny head.

"I'm happy to see you, too," she says.

"Of course you are." Dawn laughs. "You can't be anything but happy right now." She tugs on Birdie's hand. "Come on, River's baking. We're all in there, avoiding the terrible tutor. He's still sleeping, lazybones."

In the kitchen, Birdie's greeted as though returning from a long illness. Arrow folds her in a hug so tight Birdie notes never to get into a physical fight with the other girl; River kisses both her cheeks several times, laughing; Nimbus doesn't look at her but is definitely cheerful; and Lake tilts her head, squints her eyes, and murmurs "Not dead!" in a genuinely surprised tone, which is practically the same thing as a hug from her.

Everyone is so bright and shimmering, they almost hurt to look at. Birdie sits and closes her eyes, hoping they reset. One of the maids in the minister's house suffered from terrible headaches, always preceded by dancing lights only she could see. If all Birdie has to deal with after whatever happened is migraines, she thinks she got off easy.

Dawn happily chatters in her direction. Forest holds her hand. She sits and listens to her friends, the relief in the room turning the atmosphere celebratory. Birdie risks opening her eyes. Maybe they're adjusting. Arrow looks normal, at least, leaning over the counter and trying to mess up the cake River's icing.

River slaps her hand away. Arrow laughs, licking her finger. Forest strokes his thumb along Birdie's. She feels so much happiness it can't possibly be all from Dawn.

Just as River sets the cake triumphantly in the center of the table, Hawthorn steps into the kitchen. His eyes go wide and as round as his glasses. Then he coughs violently, steps back, and says, "I'm preparing things in the study and need to be left alone."

River glares at his back. "As if any of us want anything more than to leave him alone."

"In the middle of the bog," Dawn adds.

Arrow pats Dawn's head affectionately. "That's our girl."

"What did I miss?" Birdie whispers to Arrow. Arrow holds up a finger to indicate Birdie should wait, glancing meaningfully around the crowded kitchen.

After the cake is mercilessly devoured, not a crumb saved for Cook, the House Wife, or Hawthorn, Arrow claps her hands together.

"I have to get to work, since Birdie is still tired and needs to rest."

"I can take over bathroom-scrubbing duty," Dawn earnestly volunteers. "Nimbus and Lake will help, too."

Nimbus and Lake *won't* help, but they'll be out of the way and safe, which is tremendously helpful.

"Cleaning is a snake eating itself in an eternal circle," Lake grumbles, but she dutifully follows Dawn and Nimbus out.

With the young ones safely occupied, Arrow leads the others to the greenhouse. The cake helped perk her up some, but Birdie still aches, muscles protesting every movement. Forest walks slowly, a hand around her waist. She keeps her eyes on Arrow, because Arrow's still the easiest to look at. Except Arrow's already pacing and it makes Birdie feel dizzy. She leans her head against Forest's shoulder as they sit on their bench.

"What do you remember? Do you have any wounds?" Arrow doesn't wait for Birdie's answer, instead running her hands all over Birdie's head, through her hair, down to the base of her skull.

Birdie swats her away. "No. Everything hurts, but not in that way."

"Do you know what happened?" River prods.

Birdie tries to describe it. "I was asleep. And then it was like—it was like I'd been dropped off a cliff. I was drowning. But not in water. In sound, and light, and sensation. It was blasting me away, scattering me. I almost—" She stops, not wanting to go on. Half remembering it is bad, but she doesn't *want* to fully remember it.

River stares at her as though she's seeing a ghost. "That's how it felt. The day I woke up like this." She turns to Forest, and he slowly nods.

"Oh no." River leans over, holding her stomach. "It *is* contagious. You caught it from us. You're too old. You could have died. Birdie, I'm so sorry." Then her face goes pale. "Arrow, you have to leave." She steps away from Arrow, hands flying to her mouth. "You should leave *now*. Get away from us. Before it happens to you, too."

Arrow doesn't look scared. She looks thoughtful. "What happened leading up to your change, River? Tell us everything."

River wrings her hands nervously, not stepping closer to Arrow. "I was thirteen. I'd been feverish for days. My parents brought in a doctor. He got the fever to break at last, but then the next morning I had what I could only describe as the worst headache of my existence. It felt like what Birdie's describing. After that, I became a notorious dream bandit, stealing hearts and secrets." She grins rakishly, but her cheeks tremble with the effort and her smile drops off quickly.

"You were there last night," Birdie says.

River blinks back tears. "You remember?"

"You held my hand and helped me walk."

River nods, beaming. "I did. I didn't know if it made a difference, but—"

Birdie nods. "It made a difference. I think everything made a difference. Nimbus screamed, Arrow got help, Dawn kept things managed down here, you found me, and Forest—" She turns and puts her hand on Forest's cheek. "Forest did whatever he did."

He presses his lips together, a worried expression on his face.

Birdie moves on so he won't dwell on the consequences of whatever he said. "So you were sick. Forest was sick before, too. And a doctor visited him, as well."

Forest nods.

Arrow isn't pacing anymore. She's stock-still, round eyes so wide Birdie can see the whites all around them. "I'll be right back," she says, then sprints out of the greenhouse.

They wait in silent puzzlement for a few minutes. Birdie's grateful for the quiet. She closes her eyes and tries to feel present in her body. Tries to pinpoint what's different.

"Dawn said the same as River and Forest," Arrow says, returning breathless and excited. "She was sick right before she changed, too. A fever, which only broke—with a tremendous headache—*after* she was visited by a doctor. Lake and Nimbus were no help, but I don't think it's too wild an assumption to say they probably had the same experience."

"So it was getting sick that changed us? Have you been feeling ill, Birdie?" River asks.

"That's not what Arrow's getting at." Birdie can almost understand. It's like reaching for a word, circling around it, knowing it's on the tip of her tongue.

"Tell them what you told me, River. About what you saw in Hawthorn's dream," Arrow prods.

"It wasn't anything special," River says. "Just rooms with the most gaudy, terrible furniture. He has dreadful taste."

"Not that," Arrow says, bouncing impatiently on her toes.

River frowns. "He told me he was wealthy because of the procedure. I asked him to explain, and he took me to a room with a small box on a pedestal. But I've *seen* the procedure room. One of the pedantic ministers took my father on a tour once. The machine they use is enormous. Bigger than the footprint of this house and almost as tall. Even if you could hide it, you couldn't transport it. And you couldn't perform the procedure without someone knowing."

Birdie's fingers drift to her head. Hawthorn had walked into the kitchen with his usual smug expression, but then he had such a strong reaction and immediately withdrew. Because he saw someone he wasn't expecting to.

Hawthorn, who works with Dr. Bramble, who runs the procedure machine. The doctor would have no reason to interact with wealthy families, because wealthy families have no reason to need the procedure. So how did the doctor know that the workings of the House of Quiet would be disrupted? How did he know they'd need new maids and a tutor? And how did Hawthorn already know exactly who was going to be here?

They *couldn't* have known. Unless the doctor was the one making it happen.

Several things click into place at once. The first: Hawthorn tried to kill her last night. The second: He did it by performing the procedure on Birdie's too-old mind, an event that up until now has almost always resulted in death.

And the third: Everything they thought they knew about the procedure is wrong.

"I think—" Birdie starts.

"Where's Nimbus?" Cook asks, dodging around various branches and fronds. She's flushed and sweating.

"What do you mean?" Arrow demands.

"I mean, where's Nimbus? I can't find him anywhere, and the House Wife is ready to start treating him."

"No!" Birdie, River, and Arrow shout simultaneously. Forest

stands, closing the distance to Cook. She doesn't notice him looming menacingly.

Cook scowls. "You don't get to say no. This is what he's here for. What his parents want. I've let you all have too much freedom, and things are going to change around here. Now tell me where you've hidden him."

"We don't have him," Arrow snaps. But her expression changes from defiance to fear. "You really can't find him? He was cleaning bathrooms with Dawn and Lake."

"You had him cleaning bathrooms?" Cook shakes her head in disbelief. "Well, he's not down here. I looked in every room. Did you leave the stairs unlocked?"

"We're not the ones who forget to lock things. The front door," Arrow says, already rushing toward the greenhouse exit. "Is it locked?"

Birdie nods at Forest. He runs ahead with Arrow.

"He wouldn't have gone outside!" Cook shouts after them, then grumbles as she follows with Birdie and River. Birdie leans heavily on River for support.

"He almost got out once before." Birdie picks up her pace. They reach the foyer just as Forest throws open the unlocked door and bursts outside.

Which is when a club swings out and hits him in the head.

"Forest!" Birdie screams.

"Who?" Cook asks, blinking in confusion.

Arrow turns and looks at Birdie with an expression of pure terror and dread on her face. River rushes forward to help them, but before Birdie can, Cook grabs her arm.

"Not you, dear," she says.

Arrow is shoved roughly forward, revealing a young woman,

as lovely as a summer day, with golden ringlets and pale cheeks flushed with a healthy pink. She smiles brightly as she steps over Forest's prone body.

"Hello," she says.

Arrow spins on her heel, driving a fist into the new girl's stomach. The girl doubles over with a pained exhalation. She reaches out a hand and brushes Arrow's arm. Arrow collapses to the ground, writhing and screaming. River moves to run toward her, but Arrow holds up a single hand in warning. River stays where she is.

"Forest, Forest, wake up! Please, let me go help him," Birdie says, trying to break away. Cook is so much heavier and stronger than she is.

"Help *who*?" Cook shakes her head and begins dragging Birdie back toward the House Wife's room. "Beetle! What are you doing? Help me get her to Mouse," Cook demands. The driver is bending over Forest, shoving a piece of cloth into his mouth. There's a trickle of blood at Forest's hairline. He's breathing, though.

Dr. Bramble appears, walking toward them with a cane that's purely for show. He steps over Forest's prone body and smiles. His teeth are very straight and very white, and his face is round and friendly, but his smile doesn't touch his eyes. How did Birdie not see it before?

"Dr. Bramble?" River says, confused and shocked.

The same doctor who visited her when she was so sick. Of course it's the same doctor.

"Hello, Birdie," he says, ignoring River.

Birdie lets out a low cry of despair. She can't take her eyes off Forest, lying there, so vulnerable. "I'm sorry," she whispers. "I'm sorry. I didn't know they would do this. I needed their help finding Magpie. I should have told you all about them; I should have warned you."

"Who are these people?" Cook demands, looking at the driver. "All you told me was to send the older ones outside! You didn't say anything about visitors. *What* are you doing, Beetle?"

"They promised to help." The driver ties a scarf tightly around Forest's wrists, binding them behind his back.

"We have to send this one up." Cook twists Birdie's arm as she tries to break free. "She's hurting our little Mouse."

"Who is she hurting?" Dr. Bramble asks.

"The House Wife," Cook snaps. "We need to quiet her."

"But she said I was quiet. She said—" Birdie blinks once, twice, three times. Forest shines. River shines. The terrifying new blond girl shines. And no one else does. Whatever Hawthorn did didn't succeed in killing her, but it did trigger an ability.

And now she's going to end up like Rabbit. A quick death would have been kinder.

CHAPTER FORTY-THREE

A Broken Arrow

Arrow twists, trying to dive free. Iron just laughs. All it takes is a single brush of her finger and Arrow's entire world explodes into pain again. Every nerve is on fire, agony so bad Arrow can't see or think or hear, much less fight back.

River stays where she is, tears streaming down her face as she stares at Iron. "I'm going to kill you," she says as simply as if she were stating what she had planned for their supper.

Iron bares her teeth in a smile and steps forward. Arrow grabs for her ankle and misses. She knew what Iron was, what she's capable of. She sent Iron the names of everyone here, including Beetle's. That's how they found the driver. The one man capable of navigating the bog to reach the house.

Arrow thought everyone in the south deserved pain. What Iron does felt like cosmic balance. But now Arrow knows that there are innocents everywhere. She doesn't understand why Iron is here, though, and why she's working with that doctor. Is he a termite, too?

"Don't harm River," the doctor snaps at Iron. "I need all the ones with abilities. You can do whatever you want with her, though." He steps over Arrow's prone and shaking body.

Hawthorn strides toward them. "There you are, Dr. Bramble. I have the other ones gathered in the study."

"Take River. And drag Forest in, too, driver," the doctor says, pointing at the doorway where Forest is still lying unconscious. The doctor knows what he can do, and, thanks to Arrow's pigeon missives, they knew he was here when no one else did. Without Forest, the rest of them are helpless.

"As for you." He stops in front of Birdie, eyebrows furrowed. "You performed the procedure on her last night, Hawthorn?"

"Yes," the tutor says. "I have no idea how she survived."

"Fascinating."

"I'll take her to the House Wife," Cook says, tugging on Birdie. The doctor shakes his head. "You can't have her yet. No one has survived the procedure at her age. This must be examined. Come along. Hawthorn, take care of the rest of them and then fetch the box." He takes Birdie's arm and pulls her deeper into the house. Birdie looks over her shoulder with an expression of absolute despair.

"I'm sorry," she says. But why is she sorry? This is Arrow's fault. She thought she could come here as an assassin and help the north with one swift slash. Instead, she's doomed all her friends.

"Iron, get them into the study," Hawthorn says as the driver drags Forest past.

"With pleasure." She kicks Arrow. Arrow curls into a ball, and Iron kicks her again. It's petty. Iron could do so much worse with just a brush of her fingers. She's choosing to kick Arrow for the fun of it. Arrow always knew she was cruel, but the cruelty felt like a lifeline when Arrow was drowning in grief.

"Get up," Iron says, kicking her again.

Arrow stands and limps down the hallway. River moves to help her, but Arrow holds out a hand low where Iron won't see.

Iron skips cheerily after them. "I can't wait to meet all your friends, Arrow."

"You're my only friend, Iron," Arrow says. While Iron laughs, Arrow hisses at River, "Stay by Forest." She's terrified River won't understand that Iron can't know about their feelings for each other.

"Get me a cloth for his head, Minnow," River snaps as she walks into the study. A perfect delivery for someone who's never cared about the fate or emotional state of a mere maid. River's tears could have been for Forest, which is what Iron will assume now. River's cleverer than anyone ever notices. Hopefully it keeps her safe from Iron's gleeful maliciousness.

Iron was supposed to be the north's miraculous weapon. But weapons will hurt anyone, depending on where they're pointed. So why is Iron pointed at her now? Is it because she didn't obey orders to kill Birdie?

Maybe if Arrow can explain. Maybe she can talk her way out of this still. She just has to understand what Iron is trying to accomplish.

Arrow takes off her apron and hands it to River. She marches to the other side of the room and kneels next to Forest. He's unconscious on the floor. After clubbing, gagging, and binding him, the driver dragged him in here and didn't even bother to lift him onto a sofa.

"You may go now," Hawthorn says to the driver. Then he turns to Iron. "Keep watch, and don't disturb us." He closes the door behind himself.

Arrow takes in the rest of the room. Nimbus is sitting quietly in an armchair, looking painfully small and vulnerable. His expression is one not of blank peace but of mute horror. Lake and

Dawn are standing in the middle of the room. Arrow has no idea if Lake is aware of what's going on, but Dawn is. The atmosphere is soaked in anxious fear.

"Minnow, where's—" Dawn starts, but River cuts in, trying to keep up the charade that they all consider Arrow a mere maid.

"Dawn, dear, see to Lake and make certain she doesn't try to wander off."

Dawn nods, confused. But still afraid, which means they're all afraid, too. Not that Arrow needs any help with that. Not with Iron here.

Iron prowls back and forth in front of the door. To anyone else it would look like joyful prancing, but Arrow knows better. Iron is a predator; they're all prey. Iron shoots an annoyed glance at Dawn. If she identifies Dawn as the source of the pesky emotions, Arrow doesn't like imagining what she'll do.

Arrow sidles closer to her old friend, aware of how near she is to Iron's terrible touch. "What's going on?" she hisses. "Why did you attack me? This isn't the plan. I have new information about the stolen children."

Iron turns toward her, her eyes a flat, cold blue. "That's the problem with northerners, Arrow. Everyone cares *so much*. The only way to stop losing is to stop caring. Once you realize you're the only thing that matters, it all gets so much easier. And more lucrative, too."

Arrow takes a step back, deflating. Her last hope is gone. She thought Iron loved the north; Iron loves only herself. "You're not really a termite."

Iron shrugs. "I am when it suits my needs. Or the needs of those funding me."

"How long ago did you betray us? When did you join the doctor?"

Iron laughs. "I was *always* with them. Normally our kind is given the procedure and then shipped right here. But the doctor could see I was special. Useful. Meant for bigger things."

"You never escaped."

Iron claps her hands slowly. "You're smarter than you look. Smarter than the other termites, at least. They were so thrilled to have one of the stolen children back—and to have my abilities— they never questioned how, out of all the hundreds of missing kids, only *I* returned. Silly."

"But why send me here, then?" Arrow doesn't understand. The whole plan was Iron's idea. "Why have me kill Birdie?"

"Contingencies," Iron says with another shrug. "The doctor sent in that maid to help with her sister, but when your note made it clear the sister isn't here, she was a liability. She knows Dr. Bramble and Hawthorn are connected to everything. You were supposed to kill her." She tsks reproachfully. "But you proved useful regardless, sending us the coach driver's name. It was simple enough to find him and promise we could help him and his wife save their precious daughter. I'm proud, you know. It was *my* spy who got us here." She reaches out as if to bop Arrow on the nose. Arrow flinches, which makes Iron smile.

"Why me? You could have used any of the termites."

"You can do the southern accent. That, and I never liked you," Iron says. "You got to stay at home with your mom. Why did *you* deserve that?"

"None of us deserved anything that happened to us."

"Well, be comforted knowing you don't deserve what's going to happen to you today, either." Iron smiles, baring all her teeth.

Arrow feels sick to her stomach. The doctor and his accomplices were always going to find a way in. Birdie was always going to die, and so is Arrow, all without having found Birdie's sister or helped Arrow's people. Thinking they could win was always a cruel fantasy.

She glances at Lake, wondering how much Lake has already seen. How long she's known that Arrow would die today. Lake is staring right at her, face set in determined frustration.

"No," Lake says, stomping a bare foot. "You already changed it twice. Figure out how to change it again. Choose a different target. And don't fall down the red circle."

You already changed it twice. Meaning Arrow's affected the futures Lake sees. Maybe she's not so useless. But she is if she dies.

"What is she talking about?" Iron snaps.

River shoots her an irritated look. "No one ever knows. I need supplies."

Iron flexes her fingers. "Are you giving me a command?"

"No, I'm telling you that I need medical supplies. If Forest wakes up with this head injury, the increased blood flow will trigger a swelling in his brain, causing brain matter to spill out through the fracture point, killing him instantly. I'm certain your doctor wouldn't be happy if that happened on your watch. Just get me something to help keep him asleep while his head heals. Something strong."

Any termite who had actually seen action could tell that River was lying through her teeth. And the doctor will know, too. But Iron's never really been a termite. Plus, she's impatient, and irritated, and . . . scared.

Thank you, Dawn, Arrow thinks.

"Arrow, go get the doctor's bag. He left it by the front door. If you try anything, I'll make that one suffer until she bites her own tongue off," Iron says. She points at Lake.

Arrow walks to the front door. It's wide open. The coach and the horses are right there. Arrow's confident that with their conditioning and her savvy, she could make it out of the bog. Back to Sootcity, where she could find a way to send a warning to the termites that Iron is a traitor.

But she won't risk River, and she won't abandon her friends. Her mother wanted a different life for her than living in secret and dying in pain. The termites are, by necessity, always alone and isolated. Arrow's not, and she doesn't want to be.

She gets the doctor's bag and takes it to River, then backs away to her spot next to Iron.

"Do you have what you need?" Iron demands as River rifles through.

"Yes, I think so."

Arrow's heart swells with love and admiration. River is so committed to her spoiled, entitled rich girl act that she doesn't even bother thanking her terrifying captor. River might very well be the bravest person Arrow knows.

"I don't like the way I feel." Iron glares at the residents one by one. "Which of you is making me feel this way?"

Dawn freezes, guilt written across her face. Lake points at the ceiling, drawing Iron's attention. "They keep them up there. So much crying. So much begging. You hear it now, too?"

"Don't lie to me," Iron says, at the exact same time Nimbus says, "Don't lie to me."

"What is he doing?" Iron says, at the exact same time Nimbus says, "What is he doing?"

"Make him stop doing that." But Nimbus continues, not echoing but mirroring her, a perfect match to her thoughts and words.

"That's it!" Iron and Nimbus say. "I've had it with these children."

Arrow's stomach sinks with dread. She's failed everyone, and now she'll have to watch them suffer.

CHAPTER FORTY-FOUR

A Nimbus Restored

When Birdie came into the kitchen that morning, everyone was so happy and relieved to have her back that they failed to notice a key event. Forest didn't *only* stay at Birdie's side. There was a moment when he leaned down, put his hand on Nimbus's shoulder, and said ever so softly, *"Find your way back to yourself."*

It's taken a few hours, but Nimbus at last has settled in his own mind. He knows who he is. He knows which thoughts are his, which eyes, which hands. He can still feel all the other minds, hear and see and even think them, and it's still confusing and overwhelming and more terrifying than ever thanks to the new additions, but. But. Amid all that incredible clamoring, he exists.

And, thanks to his time spent being trapped in the thoughts of others, he's seen Lake's visions of the future. River rushes Iron in an attempt to drug her. Iron ducks and throws River into the mantel, where River's head cracks against the stone. She dies, immediately.

Arrow attacks Iron. Iron triggers so much pain in Arrow's body that she can't move. The men come and retrieve the unconscious Arrow and do the procedure on her. She dies, not immediately.

Forest wakes and, enraged and confused, screams before he realizes what he's doing. They *all* die, in incredible agony.

Except Lake, who has just put plugs in her ears, having seen this happen in any number of variations. She alone will stand witness as Forest rampages through the house, discovers what he's done, and then lights the House of Quiet on fire, standing in the center, cradling Birdie's body to the last.

Nimbus doesn't like that sequence of events at all.

He loves everyone here. Well, obviously not the new additions. But he loves every resident of the house because he's *been* them. He has the compassion that comes with a perfect understanding that other people are as real as he is.

And they've taken such good care of him. Not just his old friend Birdie, but all of them. Dawn, with her determined cheerfulness to comfort him when he was so lost. Lake, who often told him she wished they could wander together instead of lonely and apart. Arrow, who came here with only anger and determination to do violence, but immediately abandoned her own schemes when she thought he was in danger. Forest, who risked his deepest fear—accidentally hurting someone again—to throw Nimbus a lifeline and lead him back to his own mind. And River, who is somehow both the sweetest and most terrifying person here, even if no one else can see it. He knows exactly how far she'll go for the people she loves, and because she loves them so fiercely, he does, too.

He even loves Cook. Poor Sable, with her tortured thoughts and broken heart, who only ever wanted to be with her daughter and chose to ignore the cost. She's absolutely guilty and culpable in all this suffering, but he understands why she did it.

He can't say that he loves the House Wife, because there's not enough of a person left in her mind to love. But he's sorry for what Mouse was turned into.

He does not, however, love Iron. So he stays in Iron's vicious, greedy, paranoid mind and mirrors her just long enough to change things. River's so confused that she doesn't rush Iron. And Iron is worked into such a baffled frenzy that she barely notices as Hawthorn comes and takes Arrow away. Arrow, who is still conscious and capable of defending herself. With Arrow gone, River waits for an opening, trying to be smart and not panic. Forest, thankfully, is still out cold. Things can be different.

Nimbus looks at Lake and winks. She rolls her eyes but smiles.

I know you all better than you know yourselves, Nimbus thinks, and holds back his own smile. Now it's time to unleash true chaos and hope against hope that the others can take advantage of it.

"If he doesn't stop, I'm killing him!" Iron snaps, but this time, Nimbus doesn't mirror her.

Instead, he says in as cold and clinical a tone as he can manage, "I think Iron's becoming a liability."

CHAPTER FORTY-FIVE

A Bird Revealed

The doctor stares at Birdie over the rectangular lenses of his glasses, bushy eyebrows sprouting in all directions. How did she ever think he was the type of man who would help her?

She was just so desperate. And she'd been raised in a community that believes in helping. She should have learned by now that those in power don't feel the same. To them, young people are an acceptable sacrifice, every time. Sent to work to help support families with almost nothing when a few families have nearly everything. Put through an unpredictable and dangerous procedure in order to have hopes of a better future—but one that's tracked and controlled. Or simply stolen and never returned, in the case of young people from the north.

"If you don't want to talk here," Dr. Bramble says, gesturing to the finely furnished bedroom around them, "I can give you to the House Wife. How did you survive the procedure?"

Birdie sits on the sofa at the end of the bed. "I don't know."

"Interesting." He opens a little pad and writes with a stubby oil pencil. It makes sense that he wouldn't assume she's lying. He doesn't understand how she survived; how could a silly maid ever know more than someone of his standing?

"And what did the procedure do to you?" he asks.

"Do you want me to describe how it made me feel?"

He waves a hand dismissively. "No, I don't care about that."

Birdie hates him. It's not a sharp or urgent hate, but a low, weary hatred. Of him, and every man like him. They don't care what anything costs, only what it produces. Only how it benefits them.

"You mean what ability I have now."

"Yes." He looks up again in intent anticipation.

"I don't have one."

"Don't lie to me," he snaps.

"It didn't do anything, after the initial burst of pain and disorientation." She puts it in absurdly mild and clinical terms, trying to sound reasonable to him.

He reaches out for her hand. She wants to flinch away from his touch, but she wants to survive even more. He notes something down. Then he reaches into his large bag and pulls out a long, thick needle. Before she has time to wonder what it does, he pokes it into her arm. This time she does flinch. He puts the needle away and writes something else. "We can rule out empathic abilities. I'm not getting any stray emotions from you, and I assume if you were feeling what your friends are feeling, you'd be insensible."

He's assuming too little steel in her spine and heart. She lets him. He pulls out a stopwatch and is quiet for a full minute as he holds her wrist, watching the seconds tick by. Then he drops her hand, replaces the stopwatch, and takes another note.

"No mind reading, either, or you'd be extremely upset by what I was thinking."

Now Birdie's pulse picks up. What is he thinking about? What can she do to protect everyone? She saw what that terrifying blond girl can do. Forest was their only hope, but the doctor dealt with him already. She has to believe Forest will be all right, but fear clings to her. She can't shake the image of him lying prone. She'd gotten used to his quiet strength.

Why couldn't the procedure have given her a weapon? As always, Birdie can only listen and watch and wait, hoping against hope she finds an advantage on her own somehow. No shortcuts for Birdie, ever.

The door opens. Hawthorn drags in Arrow and shoves her into the corner. Arrow crouches there like a wounded animal. In Hawthorn's free hand, he holds a black box, small enough to be tucked into a trunk. Or a doctor's bag as he makes house calls to wealthy families.

"Iron will hurt the others if you don't do exactly what we tell you to," Hawthorn says to Arrow. Then he turns to the doctor. "Well?"

"Nothing."

Hawthorn frowns. "She might have one of the stranger ones. They don't manifest as clearly."

"Perhaps. Or perhaps there's a simpler explanation, as there nearly always is. You didn't do the procedure correctly."

Hawthorn visibly bristles at the suggestion. "I did."

"Then why didn't you see it through to the end and take notes?"

"One of the children downstairs started screaming. I didn't want to risk discovery before you arrived."

"So what you are telling me is that you did not, in fact, do it correctly. Which explains Birdie's survival *and* lack of ability."

Hawthorn's jaw twitches. "The machine could be broken."

THE HOUSE OF QUIET

"If you have a hypothesis, let's test it. On her." Dr. Bramble points to Arrow.

"Please," Birdie says. "Arrow's too old. It will kill her."

"Or perhaps she'll be remarkable, like you." Dr. Bramble lifts an eyebrow, daring her to contradict him. So that's it. He didn't believe her after all. And he's going to sacrifice Arrow to call her bluff.

But the reason Birdie survived is unconscious in the other room. Forest won't be here to call Arrow back from wherever that terrible noise sends her. She doesn't even know if he could. He doesn't mean the same to Arrow that he does to Birdie. And River can't find Arrow in time if nothing is holding her here.

"Please don't do this," Birdie says again.

Arrow locks eyes with Birdie. Birdie knows her friend is afraid, but there's no evidence of it. Arrow's chin is up, her eyes bold, her mouth firm. Hawthorn grabs her arm and pushes her into a chair while he prepares his instruments. A handle is inserted into the box, and he cranks it rapidly for a full minute. Inside the box are wires connected to two metal prongs. Hawthorn attaches those to Arrow's temples with a sticky coating of glue. Birdie reaches up to her own temples and finds the residue. None of them noticed.

How many wealthy children did the doctor do this to in order to force the ministers to use the House of Quiet?

"Survive," Arrow says to Birdie, holding her gaze. "For Magpie. And for me."

Birdie nods, trying not to cry. She glares at the doctor and wonders how his mind works that he can do these things without caring about the damage. And then, at last, she understands what's different. Because she can *see*. Maybe her eyes have adjusted, or maybe her desperation unlocked the answer.

Dr. Bramble doesn't shimmer brightly like her friends in the other room, but there's still a hint of something there. He has channels in his mind. Dry streambeds that have always been there, old and calcified over now.

That's what the procedure does. It opens those existing channels and lets information flow freely through them. It creates abilities out of senses that were only ever meant to be subtle ways for people to love and connect with and understand each other.

But instead of a gentle trickle, the procedure creates a torrent. It takes advantage of something natural by turning it unnatural and overwhelming, and it works only on brains young enough to adapt to the trauma.

The doctor has not so much as a *drop* of energy or thought going through those channels in his mind. No part of him is curious about others' experiences, or concerned about their well-being, or willing to consider anything other than himself and his own goals.

If Birdie can see those channels even when they're not in use, though . . .

"I'll take over from here," Dr. Bramble says, standing. Hawthorn glares but moves out of the way. The innocuous-looking box is on the table next to Arrow's chair. It holds what they tried to kill Birdie with. What they'll kill Arrow with next, all so they can see what happens.

"I know what it did to me." Birdie stands and steps toward the doctor.

He turns with a smug, satisfied smile. His gambit worked. "And?"

"I'll show you." Birdie brushes a finger against his forehead. An instant is all she needs to find one very specific channel. It's the same one she saw in Dawn this morning. She needs *in*, though. Not *out*. There. With a push, Birdie blasts it open.

Just like that, Dr. Bramble now has empathy so strong he can't deny or turn away from or close himself off to others' emotions. All the feelings in this house, the power and intensity of a group of young people suffering and dreaming and hoping and loving and fearing together, slam into him like an avalanche.

He crumples to the floor, broken, his brain too old and rigid to grow around the same thing he's forced on countless children in order to line other men's pockets.

Or he might be dead. It doesn't matter. Birdie isn't sorry. Men like him look at her and see something small and fragile, but they never stop to wonder what *type* of bird she might be. Birdie isn't even her real name. It's a nickname from Magpie, who couldn't pronounce Kestrel. A falcon known for hovering silently and waiting until exactly the right moment to strike.

There's a surprised whimper. Birdie looks up to see Hawthorn holding a scalpel to Arrow's throat. "Stay there or she dies," he growls as he drags Arrow backward out of the room, slams the door, and locks it.

CHAPTER FORTY-SIX

A Deadly River

River has no idea what Nimbus is doing.

She wants to go after Arrow, but how is Nimbus talking? And why is he talking like that? First he was saying what Iron was saying as she was saying it, which ought to be impossible, and now he's saying things about Iron that River doesn't understand.

Until she does. He's the smartest person in the whole house.

"He's a mind reader!" River gasps, not even having to fake much amazement. That's why poor Nimbus was lost. His ability was so strong that he couldn't distinguish between his mind and other minds. Something changed, though. River can't worry about that now, because she's too busy trying to hide the rag she's soaking in ether.

"She's served her purpose," Nimbus says, his tone still cold and clinical. "She's expendable. Her erratic tendencies make her more of a liability than an asset at this point."

"Who's saying that?" Iron demands. "You're making that up! You're trying to trick me."

"And she stole my best pen," Nimbus adds.

Iron's face goes blank with shock. "You couldn't know that. No one could know that, but . . ." She flexes her fingers, murder on her face. "I'll show them who's expendable." She turns and flings open the door, her back to the room.

Dawn picks up the poker near the fireplace, swings, and connects with the side of Iron's head with a sickening thunk. Iron drops to the floor.

"Oh, well done," River says, shocked.

"She's not dead!" Dawn squeaks defensively, pointing. Iron's still breathing.

River feels Dawn's terror and exhilaration. It's hard to focus on her own thoughts with Dawn's emotions running all over them. If River's going to help, she needs to be fully in control.

"*Should* we kill her, though?" Dawn asks. She looks at River, and her fear spikes. None of her friends have the ruthlessness required to murder an unconscious girl. And River wouldn't put that on any of them.

"No, you already took care of her. You and Nimbus saved us."

Dawn beams. There's a flood of pride and happiness, which River also has to push aside. "Now I need you, Nimbus, and Lake to go hide. Get somewhere safe."

"Out of earshot," Lake says. "Just in case."

River doesn't understand that one, but apparently Nimbus does. He blinks, trying his hardest to look at her. His eyes almost focus. "Make sure Forest knows who and where he is when he wakes up," he says. "It's important."

"I'll do my best."

"But I can help more," Dawn insists. "I want to help."

"You already have. Now it's time to let us protect you, because you deserve to be protected. Do you understand?"

Dawn nods, tears in her eyes. She throws her arms around River in a hug, then gestures for Lake and Nimbus to follow her. When neither of them can quite manage it—Nimbus looks like he's about to fall asleep on his feet, and Lake seems to think the wall no longer exists as she bumps right into it and then scowls in frustration—Dawn huffs and takes them both by the hands.

Lake tugs back. "We have to hide on the first floor. Because of the fire."

"Well, that's not ominous," River says. "Lake's right, though. You should hide in the kitchen so you have an easy exit through the pantry." But then River has an idea. A dangerous one that keeps her from rushing to save Arrow. But she trusts that Nimbus had good reason to warn her about Forest waking up, and she trusts that her beloved can take care of herself. River has to stay here and accomplish the tasks only she can.

"One last thing before you go, Dawn." River retrieves the ether-soaked rag and holds it out. "Please press this to my face until I pass out, and then immediately remove it."

"What happens if I don't immediately remove it?" Dawn asks, curious.

River lies on the floor. "I'll die."

Dawn does as she's told. The last thing River sees is a very worried expression staring down at her.

And then River's in a dark space, pulsing with pain. The dream is fractured and lurching, because the sleep of the dreamer isn't a real sleep. But it's enough of one. Instead of Forest, River sees Iron, spinning in a slow circle, fists clenched, trying to find her way out.

A short detour won't hurt anything. Not if River's quick.

Iron sees her and screams. She puts her hand on River's arm.

Nothing happens. Iron takes a step back, fear bleeding into the rage on her face. River takes a step forward and smiles. In here, she's the one with power.

"I told you what I was going to do to you," River says. "And I keep my promises."

CHAPTER FORTY-SEVEN

An Arrow Falling

Trickles of warm blood from nicks in Arrow's skin slip down her neck and soak into her dress as Hawthorn drags her backward through the hallway.

"I can't hurt you," Arrow says.

"No, but your disgusting friends can." Hawthorn bangs on the door behind himself. Arrow closes her eyes and hopes against hope that the House Wife won't open it. It's stayed closed this long when they were all desperate to get through it. Surely it will deny Hawthorn, too.

The House Wife opens it. Arrow never did believe in luck, anyway.

"There's too much noise," the House Wife says, hands over her ears, her voice a high whine.

"Move!" Hawthorn shoves her aside and throws Arrow into the room. Then he slams the door and pushes the bolt into place. He whirls on them and gestures to the House Wife, then waves the scalpel in the general direction of a closet door. "Get over there. Open it."

The House Wife shakes her head. "There's too much noise.

We need to quiet the noise. We have to take the noise to the heart of the house."

"Shut up!" Hawthorn punches the House Wife. She sits down hard, legs splayed, head hanging. Arrow lunges, but he's expecting it. He slashes at her. She retreats, arm bleeding now, too. Arrow's aware of exactly how much blood she can afford to lose before she dies. She has to be smart and careful.

"We need quiet," the House Wife whispers.

"Useless." Hawthorn gestures toward the door and glares at Arrow. "You. Open it."

Arrow does as she's told. And not just because of the threat. She has to know what's on the hidden floor. Plus, a different environment might offer her a fighting advantage.

"Hidden staircase," Arrow whispers to herself. Behind the door is a narrow, dark set of stairs going up. She tries to put some space between herself and Hawthorn to set up an ambush, but he closes the distance and casually jabs her in the back, drawing even more blood.

"Don't try it," he growls.

At the top of the stairs, she walks out into the most disappointing reveal of her entire life. The mysteriously hidden third floor is just a *room*. Large enough she's certain there aren't any secret chambers.

There's the circular window high on the wall, now a sullen, solid red with the sunlight blocked by fog outside. Lake told her not to fall down the red circle. But how could Arrow go through the window? Unless Hawthorn throws her. She'll be sure to avoid that.

She glances around desperately for something she might have missed. There are no chains, no restraints, no cages. No children waiting for her to save them. Just a solitary desk with a chair tucked in. On the desk is a tidy stack of paper inside a leather folio with a pen resting on top. Like a station waiting for a secretary.

Arrow drifts toward the papers.

"Stop!" Hawthorn shouts. "Don't move." He's looking around the room, frantic. "It has to be here. It has to be."

"What has to be here?" Arrow asks. Hawthorn answers by stabbing her lightly in the back again. She *really* hates him. "Tell me what you're looking for, and I can help you. I'm very motivated by the idea of not dying."

"They have another machine," he says.

"To do the procedure?"

"Why would we do all this to get our hands on *another* way to do the procedure? Don't be stupid. Think, you disgusting little bogger. Didn't you wonder why the minister of finance had been here before? Why Sky's father had? What interest would they have in the House of Quiet if all it did was help poor children? You know better than that."

Arrow does know better than that. Whatever was happening here, they had the house set up to keep wealthy people comfortable for short stays, and to keep poor children locked up.

"What do they do here?" Arrow whispers. She doesn't want to know. She has to know. The paintings in the hallway downstairs haunt her. All those children with their hands raised, the euphoric looks on their faces as they were literally walked on top of.

"Whatever it is, it's worth taking bogger children and performing the procedure on them, only to send them directly here rather than try to use their abilities elsewhere. It's worth powerful men paying fortunes the likes of which you can't *fathom* for just a single visit. And it can only be operated by someone with abilities like the House Wife's. Like Birdie's sister had, which was the only reason we were helping her. So we—" He pauses, corrects. The doctor isn't his partner anymore. "So *I* am going to discover the secret, and take it, and then I'll control both the means of production and the end product. I'm going to be the most powerful man alive." He kicks the desk, sending the pen rolling. "But what are they doing here? Why hide this room if there's nothing in it?"

Arrow keeps her eyes on the window. That red window, the one that unnerved River so much. Lake warned Arrow not to fall down it. Such a strange way to phrase that. Wouldn't Arrow fall *through* or *out* a window? Plus, she kept saying that Birdie went down the stairs and then died. The hidden stairs led up. Surely going back down them wasn't any more treacherous.

Arrow looks around. The desk, the chair. The window. There are no other red circles. Then it hits her. If it were sunny, the sun would hit that window from the east. Right around the same time every morning. Exactly when the House Wife always retrieved Rabbit and Sky.

Arrow hurries toward the center of the room.

"Hey!" Hawthorn shouts.

"Let me try something." Arrow lines herself up with the window, then starts walking from the wall. She takes a step, stomps. Takes a step, stomps. Takes a step, stomps. This time it sounds different. Hollow.

Arrow crouches and feels around the seams of the floorboards until she finds a string. She tugs it up. A hole in the floor reveals a tight, circular staircase winding downward.

"I found it," Hawthorn says, triumphant, peering down shoulder to shoulder with her.

Before Arrow can elbow him in the face, someone shoves them both from behind. They tumble into the dark together.

CHAPTER FORTY-EIGHT

A Bird Descending

Dawn, Lake, and Nimbus are missing, Forest is still unconscious but breathing, and River is also unconscious but breathing. Birdie didn't bother checking on that evil blond girl, but something will have to be done to make sure she doesn't hurt anyone when she wakes up. And then there's the matter of Cook and the driver, around here somewhere, lurking.

She has to find Arrow first, though. Hawthorn will kill her. But just as she's about to sprint down the hall to start searching the house, sturdy fire poker in hand, a door opens behind her. A door she's been trying to get through since she arrived.

"This way," the House Wife says.

Birdie can't believe it. "You're letting me in?"

"Yes, yes." The House Wife grasps Birdie's hands, squeezing just a little too tight. There are tears in her eyes, like she's in pain. "We're ready for you."

She backs up and gestures for Birdie to come in.

Birdie doesn't hesitate. She steps through. She can see the House Wife clearly now, too. Around her head is a halo. It's dull, worn around the edges. Nothing like the bright, chaotic wonder of her friends. The House Wife has an ability. But what is it?

Birdie struggles not to show her revulsion. There's something disgusting about the House Wife's halo. She wants to get far away from her. But she can't. Not now that she's finally inside this room.

"Come with me," the House Wife says, more urgency in her movements than Birdie's ever seen. Gone is the drifting from one space to another. The House Wife flings herself toward the closet door. Birdie follows. The shape of Forest's suggestion gets in her way again, his original command not to go through that door lingering.

It's softened by the deeper, truer thing he said, though: *You should do what you want.*

Birdie wants to go up those stairs. She wants to so very, very badly.

But Lake told her if she went down those stairs, she'd die. And if she dies, she can't help anyone. Magpie is probably dead. Birdie can admit it to herself, at last. But her friends aren't. She owes it to the people here to stay alive and protect them. She has to choose to live, to keep going and fighting, even if it means walking away from ever finding out what happened to Magpie.

For so long her world was small, focused on a future built around her sister. But now she knows how big the world is, and how many people the men in charge of this country are hurting. Her heart cracks open. Even though she hates the thought that anything in the world could be more important than her precious little sister, she can't turn her back on everyone else.

Birdie's being pulled in too many directions. Which means prioritizing her responsibilities. Any good maid knows being overwhelmed by how much there is to do doesn't get any of it done.

So the first task at hand: Find the person in urgent, immediate trouble. And that's Arrow.

"I'm sorry." Birdie takes a step back, away from the stairs. She tightens her grip on the poker. "I have to find Arrow."

"I know where she is." The House Wife points to the floor. Sure enough, there are droplets of blood, still fresh and wet. Leading directly to the stairs.

"Show me." Birdie follows the House Wife through the door. There's a moment of strain, and then she breaks through Forest's residual command.

After all Lake's warnings, Birdie expects something dire or threatening. She knows servant stairs can be deadly, but these barely even qualify. They're sturdy and well-built. She'll be extra careful on her way back down, just in case, but she doesn't understand what Lake was so concerned about.

At the top of the stairs is an open room with a single red window. But that barely merits notice, because there's a hole in the floor. The door to that hole is a wooden circle on a hinge, with a looped leather strap in the middle so it can be pulled closed from the inside. Birdie keeps one eye on the House Wife—she's watching intently, her head tilted with one ear pressed against her shoulder like she's trying to block something out—and edges up to the opening.

Ah. Of course. *Another* set of stairs. These ones go deeper than they should, past the second and first floor to somewhere underground. Darkness pools at the bottom, shrouding whatever's down there. These are stairs worthy of Lake's grim pronouncement. They feel like a journey that goes in only one direction.

Somewhere beneath Birdie, Arrow moans in pain.

Birdie takes the first steps in a rush, reaches back up, and slams the trap door shut. She shoves the metal poker through the leather strap to jam the door. Birdie waits, ready to attack the House Wife if she gets it open.

The House Wife just knocks, gently but insistently. "You'll need me," she says, her voice muffled. "The noise has to go somewhere, once it's out of you."

Satisfied that she's safe for now, Birdie carefully navigates the steps. At the bottom, propped up against the wall, is Arrow.

Arrow squints up at her, blood trickling down the side of her head. "Forest and I had a whole secret conspiracy within our conspiracy to keep you from coming down here," she grumbles. "It was a good plan."

"I'm sure it was." Birdie crouches in front of her friend. There's a light source farther down the dank stone tunnel. Arrow's face is already bruising, and there are a few shallow cuts on her throat. Her arm is bleeding. Maybe other parts of her, too. And she's cradling her other arm.

"The House Wife shoved Hawthorn and me down the stairs. I broke my arm. My ankle hurts, too," Arrow says. "I think that's just sprained, though."

"Okay." Birdie reaches for her. "I'll help you stand, and we'll go up together."

To her surprise, Arrow shakes her head. "This house has cost us too much already. We need to know why. Also, I'd rather poke my own eyes out than let Hawthorn get answers instead of us. He's in bad shape from our fall, too. You can catch him. I'll stay here and watch your back in case the House Wife comes to finish us off."

"But you're hurt. How can you—"

Arrow holds up the scalpel, glinting with menace. She smiles, her expression glinting with that same menace. "We're not ending down here, Birdie. Forest would kill me if I let you die, and River would kill me if *I* died."

Birdie presses her forehead against Arrow's shoulder, the only spot on her body that doesn't seem to be injured. "I'm glad I met you."

"There's no one I'd rather scrub bathtubs and fight evil with."

With a choked laugh, Birdie stands. She walks down the tunnel to find out, at last, what the House of Quiet has been hiding.

Around a curve, there's an archway. A figure leans exhaustedly against it, his back to her. Hawthorn turns his head and glances over his shoulder. He sighs. "We're fools, little bird. We both lose."

Beyond him is a low-ceilinged chamber, lit by a flickering lamp. And there, bound with leather straps and lying flat on a table, emaciated and strange but undeniably familiar, is Magpie. Her sister. Here, at last. Here the whole time.

Magpie opens her eyes, turns her head toward Birdie, and lets out an agonized scream.

CHAPTER FORTY-NINE

The Heart of the House

It all hurts so much.

She has no sense of self, no sense of her own body or mind anymore. She's only sensation. The noise isn't just in her ears; it's in her brain, in her bones, in her blood, pulsing, terrorizing, demanding noise. She can't escape it. There's only quiet if she makes it, and she *has* to make it. She has to make the quiet. She has to take the noise and push it into something else.

There's always a noisy body and a quiet body, one to take the noise from and one to push it into. All she feels is the buildup of pressure so terrible she thinks she'll explode, and then the release as she siphons it away and dribbles it into a different container. The old one that absorbs the noise, instead of amplifying it.

She doesn't know anything other than the noise, always somewhere from a low hum to a horrendous crescendo. Her whole world is a cycle of pain and relief. And right now it's cycled into pain worse than any she's ever known.

She has to quiet that noise. *Now*. She reaches deep inside, finds the connection to her own hand. She'd forgotten she had hands, but she does. She stretches, grasping in the air, hoping and waiting for a hand to take hers so she can release herself from this agony once more, if only for a little while.

CHAPTER FIFTY

An Arrow Aimed

Arrow is midhop on her way to make sure Birdie is okay when an iron poker comes clanging down the spiral staircase. It's nearly inaudible over whoever is screaming down the hall.

Arrow shifts toward the stairs, scalpel in hand. Cook and the driver are coming down. Behind them is the House Wife. They stop as soon as they see Arrow.

Cook holds up her hands, leaning against the stair railing. "Please. Let me explain."

A single scalpel isn't much against three grown adults, but most people are afraid of pain or injury. It's an advantage for Arrow. She doesn't *like* pain or injury, but she knows what's survivable. And so far she's surviving.

"Stay there. Don't come down any farther," Arrow commands.

Cook obeys, sitting on a step seven or eight up. The driver stays standing behind her, and the House Wife crouches above him, looking longingly through the railing down the tunnel. The screaming lessens, but it turns into something even more upsetting. Like someone wordlessly pleading for their life.

"They don't eat," Cook says, her voice raised so it carries enough to be heard. "They don't drink. They don't sleep. They need this, or they die."

"What is *this*?" Arrow asks.

"The noise," the House Wife says, her tone anguished like she, too, is in pain.

"Our Mouse," Cook says, gesturing upward toward the House Wife, "is the same as the girl in there. Their ability almost never happens. That's part of why they do the procedure on so many bog—" She catches herself and corrects. "Children from the north. It's a numbers game. Every once in a great while, the procedure produces a gaping void in a mind. The void echoes. It's *painful*. They're in pain all the time, but it's worse around anyone with an ability. Mouse says they're too noisy."

"So noisy," the House Wife sighs.

"People like our Mouse can pull energy right out of those noisy minds. Burn it out of them. It's like the peat. Dredged up, dried out, all that life puffing into smoke. They need a place to put the noise, though. They don't want to hold on to it, just quiet it. It's an instinct. They can't help it." She looks up at her daughter, her own pain and longing written all over her expression. "When someone like Mouse happens after the procedure, they're sent here to become the heart of the house."

"So she's the heart?" Arrow juts her chin toward the House Wife.

"She was."

"It wears them down," the driver says, his voice flat and emotionless. "All that pain, all that energy coming in and going out. After a while they aren't good at the taking. But they can still hold it. So the heart gives it to Mouse, and she transfers it."

Arrow goes cold. "Transfers it where?" But she doesn't need to know. She's already heard the answer. That night the minister came with Sky's father. They've both visited the house, both benefited from it. Those disgusting paintings along the hallways were a clue all along. Old men standing on top of youth, improving as they get closer to the House Wife's room.

They're literally stealing life. Burning children like peat to warm their own blood.

"They transfer it to whoever can pay." Cook doesn't sound happy about this part, at least. "A burst of vitality. A sense of recaptured youth. It doesn't last, but they come back again and again and again."

Arrow feels sick. "You didn't just come for our forests and our mines. You were stealing the north's most precious resource so that, what, a few rich old men could have a little spring in their step?"

"It didn't start that way," Cook whispers. "It started as a way to help the children who couldn't cope with their abilities."

"But someone still benefited," Arrow snaps. "They charge poor families for the procedure even though the abilities mean the government then owns their children and can assign them to whatever job they choose. Then they charge wealthy people to visit the House of Quiet to benefit from suffering. And when that wasn't enough, they started stealing from the north to fuel even more."

"We didn't do this," the driver insists.

"*You didn't stop it*," Arrow says.

She turns her back on them and limps toward Birdie. She doesn't care about Cook and her husband and the House Wife. They don't deserve so much as her rage. If Arrow has her way, she'll forget they exist.

As she steadies herself against the damp rock wall, she tries to think about what to do next. But she doesn't need to think. Not really. She already knows what has to be done. Cook said this ability is rare. Rarer than rare. All those children from the south *and* the north, and they have only two. The House Wife, and the new heart. The House Wife is all used up, which leaves the other one.

Take her out of the picture, and the House of Quiet falls. There would be no reason to steal northern children to funnel through it. It doesn't solve everything, but at least it solves that. And wouldn't it be a mercy of sorts? The House Wife isn't even a person anymore. That's not a life. That's not a future for this heart.

She came to this house to kill someone in order to help her people. Even if Iron was lying the whole time, Arrow realizes that's still her purpose. She won't hesitate this time.

She peers inside the room. On a table in the center is a yearning, straining creature, barely human anymore. Birdie looks up at Arrow, tears streaming down her face. A face that is too similar to the one on the table.

Birdie found her sister.

"Did you hear what Cook said?" Arrow asks.

"I heard enough," Birdie whispers.

"Magpie can't live without it," Hawthorn says, his voice cold. "She'll die unless she can siphon off the noise."

He's on the other side of the room, keeping Magpie between himself and the two girls. Next to him on the floor is a girl, twelve or thirteen. Empty. Dead, just like Rabbit. *That's* what Beetle was delivering the night they were all drugged. Not just wood for burning, but a child for consuming. That's why there was a break after Sky's treatments. The house had something else to gnaw on. Someone they didn't have to be careful with.

Hawthorn shifts, wincing with pain, then clears his throat and speaks in his best tutor voice. "We find ourselves with aligned interests. Birdie wants to take care of her sister, and I want to restructure power in this country. I can do it in a way that protects your people, Arrow."

Arrow ignores him. Magpie strains, bucking against the leather straps. She's trying desperately to touch her sister. They all know what will happen if she does.

"That's not Magpie," Birdie whispers. "Not really."

"We can take better care of her than they did," Hawthorn insists. "It'll be a kindness, even. We'll go back to offering this as a treatment to make life easier for those with unbearable abilities. Like your friends upstairs. None of them wanted what was done to them."

Arrow gives him an incredulous look. "That's a strange way to say '*what we did to them.*'"

He scowls. "I didn't perform the procedure on any of them. That was the doctor."

"You tried to kill Birdie."

"Yes, well, that was a misunderstanding! Which we can all move beyond, because now we have more information. Besides, what other choice do we have? Denying Magpie the energy she needs will kill her, and—"

"Don't say her name," Birdie snaps. "You don't get to say her name." She hasn't looked away from Arrow. There's something resigned and pleading in her expression. "I can't do it. Please. I can't do it." Her eyes go down to the scalpel still grasped in Arrow's hand.

Arrow doesn't want to. It's wrong, but it's the only choice. At least Arrow knows exactly where to cut. The most painless target on the human body.

Target.

Choose a different target, Lake said.

Choose a different target.

Lake's right. This broken, tormented girl isn't the problem. The House of Quiet isn't even the problem. The whole system is. If Magpie's gone, if the house is gone, even if the procedure itself is gone, the same men who grew rich and powerful off both will still be rich and powerful. They'll find another way to grind people up and profit off the remains.

Arrows fly straight and true once loosed, so be careful where you aim. That's why her mother didn't want her to join the termites, where she'd be aimed by other people. It's time for Arrow to make her own decisions. And she knows what the first one will be. It's the decision her mother made time and again.

Save those you can.

Arrow shakes her head. "We don't start this revolution with another sacrificed child. We start this revolution so there are no more sacrificed children, ever. We'll find another way."

Birdie lets out a sob, half relief and half despair. "But I don't know what to do. I don't know how to help her."

"You should—"

Hawthorn lunges for Arrow, tackling her to the ground.

CHAPTER FIFTY-ONE

Lost in the Forest

When Forest walks out of the study, head aching but clear thanks to River nudging him awake in a dream, he sees Cook and the House Wife rush into Sky's old room, grab the portable procedure device, and shove it into a bag. But they don't see him.

"Come on," the driver calls from the front door. "We have to go."

"This will help, Mouse," Cook says. "With this, we can make our own noise. You can still take what you need."

"I can't control it, though," the House Wife says, tilting her head in his direction. She can't see him, but she can still hear him. He figured that out when Lake went missing. "I'm so tired."

He nods. He understands.

"That's fine. That's fine." Cook pats the House Wife's hand, then tugs her out the door. Forest follows them.

"We're ready," Beetle calls, checking the straps on the horses. He doesn't look up. If he did, he'd see Forest standing in the doorway to the house, watching them.

"My gentle little girl. My darling little girl." Cook urges the House Wife out toward the coach.

"Stop," Forest says.

They stop. Frozen so completely Cook and the driver can't even look at each other. Forest walks up to the House Wife and leans down so they're eye to eye.

"You can see me now," he whispers, and she blinks, pupils dilating.

"There you are."

"Mouse," he says. "Tell me what you want."

The House Wife smiles. For the first time Forest can see the girl she was, the vibrant, happy child that the procedure hollowed out and destroyed. "I can still hear them, you know. Every child who passed through me. I don't want to anymore. I want quiet. Perfect, pristine quiet, and I never want to hear anything again. I want to go to sleep at last, and I don't want to wake up."

"That sounds nice," Forest says. Mouse didn't ask for any of this. She can't change what she is now, so he'll help her the only way he can. "You should do that."

Cook screams, but the sound is trapped between her locked jaws. Mouse collapses onto the soft, spongy ground. It looks like she's falling into bed at the end of a long, awful day. Her eyes close and she breathes her last, a smile on her lips.

He turns back to the house. All his kindness was used up on Mouse. He has none left for her parents, who kept the House of Quiet running all these years. Who knowingly fed it child after child, all so they could stay close to the ghost of their own little girl, lost so long ago.

He has one last thing to say to them before he goes in to help Birdie. It's a simple command, and it's exactly what they deserve.

"Walk away."

The driver begins his march. Cook follows, not quite catching up to him. They're out of sync, unable to touch or comfort each other or look back at their daughter. They walk, away from safety and into the endless peat bog to join all the innocent bodies they helped put there.

CHAPTER FIFTY-TWO

Two Birds Freed

"Arrow!" Birdie shouts. Before she can jump in, Hawthorn goes limp.

Arrow shoves him off with an annoyed grunt. Hawthorn isn't moving, but the only thing wrong Birdie can see is a single red line on the back of his neck.

"Never give a scalpel to a rebellion surgeon's daughter," Arrow says. She flinches in pain, trying to stand without using her broken arm. Birdie moves to aid her, but Arrow shakes her head. "I'm fine. You need to figure this out. There's got to be a way to help Magpie."

Magpie's cries are getting louder. It's the most wrenching thing Birdie's ever heard. She knows Magpie wants to hold her hand. She also knows Magpie would kill her without meaning to. Because this isn't Magpie anymore.

The halo around Magpie's head is so much darker and sharper than the House Wife's, with edges clean enough to slice like Arrow's scalpel. What can Birdie do? Magpie isn't in there. Birdie can't talk her sister out of what she's been turned into. She doubts even Forest could. If they could use Dr. Bramble's device, they could try to reverse it somehow. But the doctor isn't around to tell them if it's possible because of what Birdie did to him.

But . . . if she can open channels, doesn't it stand to reason that she can close them, too?

Maybe it will work. *There are no maybes. The world isn't kind,* her mother hisses in her memory. But Birdie's mother is wrong. Arrow, a girl who grew up crushed by an occupying force, a girl who lost everything, a girl who came here specifically to kill Birdie, still believes there's a kinder way. Maybe they can find that way together.

And maybe Birdie can bring Magpie with them.

Maybe doesn't feel like a foolish word anymore. It feels like a hopeful one.

Birdie stands behind Magpie's head and studies the swirls of darkness there. It's not a channel like the others. It's a void.

"Magpie in the tree, are you looking for me?" Birdie sings. She can't be sure, but she thinks Magpie stills. Just for a second. It's a risk to touch her, but Birdie's willing to try now that she suspects Magpie heard her. She leans closer, places her fingers ever so softly on Magpie's temples, and searches. She looks for Magpie with all the determination and love she has in her. And, amid so much chaos and pain and damage, she finds what she didn't dare hope for.

Magpie's still in there.

Better yet, Birdie finds the edges of the hole they blew in her sister's mind. Slowly, carefully, with the patience only an older sister could have, Birdie tugs it shut. She takes all the edges and presses them together, smoothing them over. No more an abyss for noise to build in and torment her. Just a scar.

Magpie's not screaming anymore. She's not even whimpering.

Her breathing is even and regular. Beneath her closed eyelids, her eyes move like she's dreaming. She looks exactly how Birdie imagined she would, down to the scar in her eyebrow.

"I found you," Birdie whispers, tears streaming down her face.

Birdie doesn't know how much of her sister is left. Maybe a lot. Maybe barely anything. But it doesn't matter, because Birdie kept her promise. They're back together, and she'll make sure nothing ever hurts Magpie—or anyone like her—again.

Arrow wraps a one-armed hug around Birdie from behind. "You did it."

"*We* did it."

"We did it." Arrow laughs, crying along with Birdie. "But now how do we get her and ourselves out? Maybe *this* is how you die. You can't get me up the stairs with my ankle, and neither of us can carry Magpie, so we all starve to death down here. Lake will be pleased that she was finally right about something."

Footsteps echo toward them.

"I'll take the driver," Arrow says, voice low and urgent. "You take Cook. But if it's Iron, just run." She holds up her scalpel as though wielding a sword. Birdie braces herself, fists clenched.

Arrow's scalpel drops to the floor with a metallic clatter as River bursts through the archway with Forest close behind.

Birdie can't take her eyes off Forest. He's not dead. She didn't abandon her friends to find her sister, and they didn't abandon her, either. None of them did this alone. They never could have.

"You're bleeding!" River gasps, rushing to Arrow and taking in all her wounds.

"It's not as bad as it looks." Arrow tries to hold her arms out to hug River, then gasps in pain. "Actually, it might be as bad as it looks."

"I'm so sorry it took me this long." River uses her sleeve to wipe blood from Arrow's face. "I had to wake Forest up, and then I *also* had to wake up. Fortunately, Dawn has a light touch with the ether. I would have come right after you to begin with, but Lake and Nimbus told me I needed to make sure Forest woke up the right way, and—"

Arrow presses her lips against River's. River kisses her back fiercely, then puts Arrow's good arm around her shoulder to take the other girl's weight. "Come on. Let's get out of here."

Forest looks at Magpie, then at Birdie. Birdie nods, tears in her eyes. "It's Magpie."

Forest cuts the restraints, then picks up Magpie, carrying her like the precious thing she is. Birdie walks by his side, and they slowly make their way back up, then back down into the main house. It wouldn't do to trip and break their necks in the servant staircase after everything else they survived.

In the foyer, River eases Arrow into one of the chairs and starts fussing over her injuries. Forest frowns and looks back where they came from. He lays Magpie on the rug, then goes back into the House Wife's room. Birdie doesn't want to be apart from him, but she knows they'll always come back to each other. She stays next to Magpie, stroking her hair.

"Where's Iron?" Arrow eyes the hallway warily.

"Oh, she died." River's tone is airy and conversational, as if declaring Iron is taking a holiday on the coast.

Birdie chooses not to question how or when Iron died. It's a relief she's not lurking out there somewhere, waiting to ambush them. Arrow must share her relief, because she doesn't ask follow-up questions, either.

"And the others?" Birdie asks. "Is everyone safe?"

"Here!" Dawn appears from the direction of the kitchen with Nimbus in tow. "Lake went upstairs to get something. Nimbus said you were ready for us."

"*Nimbus* said something?" Birdie looks at him, hands over her heart.

He peers shyly around Dawn. His eyes still jump to unexpected places, but it's clear from his expression that he's back.

"Oh, Nimbus!" Birdie knows he doesn't care for hugs, so she beams at him and sends him her love that way. He smiles back, dimples she'd forgotten he had popping into place.

Lake skips down the hallway, dropping the two scarves into Birdie's lap, along with the stack of drawings. "You wanted these," she said. "You were sad you forgot them."

"I do, and I would have been. Thank you." She carefully wraps the green scarf around Magpie, warming her with the love of the people they were separated from but never left behind.

Forest reappears, carrying the portable lamp that was down in the secret room. He turns it up so the flame burns as high as possible. Then he goes to each lamp in the hallway, pinches the wicks off, and turns the gas up.

"He's making sure if anyone comes looking, all they'll find is the site of a terrible accident. They'll assume we escaped into the bog and died there," Nimbus explains. His face falls. "And . . . he put that dead girl's body on the table downstairs. So it looks like Magpie died, too."

Arrow nods, face bereft. "I'm sorry we can't bury her, but it's the smart choice."

"You can read minds?" Birdie asks Nimbus.

Lake snaps her fingers at Birdie. "I want you to. Please."

Birdie blinks, confused until she realizes Lake is accepting an offer Birdie hasn't even had time to consider yet. But of course it's an offer she'll make. Hawthorn was right. All these children suffering, and at last she has a way to help them that isn't changing or quieting them—just making it easier for them to live in their own brains.

"Do you want me to take it away?" Birdie holds Lake's gaze to make sure that the younger girl knows what she's agreeing to.

"I already told you!" Lake rolls her eyes in exasperation.

Birdie puts her hands on Lake's forehead. It's much easier than it was with Magpie. A simple task to find the channel, then pinch it from a torrent to a trickle. Lake blinks rapidly, then walks unsteadily out the front door, arms held cautiously in front of her, like she still doesn't trust the world she's seeing.

"I can take them all." Birdie looks from Forest, to Dawn, to Nimbus, to River. "If you want, I'll close the places in your mind that were pried open."

"Perhaps we should talk about this *not* in the house well on its way to exploding?" River suggests.

"My girl is so smart," Arrow says, and gasps.

Birdie hadn't realized how much pain Arrow is in, but she's barely holding it together. River helps Arrow outside, and Forest picks up Magpie. They reconvene at the coach after Forest loads Birdie's sleeping sister inside. It's a safe distance from the house, so they have time to talk.

"Well?" Birdie asks.

Dawn frowns, but shakes her head. "Maybe someday. Not yet. I can still be helpful."

River shakes her head, too, one arm around Arrow's waist. "I didn't ask for this, but it was never going to cost me my life. Not like it did so many others. I think if I stay this way, I can help make things fairer."

Nimbus tilts his head as though listening, then nods. "We're going to use what we have to help you. Both of you." He looks at Arrow, too. "We're going to use our abilities to help *everyone*, because Arrow can't do it alone."

Birdie turns toward Arrow. Arrow nods. "I don't want to just free the north. Everything needs to change, otherwise nothing will. And who better to clean up this mess than a couple of rebel maids?"

Birdie laughs. "Who better indeed."

"Don't leave the rest of us out." River pulls the leather folio from the red-window room out of her bodice. Birdie didn't even think to take it. "This is a log of every minister, minister's wife, and wealthy person who took advantage of what the House of Quiet offered, as well as everyone involved in stealing and transporting northern children. I say we start there."

"My girl is so smart," Arrow murmurs again, swaying on her feet.

"A little help?" River asks, glancing at Forest. "Her girl may be smart, but she's not that strong."

"I need to sit up front," Arrow says. "None of the rest of you can find the way out of a peat bog."

Forest obliges, lifting Arrow right up onto the driver's seat.

"I'll look after our sleeping Magpie," River says. "If I fall asleep, too, maybe I can help guide her back."

Birdie nods gratefully at her, and River climbs into the back followed by Lake, Dawn, and Nimbus.

Forest steps toward Birdie, closing the distance between them.

"You didn't answer," she says, looking up into his eyes, still startling even now. She thinks she could look at those eyes every day for the rest of her life and never get tired of them. "Do you want me to take your ability away?"

He takes her hand and presses his lips to her palm, then shakes his head. He understands they have work to do. He lifts her up to the driver's seat to sit beside Arrow, then climbs into the coach with everyone else.

"Well," Birdie says as she and Arrow look at the House of Quiet. There's a strange popping sensation, and then the windows explode outward. The red circle goes last of all, raining down like blood. Smoke begins pouring out. It won't be long before the whole place is gone.

"One house down, the world to go," Arrow says.

Birdie laughs as the coach jolts forward, moving them toward an unknown future. This time, Birdie isn't afraid. Because together, Birdie and Arrow are ready, and *no one* can make them be quiet.

ACKNOWLEDGMENTS

Thank you to Michelle Wolfson, my longtime agent, for being my partner and advocate.

Thank you to Wendy Loggia, my editor, for the incredible guidance, feedback, and patience as we dredged up this story from the depths. And thank you to Makena Cioni for making a suggestion that ruined my life for a few weeks but was definitely for the best. I only got there in the end because of you two!

Thank you to Cassie Malmo, my publicist, and Kristopher Kam, also my publicist. (It takes a village, and I'm very fortunate that the village is run by you two.)

Thank you to Casey Moses for such an incredible cover design. (I wish we'd kept your blurb; it's my favorite.) And thank you to Marcela Bolívar for the gorgeously eerie art.

Thank you to the entire team at Delacorte Press. We've done so many books together and you've always been a joy to work with. Special thanks to Colleen Fellingham and Sarah Chassé, my stalwart copy editors. Will I ever learn when to use hyphens? No.

Thank you to Cassie Clare and Josh for providing the most incredible setting for a frenzied week of finally cracking a first draft, to Carrie Ryan for letting me talk out the plot so I could realize I already had the answers, and to the whole retreat group for inspiring me with your brilliance (and also an episode of the worst show I've ever seen).

Thank you to Stephanie Perkins for fielding infinite complaints and questions and a desperate "please help me" draft. I love you. Thank you to Jade Timms for reading the entire thing in two days and providing incredible notes so I'd stop panicking. You saved me from so much anxiety and dread. And thank you to Natalie Whipple, always a voice of reason and support.

Thank you to my incredible spouse and three children for providing a constant backdrop of love, joy, and patience. I couldn't imagine a happier life, and I have a pretty good imagination. It can be tempting to slide toward apathy in the face of seemingly relentless bad news and an alarming slide backward in everything from public health to civil rights, but my kids—and all young people—inspire me to keep fighting, always, for the future they deserve.

And finally, thank you to *X-Men: The Animated Series* for starting a lifelong obsession with powers, their cost, and how they might be taken advantage of. (Rogue is the best. Fight me.)

ABOUT THE AUTHOR

Kiersten White is the #1 *New York Times* bestselling, Bram Stoker Award–winning, and critically acclaimed author of many books, including *Lucy Undying, Hide, Mister Magic, The Dark Descent of Elizabeth Frankenstein,* the And I Darken trilogy, the Camelot Rising trilogy, and *Star Wars: Padawan.* White lives with her family in San Diego, where they obsessively care for their deeply ambivalent tortoise, Kimberly.

KIERSTENWHITE.COM